MAIGRET'S PICKPOCKET
and

MAIGRET AND THE
NAHOUR CASE

MAIGRET'S
PICKPOCKET

and

MAIGRET AND THE
NAHOUR CASE

★

SIMENON

THE
COMPANION BOOK CLUB
LONDON

This edition is published by
The Hamlyn Publishing Group Ltd.
and is issued by arrangement with
Hamish Hamilton Ltd.

*Made and printed in Great Britain
for the Companion Book Club
by Odhams (Watford) Ltd.*
S.869.UBL

CONTENTS

*

MAIGRET'S PICKPOCKET

★

*Translated
from the French by*
NIGEL RYAN

CHAPTER ONE

'Sorry . . .'

'Don't mention it . . .'

It was at least the third time, since the corner of the Boulevard Richard-Lenoir, that she had over-balanced, thrust her bony shoulder into him and pressed her string shopping-bag against his thigh.

She mumbled her excuses, neither embarrassed nor apologetic, after which she resumed staring straight in front of her with a stolid and resolute air.

Maigret did not bear her any ill-will. Anyone might have thought he found it entertaining to be jostled. He was in a mood to take everything lightly that morning.

He had chanced to see a bus with an outside platform coming, which was already a source of satisfaction. These means of transport were becoming more and more rare, as they were being withdrawn from circulation, and soon he would be obliged to empty out his pipe before being swallowed up inside one of those enormous modern conveyances in which the passenger feels a prisoner.

There were the same platform buses when he arrived in Paris nearly forty years before, and in those early days he never grew tired of going up and down the main boulevards on the Madeleine-Bastille line. It had been one of his first discoveries.

And the café terraces. He never grew tired of the café terraces either, from which he could survey the ever-changing scene in the street over a glass of beer.

Yet another marvel, that first year: you could go out of

9

doors, from the end of February, without an overcoat. Not always, but on occasions. And the blossom was starting to come out along some of the avenues, in particular the Boulevard Saint-Germain.

These memories were coming back to him, bit by bit, because this year once again spring had come early, and that morning he had left home without a coat.

He felt a lightness about himself, like the sparkle in the air. The colours of the shops, the food stores, the women's dresses, were gay and lively.

He was not really thinking. Only odds and ends of thoughts which didn't add up to a coherent whole. His wife would be taking her third driving lesson at ten o'clock that morning.

It was funny, unexpected. He couldn't have said exactly how it had been decided. When Maigret had been a young clerk, there was no question of affording a car. At the time it was unthinkable. And later on, he had never seen the need for one. It was too late for him to learn to drive. There were too many other thoughts passing through his head. He wouldn't see the red lights, or else he would mistake the brake for the accelerator.

But it would be pleasant to drive to their cottage, at Meung-sur-Loire, on Sundays . . .

They had just made up their minds, all of a sudden. His wife had protested, laughing.

'Just imagine . . . Learning to drive, at my age . . .'

'I'm sure you'd manage very well . . .'

She was having her third lesson, and was every bit as nervous as a young girl studying for her exams.

'How did it go?'

'The instructor is very long-suffering.'

His fellow passenger in the bus couldn't have been a car driver. Why had she come to do her shopping in the Boulevard Voltaire area, when she lived in another part of town? It was one of those little mysteries that tend to fasten themselves in one's mind. She was wearing a hat, an increasingly rare spectacle, especially in the morning. There was a chicken in her shopping-bag, butter, eggs, leeks and celery . . .

The harder object, at the bottom, which pressed into his thigh at every jolt, must have been the potatoes . . .

Why take the bus to buy perfectly ordinary provisions miles away from home, when they were readily available anywhere? Perhaps she had once lived in the Boulevard Voltaire, grown used to her local tradesmen and remained faithful to them?

The slightly-built young man, to his right, was smoking a pipe that was too short in the stem and too large in the bowl, badly balanced, thus forcing him to clamp his teeth. Young people nearly always choose a pipe both too short and too heavy.

The standing passengers on the platform were packed tightly together. The woman ought to have sat inside. There, in a fishmonger's in the Rue du Temple, he spotted some whiting. He hadn't eaten whiting for ages. Why did whiting, all of a sudden, take on a spring-like quality as well?

Everything was spring-like, like his own mood, and it was just too bad if the woman with the chicken was sullenly staring to her front, a prey to problems beyond the ken of the ordinary mortal.

'Sorry . . .'

'Don't mention it . . .'

He hadn't the courage to say:

'Instead of persecuting everybody out here why don't you take that wretched string bag of yours and go and sit inside?'

He read the same thoughts in the blue eyes of a large man wedged between him and the conductor. They understood one another. So did the conductor, who imperceptibly shrugged his shoulders. A sort of freemasonry, between men. It was amusing.

The stalls, especially the ones belonging to the greengrocers, were overflowing on to the pavements. The green and white bus carved its way through the crowd of charwomen, secretaries and clerks hurrying to work. Life was good.

Another jolt. That bag again, with its hard lump at the bottom, potatoes or something of the sort. As he stepped back, he in turn jostled somebody behind him.

'Sorry . . .'

In turn he mumbled the word, tried to turn round, and saw the face of a man, rather young, on which he read an emotion he did not understand.

He must have been less than twenty-five years old, he was bareheaded, with dishevelled brown hair, and he was unshaven. He had the look of someone who has not slept all night, who had just been through a trying or painful experience.

Threading his way to the platform step, he jumped from the bus as it was moving. It was the corner of the Rue Rambuteau, not far from the Halles, the powerful smell of which hung in the air. The man walked fast, turned round as if he were afraid of something, then was swallowed up in the Rue des Blancs-Manteaux.

Then, for no precise reason, Maigret suddenly put his hand to his hip pocket where he was in the habit of keeping his wallet.

He just prevented himself from starting off in his turn and leaping from the bus, for the wallet had vanished.

He had reddened, but he managed to keep his head. Only the big man with blue eyes appeared to have noticed anything amiss.

Maigret smiled ironically, not so much because he had just been the victim of a pickpocket, but because it was quite impossible to catch him, and all on account of the spring, and the champagne sparkle in the air, which he had begun breathing the day before.

Another habit, a mania, which dated back to his infancy: shoes. Every year, with the first days of fine weather, he bought himself a pair of new shoes, as light as possible. This had occurred the day before.

And that morning he was wearing them for the first time. They pinched. It was torture just to walk the length of the

Boulevard Richard-Lenoir, and it had been a relief to reach the bus-stop in the Boulevard Voltaire.

He would have been quite unable to pursue his thief. And anyway the latter had had time to lose himself in the narrow streets of the Marais.

'Sorry . . .'

Her again! That woman with her shopping! He just managed to stop himself snapping at her:

'Will you kindly take your potatoes and leave us in peace?'

But he contented himself with a nod and a smile.

*   *   *

In his office, too, he found the same light as he had found in those first days, with a haze hanging over the Seine, less dense than mist, made up of thousands of tiny, brilliant, living particles, peculiar to Paris.

'How are things, chief? Anything doing?'

Janvier was wearing a light suit which Maigret had never seen before. He, too, was celebrating spring early, for it was only the fifteenth of March.

'Nothing. Or rather, yes, there is something. I've just been robbed.'

'Your watch?'

'My wallet.'

'In the street?'

'In the back of a bus.'

'Did it have much money in it?'

'About fifty francs. I seldom carry more.'

'And your papers?'

'Not only my papers, but my medallion too.'

That famous medallion of the Police Judiciaire, the nightmare of all Inspectors. In theory they are supposed to carry it with them always, so as to establish that they are Crime Squad officers.

A handsome medallion in silver, or to be more precise in

13

plated copper, for with age the thin silver coating wears through to a reddish metal underneath.

On one side the Republic's Marianne with her Phrygian bonnet, the letters 'R.F.' and the word 'Police' framed in red enamel.

On the reverse, the arms of Paris, a serial number and, engraved in small lettering, the holder's name.

Maigret's medallion bore the number 0004, number 1 being reserved for the Prefect, number 2 for the Director-General of the Police Judiciaire and number 3, for some obscure reason, for the Head of the Special Branch.

Some officers hesitated to carry their medallion in their pockets, because the same regulation also provided for suspension of one month's salary in case of loss.

'Did you see the thief?'

'Very clearly. A young fellow, thin, tired-looking, with the eyes and complexion of a person who hasn't slept.'

'Did you recognize him?'

At the time when he worked on the beat, Maigret knew all the pickpockets by sight, not only the ones from Paris, but the ones who came from Spain or London for the big fairs or popular gatherings.

It is a fairly closed profession, with its own hierarchy. The top operators only bestir themselves when it is worth their while, and they do not think twice about crossing the Atlantic for a world exhibition or, for example, for the Olympic Games.

Maigret had lost sight of them somewhat. He was ransacking his memory. He was not making a tragedy out of the incident. The lightness of the morning was still affecting his mood and, paradoxically, he laid all the blame on the woman with the shopping.

'If she hadn't spent her time jostling me . . . Women ought to be banned from bus platforms . . . Especially when she didn't even have the excuse of wanting to smoke . .'

He was more irritated than angry.

'Are you going to have a look for him in the files?'

'That's what I have in mind.'

He spent nearly an hour there, examining photographs, face-view and profile, most of them of pickpockets. There were some he had arrested twenty years before, and who after that passed through his office again ten or fifteen times, almost becoming old friends.

'You again?'

'One has to live. And you, you're still there, chief. It's quite a while since we last met, isn't it?'

Some were well-dressed and others, the shabby ones, dossed down in junkyards, on the steps of Saint-Ouen and in the Métro corridors. None of them remotely resembled the young man on the bus, and Maigret knew in advance that his search would be a waste of time.

A professional doesn't have that tired, anxious look. He only works when he knows his hands won't start to tremble. And anyway they all knew Maigret's face and profile, if only from seeing it in the newspapers.

He went down to his office again and when he ran into Janvier he gave a shrug.

'You didn't find him?'

'I'd swear he's an amateur. I even wonder if he knew, a minute earlier, what he was going to do. He must have seen my wallet sticking out. My wife never stops telling me I oughtn't to carry it in that pocket. When there was a jolt and those confounded potatoes almost knocked me over, the idea came to him . . .'

His tone changed.

'What's new this morning?'

'Lucas has got 'flu. The Senegalese was killed in a bistro near the Porte d'Italie . . .'

'Knife?'

'Naturally. Nobody's able to give us a description of the assailant. He came in, around one o'clock in the morning, just as the proprietor was going to close down. He took a few strides in the direction of the Senegalese who was having a last drink and he struck so fast that . . .'

Banal. Someone would end up by turning him in, maybe in a month, maybe in two years. Maigret went to the Director's office for the daily conference, and he was careful not to mention his little adventure.

The day promised to be a quiet one. Some red tape. Some papers to sign. Routine matters.

He went home for lunch and observed his wife, who didn't talk to him about her driving lesson. For her it was a little as if, at her present age, she had gone back to school. She felt some pleasure, a certain pride even, but also some embarrassment.

'Well, you didn't drive on the pavement then?'

'Why do you ask me that? You'll give me an inferiority complex . . .'

'On the contrary. You'll make an excellent driver and I am waiting impatiently for you to motor me along the banks of the Loire . . .'

'That won't be for at least another month.'

'Is that what the instructor said?'

'The examiners are getting more and more strict and it's best not to be failed first time. Today we went on the outer boulevards. I would never have believed there was so much traffic on them, or that people drove so fast. Anybody would think . . .'

Fancy! They were eating chicken, as, no doubt, they would be in the house of the woman on the bus.

'What are you thinking about?'

'My pickpocket.'

'Did you arrest a pickpocket?'

'I didn't arrest him, but he relieved me of my wallet.'

'With your medallion?'

She thought of it at once, too. A serious hole in the budget. True, he would get a new medallion without the copper showing through.

'Did you see him?'

'As plainly as I see you.'

'An old man?'

'A young one. An amateur. He looked as if . . .'

Maigret was thinking about it more and more, without really wanting to. The face, instead of becoming blurred in his memory, was becoming clearer. He was recapturing details which he was unaware he had recorded in the first place, such as the fact that the unidentified man had thick eyebrows forming a veritable barrier above his eyes.

'Would you recognize him?'

He thought about it more than a dozen times during the course of the afternoon, lifting his head and staring at the window as though some problem were puzzling him. There was something about the story, the face, the getaway, which wasn't quite natural; he didn't quite know what.

Each time it seemed that a new detail, which would convey something to him, was on the point of coming back, then he would turn again to his work.

'Good-night, boys . . .'

He left at five minutes to six, when there were still half a dozen Inspectors left in the next office.

'Good-night, chief . . .'

They went to the cinema, he and his wife. In a drawer he had found his old brown wallet, too large for his hip pocket, so he put it in his coat.

'If you'd kept it in that pocket . . .'

They went home arm-in-arm, as usual, and the air was still warm. Even the smell of petrol was not disagreeable that evening. It, too, was part of the spring in the air, in the same way as the smell of melting tarmac is part and parcel of summer.

In the morning, he found the sun still there and had the window open for his breakfast.

'It's funny,' he said. 'There are women who cross half Paris in a bus to do their shopping . . .'

'Perhaps because of the TV Sales Guide . . .'

17

He looked at his wife with a puzzled frown.

'Every evening the television says where you can buy different things at the best prices . . .'

It had never occurred to him. It was so simple. He had wasted hours on a little problem which his wife had solved in an instant.

'Thank you.'

'Does that help you?'

'It saves me having to go on thinking about it.'

He added, philosophically, grabbing his hat:

'One doesn't think about the things one wants to . . .'

The mail was waiting for him at the office and, on top of the pile, there was a large brown envelope on which his name, his rank and the address of the Quai des Orfèvres were inscribed in block capitals.

He knew before he opened it. It was his wallet, being returned. And a moment later he discovered that there was nothing missing, neither the medallion, nor the papers, nor the fifty francs.

Nothing else. No message. No explanation.

It irked him.

*   *   *

It was just past eleven o'clock when the telephone rang.

'There's someone who insists on speaking to you personally but refuses to give his name, Superintendent. It seems you are expecting the call and would be angry if I didn't put it through. What do I do?

'All right, put it through . . .'

And, using one hand to strike a match to relight his pipe: 'Hallo! . . .'

There was a longish pause, and Maigret might have thought he had been cut off if he hadn't heard breathing on the other end of the line.

'Hallo! . . .' he said again.

Another silence, then:

"It's me . . .'

A man's voice, quite deep, but by the tone it might have been a child hesitating before confessing to an act of disobedience.

'My wallet?'

'Yes.'

'Didn't you know who I was?'

'Of course not. Otherwise . . .'

'Why are you telephoning?'

'Because I have got to see you . . .'

'Come to my office.'

'No. I can't go to the Quai des Orfèvres.'

'Are you known here?'

'I've never set foot inside the door.'

'What are you afraid of?'

Because the anonymous voice betrayed a note of fear.

'It's private.'

'What's private?'

'What I wanted to see you about. This solution came to me when I saw your name on the medallion.'

'Why did you steal my wallet?'

'Because I needed money at once.'

'And now?'

'I've changed my mind. I'm still not quite sure about it. The best thing would be for you to come as quickly as possible, before I get other ideas . . .'

There was something unreal about this conversation, in the voice, and yet Maigret was taking it quite seriously.

'Where are you?'

'Are you coming?'

'Yes.'

'Alone?'

'Do you insist that I come alone?'

'Our conversation must remain private. Do I have your word?'

'It depends.'

19

'On what?'

'On what you have to tell me.'

Another silence, seemingly heavier than the one at the start.

'I want you to give me a chance. After all it was me that called you. You don't know me. You have no way of tracing me. If you don't come, you'll never know who I am. So it's worth, to you . . .'

He couldn't find the word.

'A promise?' Maigret prompted him.

'Wait. After I've spoken to you, presently, you must give me five minutes to disappear if I ask for them . . .'

'I can't give any undertakings without knowing more about it. I am a police officer and . . .'

'If you'll only believe me, it'll be all right. If you don't believe me, or if you have any doubts, you could manage to look the other way, to give me time to leave, and afterwards you can call up your men . . .'

'Where are you?'

'Do you agree?'

'I'm prepared to come and join you.'

'Under my conditions?'

'I shall be alone.'

'But you promise nothing?'

'No.'

It was impossible for him to act otherwise, and he awaited the reaction of the other man with some anxiety. The latter was in a public telephone box, or else in a café, because he could hear the noise in the background.

'Have you made up your mind?' said Maigret, growing impatient.

'Now that I've come this far . . . What the newspapers say about you gives me hope. Are they true, these stories?'

'What stories?'

'That you are capable of understanding things which normally policemen and judges don't understand and that, in certain cases, you've even . . .'

20

'Even what?'

'Perhaps it's a mistake for me to talk so much. I don't know any longer. Have you ever been known to turn a blind eye?'

Maigret preferred not to answer.

'Where are you?'

'A long way from the P.J. If I tell you now you'll have time to have me arrested by the local police. One quick call, and you've got my description . . .'

'How do you know I saw you?'

'I turned round. Our eyes met, as you know. I was very scared.'

'Because of the wallet?'

'Not just that. Listen. Drive to the bar called Le Métro, on the corner of the Boulevard de Grenelle and the Avenue de La-Motte-Picquet. That'll take you around half an hour. I will call you there. I won't be far off and I will be with you almost immediately.'

Maigret opened his mouth, but the other man had hung up. He was quite as intrigued as he was angry, for it was the first time a complete stranger had treated him with such lack of deference, not to say cynicism.

And yet he couldn't bring himself to feel any animosity towards him. Throughout their fitful conversation he had sensed an anguish, a desire to find a satisfactory way out, a need to come face to face with the Superintendent who, in the unknown man's eyes, figured as his only hope of salvation. All because he had stolen his wallet, without realizing who he was!

'Janvier! Have you got a car downstairs? I want you to drive me to the Boulevard de Grenelle.'

Janvier was surprised, there being no case in hand in that area.

'A private meeting with the character who lifted my wallet.'

'Have you got it back?'

'The wallet, yes, in this morning's post.'

'And your medallion? That would surprise me, as it's the sort of thing anybody would like to keep as a souvenir.'

'My medallion was there, my papers, the money . . .'

'Was it a joke?'

'No, on the contrary, I have the impression that it's something very serious. My pickpocket has just rung to say he's waiting for me.'

'Shall I come too?'

'As far as the Boulevard de Grenelle. Then you must disappear, because he wants to see me alone.'

They followed the river bank as far as the Bir-Hakeim bridge and Maigret contented himself with silently contemplating the Seine as it flowed by. There were street repairs going on everywhere, with barriers and road-up areas, just as there had been in the first year he came to Paris. In fact, it used to happen in ten year cycles, each time that Paris started once again to choke itself.

'Where shall I drop you?'

'Here.'

They were on the corner of the Boulevard de Grenelle and the Rue Saint-Charles.

'Shall I wait?'

'Wait for half an hour. If I'm not back, go back to the office, or have lunch.'

Janvier was intrigued, too, and watched the Superintendent's retreating silhouette with a quizzical look.

The sun was beating down full on the pavement where hot gusts and colder gusts alternated, as if the air as a whole had not yet had time to settle down to its spring temperature.

A small girl was selling violets outside a restaurant. Maigret spotted the bar on the corner, from a long way off, surmounted by the words Le Métro, which would have been lit up in the evening. It was just an ordinary place, without personality, one of those tobacco-bars where one goes to buy cigarettes, or have a drink at the counter, or else to sit and wait for a date.

His eyes travelled round the place, which had only about

22

twenty tables on either side of the bar, most of them un-occupied.

Of course his pickpocket of the day before was not there, and the Superintendent went and sat down at the very back of the room, by the window, and ordered a half of draught.

In spite of himself he kept an eye on the door, and the people who came up to it, pushed it open, and went up to the cash desk behind which the cigarettes were stacked on the shelves.

He was beginning to wonder whether he had not been too gullible when he recognized the silhouette, on the pavement, then the face. The young man was not looking in his direction, was heading for the copper bar, putting his elbows on it, ordering:

'A rum . . .'

He was agitated. His hands moved ceaselessly. He didn't have the nerve to turn round and he was waiting impatiently to be served, as he needed a drink badly.

Seizing his glass, he gestured to the barman not to put the bottle away.

'The same again . . .'

This time, he turned in Maigret's direction. He knew, before going in, where he was. He must have spotted him from outside, or from the window of a nearby house.

He had an air of apologizing, of saying that he had no choice, that he was coming over right away. With still trembling hands he counted out some small change and put it on the counter.

Finally he came over, seized a chair, and collapsed into it.

'Have you got a cigarette?'

'No. I only smoke . . .'

'A pipe. I know. I haven't got any cigarettes, or any money to buy them.'

'Waiter! A packet of . . . What kind do you like?'

'Gauloises.'

'A packet of Gauloises and a glass of rum.'

23

'No more rum. It makes me sick . . .'

'A beer?'

'I don't know. I didn't eat anything this morning, or . . .'

'A sandwich?'

There were several platters at the bar.

'Not straight away. My chest is all constricted. You wouldn't understand . . .'

He was well dressed, in grey flannel trousers and a tartan sports jacket. Like lots of young men, he was wearing no tie, but a high-necked jersey.

'I don't know if you're at all the way one imagines you . . .'

He wasn't looking at Maigret in the face, but shot him a series of sidelong glances before fastening his gaze once more upon the floor. It was tiring to follow the incessant movement of his long thin fingers.

'Weren't you surprised to get the wallet?'

'After thirty years of detective work, one doesn't surprise easily.'

'And to find the money intact?'

'You needed it badly didn't you?'

'Yes.'

'How much did you have in your pocket?'

'About ten francs . . .'

'Where did you sleep last night?'

'I didn't sleep. I didn't eat either. I drank with my ten francs. You just saw me spend the last of the change. There wasn't enough left to get drunk on . . .'

'And yet, you live in Paris,' Maigret observed.

'How do you know?'

'And in this very area.'

There was nobody at the nearby tables, so they just spoke in muted voices. The sound of the door opening and shutting, nearly always for tobacco or matches, came to their ears.

'But you didn't go home . . .'

The other was silent for a moment, as on the telephone. He was pale, exhausted. One could feel that he was making

24

a desperate effort to respond and trying, warily, to smell out any traps that might be laid for him.

'Just as I thought . . .' he growled, finally.

'What did you think?'

'That you would guess, that you'd get it more or less in one, and that once you were on the scent . . .'

'Go on . . .'

He grew angry all of a sudden, raised his voice, forgetting that he was in a public place.

'And that once you were on the scent, I'd had it!'

He looked at the door which had just opened, and for one moment the Superintendent thought he was going to bolt. He must have been tempted. There was a fleeting gleam in his brown pupils. Then he stretched a hand out to his glass of beer and emptied it in one gulp, his eyes fixed on the other man over his glass, as though sizing him up.

'Is that better?'

'I don't know yet.'

'Let's get back to the wallet.'

'Why?'

'Because that's what made you telephone me.'

'Anyway, there wasn't enough.'

'Not enough money? What for?'

'To get away . . . To go anywhere, Belgium or Spain . . '

And, overcome once again by suspicions:

'Did you come by yourself?'

'I don't drive. One of my Inspectors brought me and he's waiting at the corner of the Rue Saint-Charles.'

The man lifted his head with a jerk.

'Did you identify me?'

'No. Your photo isn't on our files.'

'So you did have a look?'

'Of course.'

'Why?'

'On account of my wallet, and even more on account of my medallion.'

25

'Why did you stop at the corner of the Rue Saint-Charles?'

'Because its just nearby and we were passing that way.'

'You haven't had any report?'

'What about?'

'Nothing has happened in the Rue Saint-Charles?'

Maigret was hard put to it to follow the successive expressions registered on the young man's face. Seldom had he seen anyone so anxious, so tortured, clinging to God knew what last hope.

He was afraid, obviously. But of what?'

'Didn't the local police station alert you?'

'No.'

'Do you swear that?'

'I only swear in the witness-box.'

And the other's eyes seemed to bore into him.

'Why do you think I asked you to come?'

'Because you need me.'

'Why do I need you?'

'Because you've got yourself into a mess and you don't know how to get out of it.'

'That's not true.'

The voice was trenchant. The unidentified man raised his head, as though relieved.

'It's not me who's in trouble and that, witness-box or no witness-box, I can swear to without hesitation. I'm innocent, understand that!'

'Not so loud . . .'

He glanced round. A young woman was putting some lipstick on, looking at herself in a mirror, then turning towards the pavement in the hope of seeing the person she was waiting for. Two middle-aged men, crouched over a table, were talking in undertones, and from a few words he guessed at rather than actually heard, Maigret gathered the subject was racing.

'Tell me instead who you are and what you claim to be innocent of.'

'Not here. Presently . . .'

26

'Where?'

'At my house. Can I have another beer? I will be in a position to pay you back presently, unless . . .'

'Unless what?'

'Unless her bag . . . Anyway . . . A beer?'

'Waiter! Two halves . . . And let me know what I owe.'

The young man dabbed himself with a handkerchief which was still moderately clean.

'Twenty-four years old?' the Superintendent asked him.

'Twenty-five.'

'Have you been in Paris long?'

'Five years.'

'Married?'

He was avoiding questions that would be too personal, too inflammatory.

'I was. Why do you ask that?'

'You don't wear a ring.'

'Because I couldn't afford one when I got married.'

He was lighting a second cigarette. He had smoked the first one inhaling deeply, and only now did he pause to savour the tobacco.

'The fact is, all the precautions I took are useless.'

'What precautions?'

'As far as you are concerned. You've got me, fairly and squarely, whatever I do. Even if I tried to make a break, now that you've seen me and know I come from this area . . .'

He had a bitter, ironical smile, an irony directed against himself.

'I always overdo everything. Your inspector with the car, is he still at the corner of the Rue Saint-Charles?'

Maigret consulted the electric clock. It showed three minutes to twelve.

'Either he's just left, or else he's on the point of leaving, as I told him to wait half an hour for me, and if I'm not there then, to go and have lunch.'

'It doesn't matter, does it?'

Maigret didn't answer and when his companion rose, he followed. The two of them set off towards the Rue Saint-Charles, on the corner of which stood a fairly new and modern block. They took the pedestrian crossing, started down the street, but only covered about thirty yards.

The young man stopped in the middle of the pavement. An open door led into the courtyard of the big block giving on to the Boulevard de Grenelle and, under an arch, motor-cycles and children's prams could be seen.

'Is this where you live?'

'Listen, Superintendent . . .'

He was paler and more nervous than ever.

'Have you ever trusted a person, even when all the evidence was against him?'

'I've been known to.'

'What do you think of me?'

'That you are rather complicated and there are too many pieces missing for me to judge you.'

'Because you will be judging me?'

'That's not what I mean. Let's say, form an opinion.'

'Do I look the part for a villain?'

'Certainly not.'

'Or a man capable of . . . No . . . Come on . . . Best get it over quickly.'

He took him into the courtyard and led him towards the left-hand wing where, on the ground floor, a line of doors could be seen.

'That's what they call studios . . .' he grumbled.

And he took a key from his pocket.

'If you force me to go in first . . . I'll do it, whatever it costs me . . . But if I pass out . . .'

He pushed on the polished oak door. It gave on to a minute hall. An open door, on the right, revealed a bathroom with what is called a hip-bath, or a slipper-bath. It was in a mess. Towels were strewn over the tiling.

'Open it, will you?'

28

The young man was indicating to Maigret the door directly in front which was shut, and the Superintendent did what he asked.

His companion didn't bolt. But the smell was nauseating, in spite of the open window.

Beside a divan which made up into a bed at night, a woman was stretched on the Moroccan carpet with multi-coloured pattern, and blue-bottles were circling and buzzing in the air around her.

CHAPTER TWO

'HAVE YOU GOT A TELEPHONE?'

It was a ridiculous question, which Maigret put automatically, because he could see one on the floor in the middle of the room, about a yard from the body.

'I beseech you . . .' muttered his companion, leaning for support against the door-frame.

He was already at the end of his tether. For his part, the Superintendent was not sorry to leave this room where the smell of death had become unbearable.

He propelled the young man out, closed the door again behind him, and paused for a moment to readjust himself to the real world.

Children were returning from school, swinging their satchels, making their way to the various apartments. Most of the windows in the vast building were open. Several radios could be heard simultaneously, voices, music, women calling their husbands or their sons.

On the first floor a canary fluttered about in its cage, and somewhere else there was some laundry hanging out to dry.

'Are you going to be sick?'

His companion shook his head but still didn't dare open his mouth. He was clutching his chest with both hands, deathly pale, on the point of a breakdown, to judge by the near-convulsive movement of his fingers, and the uncontrollable shuddering of his lips.

'Take your time . . . Don't try to talk . . . Would you like to come and have a drink in the café on the corner?'

Again a shake of the head.

'It's your wife, isn't it?'

The man's eyes said that it was. Finally he opened his mouth to take a deep breath, but only succeeded after a long pause, as though his nerves were clamped in knots.

'Were you there when it happened?'

'No . . .'

In spite of everything, he had managed to utter the single syllable.

'When did you see her last?'

'The day before yesterday . . . Wednesday . . .'

'In the morning . . .? In the evening . . .?'

'Late in the evening . . .'

They were walking, automatically, across the great sun-bathed courtyard all round which people were leading their daily lives in different compartments in the building. Most of them were eating, or just about to do so.

Fragments of sentences reached their ears:

'Have you washed your hands . . .?'

'Careful . . . It's very hot . . .'

Kitchen smells, particularly leeks, mingled here and there with the already spring-like air.

'So you know how she died?'

The young man nodded, short of breath once again.

'When I got back . . .'

'One moment . . . You left the flat on Wednesday evening . . . Keep walking . . . Standing still won't do you any good . . . What time, roughly?'

'Eleven o'clock . . .'

'Was your wife still alive . . .? Was she in her dressing-gown when you left her . . .?'

'She hadn't undressed yet . . .'

'Do you work at night?'

'No . . . I was going out to look for some money . . . We needed some . . .'

The pair of them glanced in, unthinkingly, at the open

31

windows as they passed by, and at some of them the occupants stared back, doubtless wondering what they were doing, walking about in this fashion.

'Where were you going to look for the money?'

'Friends' houses . . . Anywhere . . .'

'Didn't you find any?'

'No . . .'

'Did any of these friends see you?'

'At the Vieux-Pressoir, yes . . . I still had about thirty francs in my pocket . . . I looked in at various places where there was a chance of finding somebody I knew . . .'

'On foot?'

'In my car . . . I didn't abandon it until I ran out of petrol, on the corner of the Rue François Premier and the Rue Marbeuf . . .'

'What did you do then?'

'I walked . . .'

The young man Maigret had on his hands was exhausted, his nerves now like those of a person who has been flayed alive.

'How long have you been without food?'

'Yesterday I ate two hard-boiled eggs in a bistro . . .'

'Come with me . . .'

'I'm not hungry . . . If you are thinking of giving me lunch I may as well tell you right away . . .'

Maigret wasn't listening, but made for the Boulevard de Grenelle and went into a small restaurant where there were several tables free.

'Steak and chips for two . . .' he ordered.

He wasn't hungry either, but his companion was in need of sustenance.

'What's your name?'

'Ricain . . . François Ricain . . . Some people call me Francis . . . It was my wife who . . .'

'Listen, Ricain . . . I have got to make a couple of telephone calls . . .'

'To bring your men here?'

'Before I do anything I've got to call the local Chief-Inspector, to let Headquarters know what's happening. Do you give your word you won't budge from here?'

'Where would I go?' Ricain replied bitterly. 'In any case you'll arrest me and put me in prison . . . I won't be able to stand it . . . I would rather . . .'

He didn't finish, but his meaning was clear.

'A half-bottle of Beaujolais, waiter . . .'

Maigret went over to the cash-desk to get some telephone counters. As he anticipated, the local Chief-Inspector was out to lunch.

'Do you want me to get a message to him right away?'

'What time will he be back?'

'Around two o'clock . . .'

'Tell him I'll be waiting for him at half past two in the Rue Saint-Charles, by the entrance of the block on the corner with the Boulevard de Grenelle . . .'

At the Parquet, he only got through to a junior clerk.

'A crime has apparently been committed in the Rue Saint-Charles . . . Take down the address . . . When one of the officers on duty comes back, tell him I will be outside the entrance at a quarter past two . . .'

Finally the P.J., where Lapointe took the call:

'Would you come to the Rue Saint-Charles in an hour's time? . . . Warn Records . . . Tell them to be at the same address around two o'clock . . . Tell them to bring something to disinfect a room where the smell is so strong you can't get in . . . Warn the pathologist . . . I don't know who's on duty today . . . See you there . . .'

He went and sat down opposite Ricain, who hadn't moved and was staring around himself as if unable to believe that this routine spectacle was real.

It was a modest restaurant. Most of the customers worked in the area and ate alone, reading newspapers. The steaks were ready, and the fried potatoes quite crisp.

'What's going to happen next?' asked the young man,

automatically picking up his fork. 'Have you alerted everybody? Is the pantomime about to start?'

'Not before two o'clock . . . From now till then, we've got time to chat . . .'

'I don't know anything . . .'

'People always think they don't know anything . . .'

He mustn't push him. After a few moments, as Maigret was putting a piece of meat to his lips, François Ricain began, unthinkingly, to cut up his steak.

He had stated that he would be unable to eat. Not only was he eating, but he drank, and a few minutes later the Superintendent had to order a second half-bottle.

'Even so you can't possibly understand . . .'

'Of all the sentences that people utter that's the one I have heard the most often during my career . . . But nine times out of ten I have understood . . .'

'I know . . . You'll be teaching me to blow my nose next . . .'

'Does it need blowing?'

'It's not a laughing matter . . . You've seen, like I have . . .'

'The difference being that you had already seen it before. Isn't that right?'

'Certainly.'

'When?'

'Yesterday, at about four o'clock in the morning.'

'Hold on a minute while I get this straight. The day before yesterday, that's to say Wednesday, you went out of your flat at about eleven o'clock in the evening and you left your wife behind . . .'

'Sophie pressed me to take her too. I made her stay because I don't like begging for money in her presence. It would have looked as if I were using her . . .'

'Right! You left by car. What sort of car?'

'A Triumph convertible.'

'If you needed money so badly, why not sell it?'

'Because I wouldn't have got a hundred francs for it. It's an ancient car I bought second-hand and it's passed through

34

God knows how many owners. It hardly stands upright on its four wheels . . .'

'You looked for any friends who might be able to lend you money and you didn't find any?'

'The ones I found were almost as broke as I was . . .'

'You returned home, on foot, at four o'clock in the morning. Did you knock?'

'No. I opened the door with my key . . .'

'Had you been drinking?'

'A certain amount, yes. At night, most of the people I mix with hang around bars or nightclubs . . .'

'Were you drunk?'

'Not to the extent that . . .'

'Depressed?'

'I was at my wit's end . . .'

'Did your wife have any money?'

'No more than I did . . . There must have been twenty or thirty francs left in her bag . . .'

'Go on . . . Waiter! Some more chips, please . . .'

'I found her on the floor . . . When I went over to her, I saw that half her face had sort of . . . gone . . . I think I saw brains . . .'

He pushed his plate away, and gulped down his fourth glass of wine.

'I'm sorry . . . I'd rather not talk about that . . .'

'Was there a weapon in the room?'

Ricain stopped short, looking narrowly at Maigret, as though the crucial moment had come.

'A revolver? An automatic?'

'Yes.'

'An automatic?'

'Mine . . . A 6.35 Browning made in Hertal . . .'

'How did you come to have this weapon in your possession?'

'I was waiting for that question . . . And you probably won't believe me . . .'

'You didn't buy it at a gunsmith's?'

35

'No . . . I had no reason to buy a gun . . . One night there were several of us, just friends, in a small restaurant in La Villette . . . We'd had a lot to drink . . . We were showing off and pretending to be tough . . .'

He had reddened.

'Especially me . . . The others will bear me out . . . It's a complex of mine . . . When I drink, I think I'm really somebody . . . Some people we didn't know attached themselves to us . . . You know how these things can go on into the small hours . . . It was in winter, two years ago . . . I was wearing a sheepskin jacket . . . Sophie was with me. She had been drinking as well, but she never completely loses her head . . .

'Next day, around noon, when I went to put on my jacket, I found an automatic in the pocket . . . My wife told me I'd bought it the night before, in spite of her pleas . . . I was insisting, apparently, that I absolutely had to kill someone who had a grudge against me . . . I kept repeating:

' "It's him or me, you see, old boy." '

Maigret had lit his pipe and was looking at his companion without betraying any signs of what he was thinking.

'Can *you* understand?'

'Go on . . . We were at Thursday, four a.m. I suppose nobody saw you come home?'

'Of course not.'

'And nobody saw you go out again?'

'Nobody . . .'

'What did you do with the weapon?'

'How do you know I got rid of it?'

The Superintendent shrugged.

'I don't know why I did it . . . I realized I'd be accused . . .'

'Why?'

Ricain looked at his questioner in amazement.

'It's obvious, isn't it? . . . I was the only person with the key . . . The weapon that was used belonged to me, and lived in the chest-of-drawers . . . We sometimes had fights, Sophie and me . . . She wanted me to have a steady job . . .'

'What is your profession?'

'In so far as you call it a profession . . . I'm a journalist, without being attached to any particular paper . . . In other words I place my copy where I can, mostly film reviews . . . I'm also an assistant director, and sometimes a script writer . . .'

'Did you throw the Browning into the Seine?'

'Just below the Bir-Hakeim bridge . . . Then I walked . . .'

'Did you go on trying to find your friends?'

'I didn't dare to any longer . . . Someone might have heard the shot and telephoned the police . . . I don't know . . . One isn't necessarily logical in moments like that . . .

'I was going to be hunted down . . . I would be accused and everything would be against me, even the fact that I had roamed about part of the night . . . I had been drinking . . . I was still in search of the first bar to open . . . When I found one, in the Rue Vaugirard, I drank three straight glasses of rum . . .

'If anybody were to question me, I would be in no fit state to answer . . . I was sure to get muddled . . . They would shut me up in a cell . . . I suffer from claustrophobia, so badly that I cannot travel by underground . . . The idea of prison, with huge bolts on the door . . .'

'Was it claustrophobia that inspired the idea of running away abroad?'

'You see! You don't believe me! . . .'

'Perhaps I do.'

'You have to have been in a situation like mine to know what goes on in one's head . . . One doesn't work things out logically . . . I couldn't tell you what route I took . . . I needed to walk, to get away from the Grenelle area, where I pictured them already on my track . . . I remember noticing Montparnasse station, drinking white wine in the Boulevard Saint-Michel . . . or perhaps it was in Montparnasse station itself . . .

'My idea wasn't so much to run away . . . It was to gain time, not to be interrogated in the state I was in . . . In

Belgium, or somewhere else, I would have been able to wait
. . . I would have followed the progress of the inquiry in the
papers . . . I would have found out details that I don't know
about and which would have helped my defence . . .'

Maigret could not help smiling at such a mixture of
astuteness and naïvete.

'What were you doing in the Place de la République?'

'Nothing . . . I wound up there, just as I might have wound
up somewhere else . . . I had one ten franc note left in my
pocket . . . I let three buses go by . . .'

'Because they were completely closed-in ones?'

'I don't know . . . I swear, Superintendent, that I don't
know . . . I needed money to take the train . . . I got on the
platform . . . There were a lot of people and we were packed
tightly together . . . I saw you from behind . . .

'At one moment you stepped back and you nearly over-
balanced . . . I noticed the wallet sticking out of your pocket
. . . I grabbed it, without thinking, and when I looked up I
saw a woman looking straight at me . . .

'I can't think why she didn't give the alarm there and then
. . . I jumped from the bus as it was moving . . . Luckily it
was a very busy street, with a jumble of narrow streets all
around it . . . I ran . . . I walked . . .'

'Two mille-feuilles, waiter . . .'

It was half past one. In forty-five minutes, justice would
don its usual trappings, and the studio in the Rue Saint-
Charles would be invaded by officials, while police outside
would keep onlookers away.

'What are you going to do with me?'

Maigret didn't answer immediately, for the good reason
that he hadn't yet made up his mind.

'Are you arresting me? . . . I realize you can't do anything
else, but I swear to you once more . . .'

'Eat up . . . Will you have a coffee?'

'What are you doing this for?'

'What am I doing that's so extraordinary?'

38

'You're making me eat, and drink . . . You aren't pushing me around. On the contrary, you are patiently listening . . . Surely that's not what you call grilling a person?'

Maigret smiled.

'Not exactly, no . . . I'm just trying to get the facts into some sort of order . . .'

'And get me talking . . .'

'I haven't pressed you overmuch . . .'

'Well, I do feel a bit better . . .'

He had eaten the mille-feuilles seemingly without noticing, and he was lighting a cigarette. A little colour had returned to his cheeks.

'Only, I couldn't go back there, and see . . . smell . . .'

'How about me?'

'That's your job . . . It isn't your wife . . .'

He passed without transition from nonsense to sense, from blind panic to lucid reasoning.

'You're a strange creature . . .'

'Because I'm straightforward?'

'I'm not anxious, either, to have you getting in my way when the forensic department descends and I'm even less keen on reporters pestering you with questions . . .

'When my Inspectors arrive at the Rue Saint-Charles— in fact they must be there by now waiting for us—I'll get them to take you to the Rue des Orfèvres . . .'

'To the cells?'

'To my office, where you will wait for me quietly . . .'

'And then? What happens after that?'

'That depends . . .'

'What do you hope to find out?'

'I have no idea . . . I have even less idea than you have, because I haven't studied the body closely and I haven't seen the weapon . . .'

This whole conversation had been accompanied by the sound of glasses, knives and forks, the buzz of voices, the bustle of waiters and the high-pitched tinkle of the cash register bell.

39

The far side of the pavement was getting the sun and the shadows of the passers-by were short and squat. Cars, taxis, buses came past, doors were slammed.

The two men paused, as if hesitating, on leaving the restaurant. In their corner in the bistro, they had been separated for a good while from other people, from the life that flowed by, from familiar noises, voices and images.

'Do you believe me?'

Ricain put the question without daring to look at Maigret.

'The moment for believing or not believing hasn't come yet. Look! My men are here . . .'

He could see one of the black cars of the P.J. in the Rue Saint-Charles, and the van of the Records Department, and recognized Lapointe in the little group chatting on the pavement. Big Torrence was there too, and it was to him that the Superintendent entrusted his companion.

'Take him to the Quai. Sit him down in my office, stay with him and don't be surprised if he falls asleep. He hasn't had a wink for two nights.'

*   *   *

Shortly after two o'clock, a van of the Paris City Health Department was seen arriving, as Moers and his men did not have the necessary equipment.

In the courtyard at the time there were groups of men waiting outside the studio doors whom the bystanders, kept at a distance by uniformed police, were observing attentively.

On one side, Dréville, the Assistant Public Prosecutor, and Camus, the magistrate, were chatting with Chief-Inspector Piget of the XVth *arrondissement*. All of them had come straight from the lunch table and a pretty massive meal, and as the task of disinfecting dragged on, they kept glancing at their watches.

The pathologist was Doctor Delaplanque, relatively new to the job, but whom Maigret liked and was now asking a few questions. Delaplanque had not hesitated, despite the smell

40

and the flies, to go into the room and make a preliminary examination.

'I'll be able to tell you a bit more presently. You mentioned a 6.35, which surprises me as I would have been prepared to bet the wound was made with a heavier weapon.'

'How about the range?'

'On first inspection, there was no burn, no powder marks. Death was instantaneous, or almost, as the woman lost very little blood. Who is she, by the way?'

'The wife of a young journalist . . .'

For everybody, Moers and the experts from Records, it was routine work carried out without personal feeling. They had all heard one of the men from the Health Department exclaiming a little while earlier, as he went into the room: 'She doesn't half stink!'

Some of the women had babies in their arms, others, strategically placed to see everything without having to move, were leaning on their elbows at their windows, and their comments were bandied from flat to flat.

'Are you sure it isn't the bigger one?'

'No, I don't know the big one . . .'

They were referring to Lourtie. It was Maigret the two women were looking out for.

'There he is! . . . The one smoking the pipe . . .'

'There are two of them smoking pipes . . .'

'Not the very young one, silly . . . The other one . . . He's going up to the men from the Ministry . . .'

Dréville, the Assistant Prosecutor, was asking the Superintendent:

'Have you got any idea what it's all about?'

'The dead woman is a girl of twenty-two, Sophie Ricain, maiden name Le Gal, born in Concarneau, where her father is a watchmaker . . .'

'Has he been informed?'

'Not yet . . . I'll see to that presently . . .'

'Married?'

'For three years, to François Ricain, a young journalist who dabbles in the cinema and is trying to make his way in Paris . . .'

'Where is he?'

'In my office.'

'Do you suspect him?'

'Not so far. He's in no condition to attend the Coroner's investigation, and he'd only get in our way.'

'Where was he when the crime was committed?'

'Nobody knows the time of the crime.'

'And you, doctor, can't you establish it approximately?'

'Not for the moment. Perhaps after the autopsy, if you can tell me what time the victim had her last meal and what she ate.'

'What about the neighbours?'

'You can see some of them watching us. I haven't questioned them yet, but I doubt whether they'll have anything interesting to tell us. Notice that you can get to these studios without passing the porter's lodge, which is at the Boulevard de Grenelle entrance.'

A thankless task. They hung about. They uttered phrases which seemed to have no rhyme or reason, and Lapointe followed in his master's steps, without opening his mouth, with the look and the demeanour of a faithful dog.

The disinfectant people were bringing out from the studio a large flexible tube, painted grey, which they had brought in a quarter of an hour before. The foreman of the team, wearing a white smock, signalled that they could now go in.

'Don't stay too long inside the room,' he advised Maigret. 'There's still formol in the air.'

Doctor Delaplanque knelt beside the body, which he examined with a little more attention than he had the first time.

'As far as I'm concerned, they can take it away.'

'And you, Maigret?'

Maigret had seen all he had to see, a huddled corpse in a

42

silk flowered dressing-gown. A red slipper still clung to one foot. It was impossible to tell from her position in the room what the woman had been doing, or even exactly where she was standing when she was hit by the bullet.

As far as it was possible to judge, the face was fairly ordinary, moderately pretty. Her toe-nails were painted red but had not been attended to for quite a long time because the varnish was cracked and the nails were not scrupulously clean.

The clerk was writing away, beside his boss, as was the Superintendent's secretary.

'Bring the stretcher in . . .'

They trod on dead flies. One by one, the people who were crowded in the room pulled out their handkerchiefs and put them to their eyes, on account of the formol.

The body was taken away, while a respectful silence reigned for a few moments in the courtyard. The men from the Public Prosecutor's office withdrew first, then Delaplanque, while Moers and the experts waited to begin their work.

'Do we search everything, chief?'

'It's best. You never know.'

Perhaps they were up against a mystery, and perhaps, on the other hand, it would turn out to be quite straightforward. It is always that way at the start of a case, or nearly always.

His eyelids stinging, Maigret pulled open a drawer in the chest-of-drawers, which contained a wide assortment of objects: an old pair of binoculars, some buttons, a broken pen, pencils, photographs taken during the making of a film, sun glasses, bills . . .

He would come back when the smell had had time to dissipate, but despite it he still noted the way the studio was decorated. The floor was varnished black and the walls painted, like the ceiling, in bright red. The furniture, on the other hand, was chalky white, which lent an air of unreality to the whole room. It was like a stage set. Nothing seemed solid.

'What do you think of it, Lapointe? How would you like to live in a room like this?'

'It'd give me nightmares.'

They went out. There were still some bystanders hanging about in the courtyard and the police had let them come a little nearer.

'Didn't I tell you it was him . . . I wonder if he'll be back . . . They say he does it all himself, and as like as not he'll be questioning all of us.'

The speaker, an insipid blonde with a baby in her arms, was gazing at Maigret with a smile on her face that a film star might have inspired.

'I'm going to leave you Lourtie . . . Here is the key to the studio . . . When Moer's men have finished, shut the door again and start questioning the neighbours . . . The crime wasn't committed last night, if it was a crime, but the night of Wednesday to Thursday . . .

'Try and find out whether the neighbours heard any coming and going . . . Divide up the residents between Lourtie and yourself . . . Then question the local shopkeepers . . . There is a heap of bills in the drawer . . . You'll find the addresses of the stores where they did their shopping . . .

'I was forgetting . . . Will you make sure the telephone is still working? . . . I have a feeling that when I saw it at noon it was off the hook . . .'

The telephone was working.

'Don't come back to the Quai, you two, without giving me a ring first . . . Keep smiling . . .'

Maigret went off in the direction of the Boulevard de Grenelle and vanished into the Métro. Half an hour later he emerged into the fresh air and the sun, then went back in again to his office, where François Ricain was waiting patiently, while Torrence was reading a paper.

'Aren't you thirsty?' he asked Ricain, taking off his hat and opening the window a little wider. 'Anything new Torrence?'

'A reporter just rang.'

'I was surprised not to see them over there . . . Their tip-

44

off system must be badly organized in the XVth *arrondissement*. It's Lapointe who'll have them on his back . . .'

His eyes turned to Ricain, to his hands, and he said to the Inspector:

'Take him to the laboratory, just in case . . . Have a paraffin test done . . . It doesn't prove anything in the event, as it's almost two days since the crime was committed but it will avoid awkward questions . . .'

They would know, within a quarter of an hour, whether Ricain had powder marks on his fingers. The absence of them would not be conclusive proof that he had not fired the gun, but it would be a point in his favour.

'Hallo! . . . Is that you? . . . I'm sorry . . . Of course. If it hadn't been work, I would have been back for lunch . . . Yes, I ate something, beefsteak and chips, with an over-excited young man . . . I promised myself I'd ring you, as we were going into the restaurant, then we got talking and I must confess, I clean forgot . . . You aren't cross with me, are you? . . . No, I can't tell . . . We'll have to see . . .'

That evening he might or might not be at home for dinner, he couldn't tell yet. Especially with a young man like François Ricain, who changed his mood within the space of a few seconds.

Maigret would have been hard put to it to formulate an opinion of him. Intelligent, that he certainly was, even keenly so, as some of his answers revealed. At the same time there was a rather naive, or childish side to him.

How should he judge him at that moment? He was in a lamentable physical and mental state, a nervous wreck torn between conflicting emotions.

If he hadn't killed his wife, and if he really had toyed with the idea of absconding to Belgium or somewhere else, it revealed a state of total inner confusion which the claustrophobia he suffered from was not by itself enough to explain.

Probably it was he who had thought up and done the decoration in the studio, the black flooring, the red walls and ceiling, the livid furniture which stood out as though floating in space.

It gave the impression that the ground under one's feet was unstable, that the walls were going to advance or recede as in a cinema set, that the chest-of-drawers, the divan, the table, the chairs, were imitation ones made of papier-mâché.

Did he not himself seem rather like an imitation person? Maigret imagined the faces of the Assistant Prosecutor, or the magistrate Camus, if they had been able to read, from end to end, the words the young man had spoken, firstly in the café at La-Motte-Picquet, then in the little local restaurant afterwards.

He would have been interested to have Doctor Pardon's impressions of him.

Ricain came back, followed by Torrence.

'Well?'

'Result negative . . .'

'I've never fired a shot in my life, except at a fair . . . I'd have a job to find the safety catch . . .'

'Sit down . . .'

'Have you seen the magistrate?'

'The magistrate and the Assistant Prosecutor.'

'What have they decided to do? . . . Am I going to be arrested? . . .'

'It's at least the tenth time I've heard you pronounce that word . . . Up till now, I would only have one reason to make an arrest: the theft of my wallet, and I haven't laid a charge against you . . .'

'I returned it to you . . .'

'Precisely. Now we're going to try to clear up one or two things you have told me, and others which I don't yet know about. You can go, Torrence. Tell Janvier to come in . . .'

A few moments later Janvier was settling himself down at the far end of the desk and taking a pencil from his pocket.

'Your name is François Ricain. You are twenty-five years old. Where were you born?'

'In Paris, in the Rue Caulaincourt.'

A bourgeois, almost provincial street, behind the Sacré-Coeur.

'Are your parents still alive?'

'My father . . . He's a driver, in the Railways.'

'How long have you been married?'

'A little over three and a half years. Four years ago this June . . . The 17th . . .'

'So you were twenty-one and your wife was . . .'

'Eighteen . . .'

'Was your father already a widower?'

'My mother died when I was fourteen . . .'

'Did you go on living with your father?'

'For a few years . . . At seventeen I left . . .'

'Why?'

'Because we didn't get on . . .'

'Was there any special reason?'

'No . . . I was bored . . . He wanted me to go into the railways like him, and I refused . . . He thought I was wasting my time reading and studying . . .'

'Did you pass your *baccalauréat* exam?'

'I left two years before . . .'

'What for? . . . Where did you live? . . . On what? . . .'

'You're rushing me,' complained Ricain.

'I'm not rushing you. I'm putting elementary questions to you.'

'There were different periods . . . I sold newspapers in the street . . . Then I was an errand boy in a printing firm in the Rue Montmartre . . . For a while I shared a room with a friend . . .'

'His name and address . . .'

'Bernard Fléchier . . . He had a room in the Rue Coquillière . . . I lost touch with him . . .'

'What did he do?'

'He drove a delivery van . . .'

'Then?'

47

'I worked for six months in a stationer's . . . I wrote short stories which I peddled to newspapers . . . One was accepted and I got a hundred francs . . . The man I dealt with was surprised to see how young I was.'

'Did he accept any other stories?'

'No. The others were rejected . . .'

'What were you doing when you met your wife—I mean the girl who was to become your wife, Sophie Le Gal—that's right, isn't it?'

'I was third assistant director on a film which the censors have banned, a film about war made by some young people . . .'

'Was Sophie working?'

'Not regularly . . . She did walk-on parts . . . She sometimes did a bit of modelling . . .'

'Was she living alone?'

'In a hotel room, in Saint-Germain-des-Près . . .'

'Love at first sight?'

'No. We slept together, because after one wild party we wound up together in the street at three o'clock in the morning . . . She let me take her home . . . We stayed together for several months, then one fine day we had the idea of getting married . . .'

'With her parent's consent?'

'They hadn't much to say . . . She went to Concarneau and came back with a letter from her father authorizing the marriage . . .'

'And you?'

'I saw my father, as well.'

'What did he say?'

'He shrugged his shoulders . . .'

'Didn't he come to the wedding?'

'No . . . Just friends, three or four . . . In the evening we all ate together at the Halles . . .'

'Before meeting you, did Sophie have any affairs?'

'I wasn't the first one, if that's what you mean . . .'

'She didn't live for any length of time with a man who

48

might have been enough in love with her to try to see her again?'

He seemed to be searching in his memory.

'No . . . We did meet some former friends of hers, but no great lovers. You know, in four years we had time to mix in various different circles . . . Some people were our friends for six months, then dropped out of sight . . . Others took their place, and we saw them every now and then . . . You ask questions as if it was all clear cut . . . They're writing down my answers . . . I've only got to make one mistake, or get muddled up or leave out some detail and you'll jump to God knows what conclusion . . . You must admit it's not very fair . . .'

'Would you rather be questioned in the presence of a lawyer?'

'Have I the right?'

'If you consider yourself to be a suspect . . .'

'And you? . . . What do you consider me as? . . .'

'As the husband of a woman who has died, died a violent death . . . As a young man who panicked and stole my wallet and then returned it to me with its contents . . . As a very intelligent but not very stable character . . .'

'If you'd just spent two nights like I have . . .'

'We'll come to that . . . So, you've held down different jobs, each one for a short time . . .'

'It was only to earn my living while I was waiting . . .'

'Waiting to do what?'

'To start my career . . .'

'What career?'

He frowned and looked hard at Maigret, as if to ensure there was no trace of sarcasm in his voice.

'I'm still in two minds . . . Perhaps I'll do both . . . Anyhow, I want to write, but I don't know if it will be in the form of film scripts or novels . . . Film directing tempts me, on condition I do the whole film myself . . .'

'Do you mix with film people?'

49

'At the Vieux-Pressoir, yes . . . You can meet people starting out like myself there, but a producer like Monsieur Carus isn't too grand to come and dine with us . . .'

'Who is Monsieur Carus?'

'A producer, I told you. He lives in the Hotel Raphael, and his office is at 18b de Bassano, off the Champs-Elysées . . .'

'Has he financed any films?'

'Three or four . . . In co-operation with the Germans and Italians . . . He travels a lot . . .'

'What sort of age is this gentleman?'

'About forty.'

'Married?'

'He lives with a young girl, Nora, who has been a model.'

'Did he know your wife?'

'Of course . . . It's a very informal circle . . .'

'Has Monsieur Carus got plenty of money?'

'He raises it for his films . . .'

'But he doesn't have a private income?'

'I told you he lives at the Raphael, where he has a suite . . . It's pretty expensive . . . At night he goes round the smartest clubs . . .'

'He wasn't the one you were looking for on the night of Wednesday to Thursday?'

Ricain blushed.

'Yes . . . Him or someone else . . . Preferably him because he nearly always has wads of notes on him . . .'

'Do you owe him money?'

'Yes . . .'

'A lot?'

'Upwards of two thousand francs . . .'

'Doesn't he ask for it back?'

'No . . .'

A very slight change, hard to pinpoint, was taking place in the young man and Maigret observed him more closely.

But he had to remain cautious, for he was still prepared at any moment to retreat into his shell.

CHAPTER THREE

WHEN MAIGRET GOT UP, Ricain began to tremble and looked at him apprehensively, still apparently expecting some blow of fate, or a trick. The Superintendent went and stood for a moment by the open window, as if to steep himself in reality by watching the passers-by and the cars on the Saint-Michel bridge, and a tug with a big clover-leaf marking on its funnel.

'I'll be right back . . .'

From the Inspectors' room, he asked for the pathologists' laboratory.

'Maigret here . . . Would you see if Doctor Delaplanque has finished the autopsy . . .'

He had to wait quite a long time before he heard the pathologist's voice on the other end of the line.

'You've called at just the right moment, Superintendent. I was going to ring you. Have you been able to find out what time the young woman had her last meal, and what it consisted of?'

'I'll tell you in a moment. How about the wound?'

'As far as I can judge the shot was fired at a distance of, say, between a yard and a yard and a half.'

'From the front?'

'From the side. The victim was standing up. She must have staggered back a step or two before falling on the carpet. The laboratory, which found patches of blood, will confirm my words. Another thing. The woman had begun a pregnancy which had been terminated towards the third or fourth month by the crudest possible methods. She smoked a lot, but was in quite good health . . .'

51

'Do you mind hanging on a moment?'

He went back to his office.

'Did you have dinner with your wife on Wednesday evening?'

'Around half-past eight, at the Vieux-Pressoir . . .'

'Do you remember what she ate?'

'Wait . . . I wasn't hungry . . . I just had some cold meat . . . Sophie ordered a fish soup which Rose recommended, then some beef . . .'

'No pudding?'

'No . . . We drank a carafe of Beaujolais . . . I had some coffee; Sophie didn't want any . . .'

Maigret went into the next room and repeated the menu to Delaplanque.

'If she ate at half-past eight, I can put the death at somewhere around eleven o'clock in the evening, for the food was almost completely digested . . . I'll tell you more after the chemical analysis, but it'll take a few days . . .'

'Did you do the paraffin test?'

'Yes, I saw to that . . . There wasn't any trace of powder on the hands . . . You'll get my preliminary report in the morning . . .'

Maigret took up his place again in his office and arranged the five or six pipes which lived there in order of size.

'I've got some more questions to put to you, Ricain, but I hesitate to do so today. You're worn out and you're only keeping going on your nerves . . .'

'I'd rather get it over with now . . .'

'As you wish. So, if I've understood you correctly, you've never, up till now had any fixed job, or regular income?'

'There are tens of thousands of us in the same boat, I imagine . . .'

'To whom did you owe money?'

'To all the shopkeepers . . . Some of them won't supply us any more . . . I owe another five hundred francs to Maki . . .'

'Who's he?'

'A sculptor, who lives in the same block . . . He's abstract, but to make a bit of money he does busts every now and then . . . This had happened a fortnight ago . . . He made four or five thousand francs and bought us dinner . . . Over the dessert I asked him to make me a small loan . . .'

'Who else?'

'There's a stack of them . . .!'

'Did you plan to pay them back?'

'I'm sure one day I'll make a lot of money . . . Most directors and well-known writers began like me . . .'

'Let's turn to something else. Were you jealous?'

'Of whom?'

'I'm referring to your wife. I presume that sometimes some of your friends used to try to make up to her?'

Ricain fell silent, embarrassed, and shrugged his shoulders.

'I don't think you'll be able to understand . . . You belong to a different generation . . . We young people don't attach so much importance to these things . . .'

'Do you mean you allowed her to have intimate relations with other people?'

'It's difficult to reply to such a crude question . . .'

'Even so, try.'

'She posed in the nude for Maki . . .'

'And nothing happened?'

'I never asked them.'

'And Monsieur Carus?'

'Carus has as many girls as he wants, all the ones who want to get into films or television . . .'

'Does he exploit the situation?'

'I believe so . . .'

'Didn't your wife try to get into films?'

'She had a small speaking part three months ago . . .'

'And so, you weren't jealous?'

'Not in the way you mean . . .'

'You told me Carus had a mistress . . .'

'Nora . . .'

'Is she jealous?'

'That's not the same thing . . . Nora is an intelligent woman, and ambitious . . . She looks down on the cinema . . . What she cares about is becoming Madame Carus and having plenty of money at her disposal . . .'

'Did she get on well with your wife?'

'As well as with anyone . . . She was condescending to all of us, men and women alike . . . What are you driving at?'

'Nothing.'

'Are you planning to interrogate everybody I was in touch with?'

'Possibly. Someone killed your wife. You state that it wasn't you and until I have proof to the contrary I'm inclined to believe you.

'An unknown person got into your house on Wednesday evening, when you had just gone out. This person had no key, which leads one to suppose that your wife let him into the studio without being suspicious.'

Maigret was looking heavily at the young man, who was becoming visibly impatient, trying to get a word in.

'One moment! Who, among your friends, knew of the existence of the gun?'

'Nearly all of them . . . In fact, all . . .'

'Did you sometimes carry it on you?'

'No. But sometimes when I was in funds, I would ask my friends round . . . I would buy some cold meat and salmon and things like that and everybody brought a bottle of wine or whisky . . .'

'What time did these little parties finish?'

'Late . . . We drank a great deal . . . Sometimes people fell asleep and stayed till morning . . . Occasionally I would play with the revolver, as a joke . . .'

'Was it loaded?'

Ricain didn't answer at once, and at these moments it was difficult not to have suspicions about him.

'I don't know . . .'

54

'Listen. You speak of parties when everyone was more or less drunk. You would grab a gun, just for fun, and now you tell me you didn't even know whether it was loaded. Earlier on you told me you didn't know where the safety catch was. You could have killed one of your friends without meaning to.'

'It's possible . . . When one is drunk . . .'

'Were you often drunk, Ricain?'

'Quite often . . . Not so drunk I didn't know what I was doing, but I drink neat spirits, like most of my friends . . . When we meet up, especially in clubs and cafés . . .'

'Where did you lock up your gun?'

'It wasn't locked up. It was kept in the top of the chest-of-drawers with old bits of string, nails, drawing-pins, bills, all the things we couldn't find a place for anywhere else . . .'

'So any one of the people who used to spend the evening with you could have taken the weapon and used it?'

'Yes . . .'

'Do you have any suspicions?'

A moment's hesitation once again, a sidelong glance.

'No . . .'

'Nobody was properly in love with your wife?'

'I was . . .'

Why did he say it with a note of sarcasm in his voice?

'In love but not jealous?'

'I've already explained . . .'

'And Carus?'

'I told you . . .'

'Maki?'

'He's a big brute to look at, but he's as gentle as a lamb and women frighten him . . .'

'Tell me about the others, the people you saw, the ones you met up with in the Vieux-Pressoir and who used to round off their evenings with you, when you were solvent . . .'

'Gérard Dramin . . . He's an assistant director . . . He was the one I worked with on a script, and I was third assistant on the film.'

'Married?'

'At the moment he's living apart from his wife . . . It isn't the first time . . . After a few months they always go back to each other again . . .'

'Where does he live?'

'All over the place, always in hotels . . . He boasts openly of possessing nothing of his own except a suitcase and its contents . . .'

'Are you noting this down, Janvier?'

'I'm with you, chief . . .'

'Who else, Ricain?'

'A photographer, Jacques Huguet, who lives in the same block as me, in the centre building . . .'

'How old?'

'Thirty.'

'Married?'

'Twice. Divorced both times. He has one child by his first wife, two by the second. She lives on the same floor.'

'Does he live by himself?'

'With Monique, a nice girl, seven or eight months pregnant . . .'

'That makes three women in his life. Does he still see the first two?'

'The girls get on well together.'

'Go on.'

'Go on with what?'

'The list of your friends, the regulars at the Vieux-Pressoir.'

'They keep changing, I told you before . . . There's Pierre Louchard . . .'

'What does he do?'

'He's over forty, he's queer, and he runs an antique shop in the Rue de Sèvres . . .'

'What does he have in common with your group?'

'I don't know . . . He's a regular customer at the Vieux-Pressoir . . . He follows us about . . . He doesn't talk much, and seems to feel at home with us . . .'

'Do you owe him money?'

'Not much . . . Three hundred and fifty francs . . .'

The telephone bell rang shrilly and Maigret picked up the receiver.

'Hallo, chief. Lapointe would like a word with you. Shall I put him through to your office?'

'No, I'll come round . . .'

He went back into the Inspectors' room.

'You asked me to ring when we were through, chief. Lourtie and I have questioned all the neighbours who could have heard anything, especially the women, as most of the men are still at work.

'Nobody remembers a shot. They are accustomed to noises coming from the Ricains' flat at night. Several of the tenants had complained to the porter about it and were planning to write to the landlords.

'Once at about two o'clock in the morning an old lady who was suffering from tooth-ache was standing by her window when she saw a naked girl burst out of the studio and run into the courtyard pursued by a man.

'She wasn't the only one who said that orgies used to take place in the Ricains' studio.'

'Did Sophie have visitors when her husband was away?'

'Well, the fact is, chief, the women I spoke to weren't very precise. The words that came up most often were: savages, not properly brought up, immoral living. As for the concierge, she was waiting for their lease to come up to give them notice to quit as they were six months behind with the rent and the landlord decided to get rid of them if they didn't pay up. What shall I do?'

'Stay put at the studio until I get there. Keep Lourtie with you, as I may need him.'

He went back to his office where Janvier and Ricain were waiting in silence.

'Listen to me, Ricain. At this stage, I don't want to ask the magistrate for a warrant against you. On the other hand,

I don't suppose you want to sleep in the Rue Saint-Charles tonight.'

'I couldn't . . .'

'You haven't got any money. I would rather not see you let loose again in Paris trying to find a friend who'll lend you some money.'

'What are you going to do with me?'

'Inspector Janvier is going to take you to a small hotel, not far from here, in the Ile Saint-Louis . . . You can have food sent up to you . . . If you pass a drugstore or a chemist buy yourself some soap, a razor and a toothbrush . . .'

The Superintendent gave Janvier a wink.

'I'd rather you didn't go out. Besides I must warn you that if you should happen to . . .'

'I'll be followed . . . I realized that already . . . I'm innocent . . .'

'So you said . . .'

'Don't you trust me?'

'It's not my job to trust people. I'm content to wait. Goodnight.'

Alone once again, Maigret paced his office for a few minutes, pausing every now and then in front of the window. Then he picked up the telephone to tell his wife that he would not be home for dinner.

A quarter of an hour later, he was back in the Métro on his way to Bir-Hakeim. He knocked on the studio door and Lapointe let him in.

The smell of formol still hung in the air. Lourtie, seated in the only armchair, was smoking a small, exceptionally strong cigar.

'Do you want to sit down, chief?'

'No thank you. I presume you found nothing new?'

'Some photos . . . Here's one of the Ricains together on the beach . . . Another in front of their car . . .'

Sophie wasn't bad looking. She had that slightly sulky look fashionable among young people and a *bouffant* hair style.

58

In the street one might have taken her for any one of thousands with the same mannerisms and the same way of dressing.

'No wine, or spirits?'

'A bottle with some whisky dregs in that cupboard.'

An old cupboard without character, like the cabinet and the chairs, but made original by the matt white paint which contrasted with the black floor and red walls.

Maigret, hat on head, pipe in mouth, pulled open the doors and drawers. Very few clothes. Three dresses altogether, cheap, garish. Some trousers, polo-necked jersey . . .

Next to the bathroom the kitchenette was scarcely larger than a cupboard, with its gas ring and miniature refrigerator. In the latter he found an opened bottle of mineral water, a quarter of a pound of butter, three eggs, a cutlet in a congealed sauce.

Nothing was clean, neither the clothes nor the kitchen, or the bathroom in which the dirty laundry was strewn about.

'Has nobody rung?'

'Not since we've been here.'

By now the crime must have found its way into the evening papers, or would be doing so at any moment.

'Let Lourtie go and have a bite, then come back here and settle down as comfortably as possible. All right, Lourtie, old boy?'

'All right, chief. Am I allowed a nap?'

As for Maigret and Lapointe, they set out on foot for the Vieux-Pressoir.

'Have you arrested him?'

'No. Torrence has taken him off to the Cigognes, in the Ile Saint-Louis.'

It was not the first time that they had put a customer they had been anxious to keep an eye on in there.

'Do you think he killed her?'

'He is both intelligent enough and stupid enough to have done it. On the other hand . . .'

Maigret struggled for words, but could not find them. He

59

had seldom been so intrigued by a person as he was by this François Ricain. At first sight, he was just an ambitious young man of the kind one runs into every day in Paris and any other capital city.

A future failure? He was only twenty-five. Men who later became famous were still walking the streets at his age. At moments the Superintendent was inclined to trust him. Then, immediately afterwards, he would give a discouraged sigh.

'If I were his father . . .'

What would he do with a son like Francis? Try to bring him to heel, guide him back on to the rails?

He resolved to go and see the father in Montmartre. Unless he came round to the P.J. of his own accord when he read the papers.

Lapointe, who was walking beside him in silence, was little more than twenty-five years old. Maigret mentally compared the two men.

'I think it's there, chief, on the other side of the boulevard, near the Air Terminal Métro.

They found themselves gazing at the entrance door flanked by two worm-eaten wine-presses, with heavily curtained windows through which filtered the pink light of the lamps, which were already lit.

It wasn't yet time for apéritifs, much less for dinner, and there were only two people in the room, a woman, on the customers' side of the bar, perched on a high stool and drinking through a yellowish straw, and the proprietor on the other, bent over a newspaper.

The lights were pink, the bar was supported by wine-presses, the massive tables were covered with check cloths, and the walls three-quarter panelled with dark woodwork.

Maigret, walking ahead of Lapointe, frowned as he caught sight of the man with the newspaper, as if he were trying to remember where he had seen him before.

The proprietor, for his part, raised his head, but it only took him an instant to recognize the Superintendent.

'What a coincidence . . .' he remarked, tapping, the still fresh print. 'I was just reading that you were in charge of the case . . .'

And, turning to the girl:

'Fernande, meet Superintendent Maigret in person . . . Sit down, Superintendent . . . What can I offer you . . .?'

'I didn't know you had taken to the catering profession.'

'When you begin to get on a bit . . .'

And it was true that Bob Mandille must have been about Maigret's age. He was much talked about, in the old days, when he used to devise some new exploit every month, walking along the wing of an aeroplane in flight, parachuting over the Place de la Concorde and landing a few feet from the Obelisk, or leaping from a galloping horse into a racing car.

The cinema had turned him into one of its most celebrated stunt-men, after trying in vain to make him a male lead. People had lost count of the accidents he had had, and his body must have been a mass of scars.

He had kept his figure, and his elegance. There was just the suggestion of stiffness in his movements, which recalled an automaton. As for his face, it was just a little too smooth, with slightly too regular features, probably the result of plastic surgery.

'Scotch?'

'Beer.'

'Same for you, young man?'

Lapointe wasn't at all pleased to be addressed in this way.

'You see, Monsieur Maigret . . . I've had enough. The insurance companies tell me I'm too old to be a good risk and all of a sudden they don't want me in films any more . . . So I married Rose and turned publican . . . You're looking at my hair? Do you remember my picture, when I was scalped by the blades of a helicopter and my head was as bald as an egg . . .? A wig, that's all there is to it . . .'

He raised it, gallantly, as if it were a hat.

'You know Rose, don't you . . .? She sang for a long time

61

at the Trianon-Lyrique . . . Rose Delval, as she was called then . . . Her real name is Rose Vatan, which didn't sound right on a billboard . . .

'Well, what do you want to talk about?'

Maigret glanced in the direction of the girl called Fernande.

'Don't worry about her . . . She's part of the furniture . . . In two hours she'll be so drunk she won't be able to move and I'll put her into a taxi . . .'

'You know Ricain, of course?'

'Of course . . . Your health . . . I only drink water, so excuse me . . . Ricain comes to dine here once or twice a week . . .'

'With his wife?'

'With Sophie, naturally . . . It's unusual to see Francis without Sophie . . .'

'When did you see them last?'

'Wait . . . What day is it? Friday . . . They came on Wednesday evening . . .'

'With friends?'

'There were none of the band that night . . . Except for Maki, if I'm not mistaken . . . I seem to remember Maki eating in his corner . . .'

'Did they sit down with him?'

'No . . . Francis pushed the door half-open, and asked me if I'd seen Carus and I said no, I hadn't seen him for two or three days . . .'

'What time did they leave?'

'They didn't come in . . . They must have eaten somewhere else . . . Where is he now, Francis? I hope you haven't put him inside . . .?'

'Why do you ask?'

'I've just read in the paper that his wife was shot dead with a revolver and that he's disappeared . . .'

Maigret smiled. The police of XVth *arrondissement*, who didn't know the full story, had misled the reporters.

'Who told you about my restaurant?'

'Ricain.'

'So he's not on the run?'

'No.'

'Arrested?'

'Not arrested, either. Do you think he would have been capable of killing Sophie?'

'He's incapable of killing anything . . . if he was going to, it would be himself . . .'

'Why?'

'Because there are times when he loses his self-confidence and starts hating himself . . . That's when he drinks . . . After a few glasses he becomes desperate, convinced that he's a failure who's going to let his wife down . . .'

'Does he pay you regularly?'

'He's chalked up quite a bill . . . If I listened to Rose, I'd have given up letting him have credit a long while ago . . . For Rose, business is business . . . True, her job is harder than mine, at the stove all day . . . She's there now, and she'll still be there at ten o'clock tonight . . .'

'Did Ricain come back that night?'

'Wait . . . I was busy with a table later on . . . I felt a draught and I turned to the door . . . It was open and I thought I saw him there looking for someone . . .'

'Did he find them?'

'No.'

'What time was this?'

'Around eleven o'clock . . . You were right to press me . . . It was that evening that he came back a third time, later on . . . Sometimes, when the dinners are finished we stay on for a chat with the regulars . . . It was past midnight, on Wednesday, when he came back . . . He stayed by the door and signalled me to come over . . .'

'Did he know the customers you were with?'

'No . . . They were old friends of Rose, theatre people, and Rose had joined us, in her apron . . . Francis is scared stiff of my wife . . .

63

'He asked me if Carus had come . . . I told him he hadn't . . . And Gérard? . . . Gérard, that's Dramin, who's going to make a name for himself one day in the cinema . . . He hadn't come, either . . . Then he blurted out that he needed two thousand francs . . . I made it clear that I couldn't help. A few dinners, all right . . . A fifty or a hundred franc note, every now and then when Rose is looking the other way, that I can manage . . . But two thousand francs . . .'

'He didn't say why he needed it so badly?'

'Because they were going to turn him out of the studio and sell everything he owned . . .'

'Was it the first time?'

'No, and that's the point . . . Rose isn't so very wrong: he's an habitual sponger . . . But not a cynical one, if you see what I mean . . . He does it in good faith, always quite convinced that tomorrow or next week he will be signing a big contract . . . He is so ashamed of asking that one is ashamed of refusing . . .'

'Is he a nervous person?'

'Have you seen him?'

'Of course.'

'Nervous or calm?'

'A bundle of nerves . . .'

'Well, I've never seen him any other way . . . Sometimes it's quite exhausting to watch . . . He clenches his fists, pulls faces, flies into a fury over nothing, or else he goes all embittered, or gets on his high horse . . . And yet, you know, Superintendent, he is basically sound, and I wouldn't be surprised if he does something one day . . .'

'What do you think of Sophie?'

'They say you mustn't speak ill of the dead . . . The Sophies of this world, you run into them by the dozen if you see what I mean . . .'

And with a glance he indicated the girl sitting at the bar, lost in contemplation of the bottles in front of her.

'I wonder what he saw in her . . . There are thousands of

64

them, all dressed alike, with the same make-up, dirty feet, worn out heels, wandering about in the mornings in trousers too tight for them and living on salads . . . All hoping to become models or film stars . . . My eye . . .'

'She had a bit part . . .'

'Ah yes, through Walter . . .'

'Who is Walter?'

'Carus . . . If you totted up the number of girls who have earned their right to a bit part . . .'

'What sort of a man is he?'

'Come and have dinner here and you'll probably be able to see for yourself . . . He sits at the same table one night in two, and there's always someone around to make the most of his hospitality . . . A producer . . . You know how it goes . . . The man who finds the money to start a film, then the money to continue it, and then, after months or years, the money to finish it . . . He's half English and half Turkish, which is an interesting mixture . . . A decent sort, straight, with a resounding voice, always ready to buy a round of drinks and addressing everyone as "*tu*" within five minutes of meeting them.'

'Did he call Sophie "*tu*"?'

'He addresses all women as "*tu*" and calls them his baby, his sweetheart or his turtle dove as the fancy takes him . . .'

'Do you think he slept with her?'

'I'd be surprised if he didn't . . .'

'Wasn't Ricain jealous?'

'I suspected you were coming to that . . . First of all, Carus wasn't the only one . . . I would think the others have all trodden that path . . . I could have, too, if I'd wanted, even though I could almost have been her grandfather . . . Leaving that aside . . . We had a few rows about that, Rose and me . . .

'Question Rose and you'll find she hasn't a good word to say for him. She thinks he's a good-for-nothing, living off his wits, and playing the big misunderstood act but in spite of everything is really just a little pimp . . . That's my wife's opinion . . .

'It's true of course that she spends three-quarters of her time in the kitchen so she doesn't know him as well as I do . . .

'I've tried to make her understand that Francis knew nothing of what was going on . . .'

'Do you believe that?'

The retired acrobat had very pale blue eyes that reminded one of a child's. In spite of his age and his air of experience, he had still preserved a childlike enthusiasm and charm.

'Perhaps I'm a bit naïve, but I trust the lad . . . There have been times when I haven't been so sure, and I've almost come round to Rose's way of thinking . . .

'But I always come back to my original position: He's really in love . . . Enough for her to make him believe anything . . . The proof is the way he let himself be treated by her . . . Some evenings, when she had a drop too many, she told him, cynically, that he was nothing but a failure, a minus quantity, that he had no fire in his belly, nor, saving your presence, anywhere else either, and that she was wasting her time on a half-portion like him . . .'

'How did he take it?'

'He would retire into his shell and you could see the beads of sweat on his forehead . . . Even so he would force himself to smile:

'"Come on Sophie . . . Come to bed . . . You're tired . . ."'

At the back of the room a door opened. A small, very fat woman appeared, wiping her hands on a large apron.

'Well! well! . . . The Superintendent . . .'

And, while Maigret was still trying to remember where he could have seen her before, as he had never been a regular visitor to the Tianon-Lyrique, she reminded him:

'Twenty-two years ago . . . In your office . . . You arrested the character who lifted my jewels from my dressing-room . . . I've put on a little weight since those days . . . In fact, it's thanks to those jewels that I was able to buy this restaurant . . . That's right, isn't it, Bob . . .? What have you come here for?'

66

Her husband explained, with a gesture towards the news-paper:

'Sophie's dead . . .'

'Our Sophie, the little Ricain girl?'

'Yes . . .'

'An accident? I'll bet it was him driving and . . .'

'She was murdered . . .'

'What this he's saying, Monsieur Maigret?'

'The truth . . .'

'When did it happen?'

'Wednesday evening . . .'

'They used to have dinner here . . .'

Rose's face had lost not only her good humour, which was her trade mark, as it were, but her cordiality.

'What have you been telling him?'

'I've been answering his questions . . .'

'I bet you haven't had a good word for her. Listen, Super-intendent, Bob isn't a bad character and we get along quite well together . . . But on the subject of women, you mustn't listen to him . . . To hear him you'd think they're all tarts and men are their victims . . . Now, take this poor girl, for example . . .

'Look at me, Bob . . . Who was right . . .? Was it him or her that caught it . . .?'

She paused, glaring defiantly at them, her hands on her hips.

'Same again, Bob,' Fernande mumbled slackly.

And to speed her on her way, Mandille gave her a double.

'Were you fond of her, Madame?'

'How can I put it . . .? She was brought up in the provinces . . . And at Concarneau, moreover, where her father is a clockmaker . . . I'm sure her mother goes to mass every morning . . .

'She arrives in Paris and falls in with this gang who think they're geniuses because they work in the cinema or television. I've been in the theatre myself, which is a far more difficult proposition . . . I've sung the whole repertoire but I never gave myself airs . . . While these little cretins . . .'

'Which one do you mean in particular?'

'Ricain, for a start . . . He considered himself the smartest of the lot . . . When he managed to get an article into a magazine read by a few hundred imbeciles, he imagined he was going to rock the film world on its foundations . . .

'He took the girl over . . . Apparently they actually got married . . . He might at least have fed her properly, mightn't he . . .? I don't know what they would have done for food if their friends hadn't invited them and if my half-wit of a husband hadn't given them credit . . . How much does he owe you, Bob?'

'No matter . . .'

'You see! . . . And all the while, there I am, slaving in the kitchen . . .'

She was grumbling for the sake of grumbling, which did not prevent her from looking at her husband with a certain tenderness.

'Do you think she was Carus' mistress?'

'As if he needed her! . . . He had quite enough on his hands with Nora . . .'

'Is that his wife?'

'No . . . He wanted to marry her all right, but he is already married in London and his wife won't hear of a divorce . . . Nora . . .'

'What's she like?'

'Don't you know her? . . . That one, now, I wouldn't defend . . . You can see it isn't just prejudice . . . What men see in her, I keep asking myself . . .

'She's at least thirty, and if you cleaned all her make-up off, you'd probably guess nearer forty . . . She's thin, it's true, so thin you can count her bones . . .

'Black and green round the eyes, to give them mystery it seems, but it only makes her look like a witch . . . No mouth, because she hides it under a layer of white stuff . . . And greeny white on her cheeks . . . That's Nora for you . . .

'As for her clothes . . . The other day she turned up in a silver lamé pyjama affair so tight she had to come into the kitchen to get me to sew up the seam of the trousers . . .'

'Does she do cinema work?'

'What do you take her for? . . . She leaves that to the young girls who don't count . . . Her dream is to be married to a big international producer, to be Madame the producer's wife . . .'

'You're exaggerating,' Mandille sighed.

'Less than you were a moment ago.'

'Nora is intelligent, cultivated, much more cultivated than Carus, and without her he probably wouldn't be so successful . . .'

From time to time, Maigret turned to Lapointe who was listening in silence, motionless by the bar, no doubt dumbfounded by what he heard and by the atmosphere of the Vieux-Pressoir.

'Will you stay for dinner, Monsieur Maigret . . .? If there isn't too much of a rush perhaps I'll be able to come over now and then for a chat . . . There's *mouclade* . . . I never forget that I was born in La Rochelle, where my mother sold fish, so I know some good recipes . . . Have you ever eaten *chaudrée fourrasienne*?'

Maigret rattled off, 'Soup made of eel, baby sole, and cuttlefish . . .'

'Have you been there often?'

'To La Rochelle, yes, and to Fourras . . .'

'Shall I put a *chaudrée* on for you?'

'With pleasure . . .'

When she had gone off, Maigret grunted:

'Your wife doesn't share your opinions about people. If I listened to her I would be arresting François Ricain right away . . .'

'I think you'd be making a mistake.'

'Can you suggest anyone else?'

69

'As the guilty party? . . . No . . . Where was Francis at the time?'

'Here . . . Round about . . . He claims he was roaming Paris looking for Carus or anybody who would lend him some money . . . Wait now . . . He mentioned a club . . .'

'The Club Zéro, I'll bet . . .'

'That's right . . . Near the Rue Jacob . . .'

'Carus often goes there . . . Some other customers of mine, too . . . It's one of the latest smart places to go to . . . It changes every two or three years . . . Sometimes they don't last that long, just a few months . . . It isn't the first time Francis has been short of money, or that he's been round trying to cadge the odd thousand franc note, or notes . . .'

'He didn't find Carus anywhere.'

'Did he try his hotel?'

'I imagine so . . .'

'Then he must have been at Enghien . . . Nora is a great gambler . . . Last year, at Cannes, he left her alone in the casino and when he came back for her, she had sold her jewels and lost the lot . . . Another beer? Wouldn't you prefer an old port?'

'I'd rather have a beer. How about you, Lapointe?'

'A port . . .' Lapointe mumbled, blushing.

'May I use the telephone?'

'In the back on the left . . . Wait . . . I'll give you some counters . . .'

He took a handful from the cash drawer and gave them to Maigret without counting them.

'Hallo! . . . The Inspectors' room? . . . Who's that speaking? Torrence? . . . Any news? . . . Nobody asked for me? . . . Moers? I'll call him when I've finished with you . . .

'Have you had a call from Janvier . . .? He's still at the Hotel des Cigognes? The lad's asleep? . . . Good . . . Yes . . . Good . . . You're going to take the watch over from him? . . . Okay, old man . . . Good night . . . Keep an eye open, though, even so . . .

'If he wakes up there's no telling what he may get up to . . .
One second . . . Could you telephone the River Police . . .?

'Tomorrow morning they should send some frogmen to the
Bir-Hakeim bridge . . . A little above it, forty yards at the
most, they ought to find a revolver thrown in from the bank
. . . Yes . . . Mention my name . . .'

He rang off and dialled the laboratory.

'Moers . . .? I gather you've been trying to get me . . .?
You found the bullet in the wall? What . . .? Probably a 6.35
. . . Well send it to Gastinne-Renette . . . It's possible we'll
have a weapon to show them tomorrow . . . And the prints?
. . . I expect so . . . Everywhere . . . On both of them . . .
And several different people . . . Men and women . . . It
doesn't surprise me, as they can't have cleaned the place very
often . . . Thank you, Moers . . . See you tomorrow . . .'

François Ricain was sleeping, exhausted, in a small bedroom in the Ile-Saint-Louis, as Maigret was about to settle
down to a tasty *chaudrée* in the restaurant where the young
couple used to meet up with their band of friends.

As he left the telephone booth, he could not help smiling as
Fernande, who had suddenly come to life again, was making
animated conversation with Lapointe, who did not know
quite how to react.

71

CHAPTER FOUR

IT WAS A STRANGE EVENING of covert glances, whispers, of comings and goings round the confined floor-space, with the pink light and the good smells from the Vieux-Pressoir's kitchen.

Near the entrance, Maigret had settled himself with Lapointe in a sort of niche where there was a table for two.

'It's the table Ricain and Sophie used to take when they weren't with the others,' Mandille had explained.

Lapointe had his back to the room and every now and then, when the Superintendent pointed out something of interest, he would turn round, as discreetly as possible.

The *chaudrée* was good, and was accompanied by a minor Charentes wine not usually sold commercially, the dry, hard wine used to make cognac.

The one-time tumbler comported himself as master of the house, receiving his customers like guests and shepherding them from the door. He joked with them, kissed the ladies' hands, led them to their tables, and, before the waiter had time, handed them the menu.

Almost always he would then come over to Maigret.

'An architect and his wife . . . They come every Friday, sometimes with their son, who is studying law . . .'

After the architect, two doctors and their wives, at a table for four, regulars as well. One of the doctors was expecting a telephone call, and a few minutes later he collected his bag from the hat-check girl and made his apologies to his table.

Maki the sculptor was eating with a hearty appetite, all by

himself in his corner, helping himself with his fingers more freely than is usually considered polite.

It was eight o'clock when a sallow youth with unhealthy complexion came in and shook hands with him. He didn't join him, but went and sat on a bench-seat, spreading a roneo-typed manuscript in front of him.

'Dramin . . .' Bob announced. 'He usually works while he eats. It's his latest film script, which he's already been made to start again from scratch two or three times . . .'

Most of the customers knew one another, at least by sight, and exchanged direct nods from a distance.

From the descriptions given to him, Maigret at once recognized Carus and, even more easily, Nora, who would have had difficulty in passing unnoticed.

That evening she was not wearing lamé trousers, but a dress in a material almost as transparent as cellophane, and so tight that she appeared to be naked.

Of the face, which was whitened like a clown's, one could only actually see the coal black eyes underlined not just with black and green, but with gold specks which sparkled in the light.

There was something ghostly about her profile, her look, her manner, and the contrast was all the greater with the vitality of the portly Carus, with his solidly hewn features, and his healthy smiling face.

While she followed Bob to the table, he shook hands with Maki, then Dramin, then the one remaining doctor and the two women.

When he in turn had sat down, Bob leaned forward to say a few words to him and the producer's eyes looked round in search of Maigret, coming to rest on him with curiosity. He seemed about to get up to shake hands with Maigret, but first he examined the menu which had been slipped into his hand, and began discussing it with Nora.

When Mandille came back to Maigret's corner, the latter expressed his surprise.

73

'I thought the band all sat at the same table together?'

'Sometimes they do . . . Some evenings, they stay in their own corners. Occasionally they get together over the coffee . . . On other days they all sit down together . . . The customers make themselves at home here . . . We have very little space and we don't encourage it . . .'

'Do they all know?'

'They've read the papers, or heard the news on the radio, of course . . .'

'What are they saying?'

'Nothing . . . It's given them all quite a shock . . . Your presence here must make them feel uncomfortable . . . What will you have to follow the *chaudrée*? . . . My wife recommends the leg of lamb, which is real *pré-salé* meat . . .'

'How about it, Lapointe? . . . Right, then, lamb for two . . .'

'A carafe of red Bordeaux?'

Through the curtains could be seen the lights of the boulevard, the passers-by, some walking faster than others, the occasional couple arm-in-arm, stopping every few paces to embrace or exchange amorous glances.

Dramin, as Bob had predicted, ate with an eye on his manuscript, every now and then taking a pencil from his pocket to make a correction. He was the only one of Ricain's acquaintances not to appear concerned by the presence of the policemen.

He wore a dark suit, ready-made, a nondescript tie. He might have passed for an accountant or a cashier at the bank.

'Carus is debating whether to come and talk to me or not,' declared Maigret, who was observing the couple. 'I don't know what Nora is telling him under her breath, but he doesn't agree.'

He imagined the other evenings, with François Ricain and Sophie coming in, looking round for their friends, wondering whether anybody would invite them to sit with them, or whether they would have to eat alone in their corner. They must have seemed like poor relations.

'Are you planning to question them, chief?'

'Not right now. After the lamb.'

It was very hot. The doctor who had been called to the invalid's bedside was back already, and from his gestures they gathered that he was complaining that he had been disturbed for nothing.

Where had Fernande, the big girl propped against the bar, got to? Bob must have got rid of her. He was deep in conversation, with three or four customers who had taken her place. They were being very familiar and seemed in high spirits.

'The ghost-woman is trying to persuade her husband to do something . . .'

In fact she was talking to him under her breath, without taking her eyes off Maigret, giving Carus advice. What advice?

'He is still hesitating. He is burning to come over and join us, but she's stopping him. I think I'll go over . . .'

Maigret rose heavily, after wiping his lips with his napkin, and threaded his way between the tables. The couple watched him coming, Nora impassively, Carus with visible satisfaction.

'Am I disturbing you?'

The producer rose to his feet, wiped his mouth in his turn, and held out his hand.

'Walter Carus . . . My wife . . .'

'Superintendent Maigret . . .'

'I know . . . Pray sit down . . . Can I offer you a glass of champagne? . . . My wife drinks nothing but champagne, and I must say I can't blame her for that . . . Joseph! . . . A champagne glass for the Superintendent . . .'

'Please, go on with your dinner . . .'

'I need hardly tell you I know the reason for your presence . . . I heard the news just now, on the radio, on my way to the hotel for a shower and a change . . .'

'Did you know the Ricains well?'

'Quite well . . . Here we all know one another . . . He more

75

or less worked for me, in the sense that I've got some money tied up in the film he's working on . . .'

'Didn't his wife play a bit part in another of your films?'

'I'd forgotten . . . More likely as an extra . . .'

'Did she mean to take up the cinema as a profession?'

'Not seriously . . . I don't think so . . . At a certain age most girls want to see themselves on the screen . . .'

'Did she have any talent?'

Maigret had the impression that Nora was kicking Carus under the table, as a warning.

'I must confess to you that I don't know . . . I don't think she even had a screen test . . .'

'And Ricain?'

'You are asking me whether he has any talent?'

'What sort of a person is he, professionally?'

'What would you say, Nora?'

The reply came, icily:

'Nothing . . .'

The remark seemed to fall incongruously and Carus hastened to explain:

'Don't be surprised . . . Nora is a bit psychic . . . She possesses a kind of fluid which puts her in instant contact with certain people and which, with others, has the opposite effect . . . You can take my word for it or not, but this fluid—I can't find any other word to describe it—has often been useful to me in business, even on the Stock Exchange . . .'

Under the table, the foot was at work again.

'With Francis, contact was never established . . . Personally, I find him intelligent, gifted, and I'd be willing to wager that he'll make a fine career for himself . . .

'Now take Dramin, for example, buried in his script over there . . . There's a serious worker for you, who gets the job done as competently as you could wish . . . I've read some excellent dialogues of his . . . But unless I'm completely mistaken, he will never be a big-time director . . . He needs somebody, not only to guide him, but to inject the vital spark . . .'

He was delighted with the word he had just found.

'The spark! . . . That's what is lacking most of the time, and that's essential, as much to the cinema as to television . . . Hundreds of specialists serve you up adequate work, a well-constructed story, a dialogue with no rough edges . . . Only nearly always, for want of something, the result is flat and grey . . . The spark, if you see what I mean . . .

'Well now, you can't count on Francis to provide you with the solid matter . . . His ideas are often preposterous . . . He has suggested I don't know how many ideas which would have been the ruin of me . . . On the other hand, now and then he has the spark . . .'

'In what sphere?'

Carus scratched his nose, comically.

'That's just it . . . You speak like Nora . . . One evening, after dinner, he will express himself in such a way, with such conviction and such fire that you will be persuaded you have a genius on your hands . . . Then, next day, you'll realize that what he was saying doesn't stand up . . . He's young . . . It'll all come out in the wash . . .'

'Does he work for you at the moment?'

'Apart from his reviews, which are remarkable, although somewhat over-ferocious, he doesn't work for anybody . . . He bubbles over with projects, busies himself with several films at the same time, without ever finishing any one of them . . .'

'And does he ask you for advances?'

The feet, under the table, kept up their silent conversation.

'Look, Superintendent, our profession isn't like other professions . . . We are all in search of talent, actors, script-writers and producers . . . It doesn't pay to take a known director who will make you the same film over and over again, and, as for stars, it's a question of finding new faces . . .

'Also we are obliged to gamble on a certain number of promising young people . . . To gamble modestly, otherwise we'd be ruined overnight . . . A thousand francs here, a screen test, a word of encouragement . . .'

77

'In fact, if you lent considerable sums of money to Ricain it was because you hoped to get it back one day . . .'

'Without counting on it too much . . .'

'And Sophie?'

'I had nothing to do with her career . . .

'Did she hope to become a star?'

'Don't make me say more than I already have . . . She was always with her husband and she didn't talk much . . . I think she was shy . . .'

An ironical smile appeared on Nora's pale lips.

'My wife thinks otherwise, and, as I've more confidence in her judgement than I have in my own, don't attach too much weight to my opinions . . .'

'How did Sophie and Francis get on?'

'How do you mean?'

He was feigning surprise.

'Did they seem very close to one another?'

'You seldom saw the one without the other and I don't ever remember them quarrelling in my presence.'

The smile again, enigmatic, on Nora's lips.

'Perhaps she was a bit impatient . . .'

'In what sense?'

'He believed in his star, in the future, a future which he saw as brilliant, and just round the corner . . . I suppose that when she married him she imagined she was about to become the wife of a celebrity . . . Famous and rich . . . Now after more than three years, they were still living from hand to mouth and had nowhere to turn . . .'

'Did she hold it against him?'

'Not in front of other people, as far as I know . . .'

'Did she have any lovers?'

Nora turned to Carus, as if curious to hear his answer.

'You are asking a question which . . .'

'Why not tell the truth?'

For the first time, she was no longer content with signals under the table, and was breaking her silence.

78

'My wife is referring to an incident of no importance . . .'
And Nora, bitingly:

'It depends who to . . .'

'One night we'd all been drinking . . .'

'Where was this?'

'At the Raphael . . . We set off from here . . . Maki was with us . . . Dramin too . . . Then a photographer, Huguet, who works for an advertising firm . . . I think Bob came too . . .

'At the hotel I had some champagne and some whisky sent up . . . Later I went into the bathroom and I had to pass through our room where only the bedside lights were on . . .

'I found Sophie stretched out on one of the twin beds . . . Thinking she was ill I bent over her . . .'

Nora's smile was growing more and more sarcastic.

'She was crying . . . I had the greatest difficulty in getting a few words out of her . . . She eventually admitted to me that she was in despair, and wanted to kill herself . . .'

'And how did I find the two of you?'

'I took her, automatically, into my arms, it's true, as I would to console a child . . .'

'I asked you if she had any lovers. I wasn't thinking particularly of you.'

'She posed in the nude for Maki, but I'm convinced Maki wouldn't touch the wife of a friend . . .'

'Was Ricain jealous?'

'You're asking too much of me, Monsieur Maigret . . . Your good health! . . . It all depends what you mean by jealousy . . . He wouldn't have liked to lose his hold over her, and see another man assume more importance in her eyes . . . In that sense he was jealous of his friends as well . . . If, for example, I invited Dramin to come and have coffee at our table without asking him as well, he would sulk for the rest of the week . . .'

'I think I understand . . .'

'Haven't you had any dessert?'

'I scarcely ever touch it . . .

'Nor does Nora . . . Bob! . . . What do you recommend for pudding?'

'A pancake, *flambée*, with maraschino?'

Comically, Carus considered the rounded contours of his stomach.

'A little more or less . . . Pancakes it is . . . Two or three . . . Armagnac rather than maraschino . . .'

All this time, Lapointe had been growing more and more bored in his corner, with his back to the room. Maki was picking his teeth with a match, doubtless asking himself whether his turn would come shortly to face the Superintendent across the table.

The doctors' table was the merriest and from time to time one of the women gave tongue to a piercing laugh which made Nora wince.

Rose abandoned her ovens for an interval to make a tour of the tables, wiping her hand on her apron before offering it. Like the doctors she, too, was in good spirits, which Sophie's death had done nothing to dampen.

'Well, Walter, you old rascal? . . . How come you've not been seen since Wednesday? . . .'

'I had to fly to Frankfurt, to see a business associate, and from there I went on to London . . .'

'Did you go with him too, dear?'

'Not this trip . . . I had to go for a fitting . . .'

'Aren't you frightened of letting him travel on his own?'

She moved away with a laugh and stopped by another table, then another. Bob was cooking the pancakes on a grill:

'I gather,' he said, 'that Ricain was looking for you for part of the night? . . .'

'Why was he looking for me?'

'It was the Superintendent who told me just now . . . He needed two thousand francs urgently . . . On Wednesday he came round here and asked for you . . .'

'I took the five o'clock plane . . .'

'He came back twice . . . He wanted me to lend him the money, but it was too big a loan for me . . . Then he went on to the club . . .'

'Why did he want two thousand francs?'

'The landlord was threatening to turn him out . . .'

Carus turned to the Superintendent.

'Is that true?'

'That's what he told me . . .'

'Have you arrested him?'

'No. Why?'

'I don't know. A stupid question, now I come to think of it . . .'

'Do you think he could have killed Sophie?'

The feet, still those feet! It was possible literally to follow the conversation under the table, while all the time Nora's face remained frozen.

'I can't see him killing anybody . . . What weapon was used? . . . The papers didn't say . . . The radio didn't mention it either . . .'

'An automatic . . .'

'Francis can't ever have possessed a firearm.'

'On the contrary!' the flat, precise voice of Nora cut in. 'You saw it. That night in his place, and you were scared. He had had a lot to drink. He had just described a hold-up scene to us . . .

'He put one of Sophie's stockings over his head and he began threatening us with a gun, telling us to line up against the wall, with our hands in the air . . . Everyone obeyed, for fun . . .

'You were the only one who was frightened, and asked if the gun was loaded . . .'

'You're quite right . . . It all comes back to me . . . I hadn't given it a second thought . . . I'd had a lot to drink myself . . .'

'In the end he put the gun back in the chest-of-drawers . . .'

'Who was there?' asked Maigret.

81

'The whole gang . . . Maki, Dramin, Pochon . . . Dramin was with a girl I had never seen before and about whom I can remember nothing . . . She was ill and spent an hour in the bathroom . . .'

'Jacques was there too . . .'

'With his wife, yes, who was already pregnant . . .'

'Is anybody aware that, last year, Sophie was almost certainly pregnant as well?'

Why did Nora turn sharply to Carus? The latter looked at her in surprise.

'Did you know?'

'No. If she had a child . . .'

'She didn't have it,' the Superintendent put in. 'She had it aborted between the third and fourth months . . .'

'Then it all passed unnoticed . . .'

Maki was coughing, in his corner, as if to call Maigret to order. It was quite a while since he had finished eating and he was becoming impatient.

'We've told you all we know, Superintendent . . . If you need me, come round and see me in my office . . .'

Did he really wink as he took a visiting card from his wallet and handed it to him?'

Maigret had the impression that Carus had plenty more to say, but that the presence of Nora was holding him back.

*   *   *

Settled in his corner once again, Maigret filled his pipe while Lapointe remarked, with a slight smile:

'He's still hesitating, but he'll be on his feet in a second . . .'

He was referring to Maki. Unable to look directly into the room, to which he had his back turned, the detective had spent his time observing the sculptor, the only person in his field of vision.

'At first, when you were sitting at Carus' table, he was frowning, then he shrugged. He had a carafe of red wine in front of him . . . Less than five minutes later he had emptied

it and signalled the waiter to bring him another one . . .
He didn't miss one of your gestures, or your movements
. . . It was as if he was trying to read everyone's lips . . .

'Soon he became impatient . . . At one moment he called
the proprietor over and talked to him in a low voice . . . The
two of them looked in your direction . . .

'Then he half rose to his feet, after a glance at his watch . . .
I thought he was going to leave, but he ordered an armagnac
which was brought to him in a big glass . . . He's coming
over! . . .'

Lapointe was not mistaken. Doubtless annoyed not to see
Maigret make a move, Maki had decided to approach him
instead. For a moment he stood, immense, between the two
men.

'Excuse me,' he murmured, putting his hand to his head in
a sort of salute. 'I wanted to let you know I was just leaving . . .'

Maigret lit his pipe with a series of little puffs.

'Have a seat, Monsieur Maki . . . Is that your real name?'

Sitting down heavily, the man grumbled:

'Of course not . . . I'm called Lecoeur . . . Not a name for
a sculptor . . . No one would have taken me seriously.'

'Did you know I wanted a word with you?'

'Well, I'm a chum of Francis too . . .'

'How did you hear the news?'

'When I got here . . . I hadn't read the evening paper, and
I never listen to the radio . . .'

'Was it a shock?'

'I'm sorry for Francis . . .'

'Not for Sophie?'

He was not drunk but his cheeks were flushed, his eyes
shining, his gestures exaggerated.

'Sophie was a bitch.'

He looked at them in turn as if defying them to deny it.

'What did he—Monsieur Carus—tell you?'

He pronounced the *Monsieur* ironically, as *Mossieu*, clowning
it.

83

'Naturally, he knows nothing. What about you?'

'What do you expect me to know?'

'When did you last see Francis Ricain and his wife?'

'Him, Wednesday . . .'

'Without her?'

'He was alone.'

'What time?'

'Around half-past ten . . . He spoke to me before going off to find Bob . . . I had finished my dinner and was just having my armagnac . . .'

'What did he say to you?'

'He asked me whether I knew where Carus was . . . I must explain that I, too, work, for that gentleman over there . . . Well, more or less . . . He needed a clay model for some lousy film, a horror film, and I knocked something together for him . . .'

'Did he pay you?'

'Half the agreed price . . . I'm waiting for the other half.'

'Did Francis tell you why he wanted to see Carus?'

'You know very well . . . He needed a couple of thousand francs . . . I hadn't got it . . . I offered him a drink and he went off . . .'

'And you haven't seen him since?'

'Neither him nor her . . . What did that Nora tell you?'

'Not much . . . She doesn't seem to have a very soft spot for Sophie . . .'

'She never had a soft spot for anybody . . . Perhaps that's because she's so flat-chested . . . I beg your pardon . . . That wasn't very witty . . . I can't stand the sight of her . . . Nor him, either, for all his smiles and his handshakes . . . At first sight, they make a very odd couple, he all honey, and she all vinegar, but underneath they're both the same . . .

'When somebody can be of use to them, they squeeze him dry, then they chuck him away like a bit of old orange peel . . .'

'Which is what happened to you?'

'What did they tell you about Francis? You haven't answered me . . .'

'Carus seems to think highly of him.'

'And her?'

'She doesn't like him . . .'

'Did they mention Sophie?'

'They told me a story that happened in the bedroom one night when everybody had been drinking in the Raphael . . .'

'I was there . . .'

'It appears nothing happened between Carus and Sophie . . .'

'My eye!'

'Did you see them?'

'I went into the room twice, to go to the lavatory, without them noticing . . . She tried once with me, too . . . She wanted me to make a sculpture modelled on her, me, an abstract . . . I ended by giving in to be rid of her . . .'

'Were you her lover?'

'I had to sleep with her, out of politeness. She would have held it against me if I hadn't done it . . . I didn't feel very pleased with myself, because of Francis . . . He didn't deserve to marry a tramp . . .'

'Did she talk about suicide to you as well?'

'Suicide? Her? In the first place, when a woman talks about it, you can be sure she will never do it . . . She play-acted . . . With everybody . . . With a different role for each person . . .'

'Did Francis know?'

Maigret was starting to call him Francis, as well, as if he was gradually becoming intimately acquainted with Ricain.

'If you want my opinion, he suspected it . . . He closed his eyes, but it infuriated him . . . Did he really love her? . . . There are times when I wonder . . . He pretended to . . . He had taken her on and he didn't want to let her go . . . She must have convinced him that she would kill herself if he left her . . .'

'Do you think he's talented?'

'More than talented . . . Of all of us, he's the only one who

85

will do something really important . . . I'm not bad in my field, but I know my limitations . . . Him, well, the day he really gets down to it . . .'

'Thank you, Monsieur Maki . . .'

'Just plain Maki . . . It's a name which doesn't go with the Monsieur . . .'

'Good-night, Maki . . .'

'Good-night, Superintendent . . . And this, I presume, is one of your detectives? . . . Good-night to you, too . . .'

He went off, with a heavy tread, after a wave to Bob.

Maigret mopped his brow.

'There's only one left; Dramin, with his nose in his script, but I've had enough for tonight . . .'

He looked round for the waiter, asked for the bill. It was Mandille who came running over:

'Allow me to consider both of you as my guests . . .'

'Impossible . . .' said Maigret with a sigh.

'Will you at least accept a glass of old armagnac?'

They had to go through with it.

'Have you got the information you wanted?'

'I've begun to find my way round the group . . .'

'They aren't all here . . . And the atmosphere changes from day to day . . . Some evenings it's very gay, even wild . . . Haven't you spoken to Gérard? . . .'

He was referring to Dramin, who was heading for the door, script in hand.

'Hey! Gérard . . . Let me introduce Superintendent Maigret and one of his detectives . . . Will you have a drink with us?'

Very short-sighted, he wore thick glasses and held his head bent forward.

'How do you do? . . . I beg your pardon . . . I have some work to finish . . . By the way, has Francis been arrested?'

'No, why? . . .'

'I don't know . . . Excuse me . . .'

He unhooked his hat from the hat-peg, opened the door, and set off along the pavement.

'You mustn't pay any attention to him ... He is always like that ... I think it's a pose, a way of making himself seem important ... He does his absent-minded act, the solitary figure ... Perhaps he feels resentful that you didn't go and seek him out ... I bet he hasn't read a line all evening ...'

'Your good health ...' murmured Maigret. 'For myself, I'll be glad to get to bed ...'

Even so, he passed the Rue Saint-Charles with Lapointe, and rapped on the studio door. Lourtie opened it. He had taken off his jacket and his hair was dishevelled from sleeping in the armchair. The room was lit only by a night-light and the smell of the disinfectant had still not dispersed.

'Has nobody called?'

'Two reporters ... I didn't tell them anything, except to apply to the Quari ...'

'No telephone calls?'

'There were a couple.'

'Who?'

'I don't know ... I heard the phone ring ... I picked it up and said "Hello" ... I heard breathing the other end, but the caller said nothing and soon rang off ...'

'Both times?'

'Both times.'

'What sort of times?'

'The first time around ten past eight, the second a few moments ago ...'

A few minutes later, Maigret was dozing in the small black car taking him home.

'I'm tired out,' he confessed to his wife as he started to undress.

'I hope you had a good dinner?'

'Too good ... I must take you to that restaurant ... It's kept by an old comic opera singer who has turned her hand to cooking ... She makes a *chaudrée* like you have never ...'

'What time tomorrow?'

'Seven o'clock.'

'So early?'

So early, in fact, that it was seven o'clock straight away, without any transition. Maigret did not even have the sensation that he had been asleep before he could smell coffee and his wife was touching him on the shoulder on her way over to draw back the curtains.

The sun was clear and tepid. It was a delight to open the window as he awoke and to hear the sparrows chattering.

'I suppose I shouldn't expect you at lunch time?'

'I probably won't have time to come back to eat . . . It's a strange case . . . Strange people . . . I'm in the film world, and as in the films, everything started with a gag, with the theft of my wallet . . .'

'Do you think he was the killer?'

Madame Maigret, too, who only knew the case from the newspapers and the radio, was annoyed with herself for asking the question.

'I'm sorry . . .'

'In any case, I would be hard put to it to answer you . . .

'Aren't you going to put on your light coat?'

'No . . . The weather is the same as yesterday's and yesterday I wasn't cold . . . Not even on my way home last night . . .'

He didn't wait for the bus, but hailed a taxi and had himself dropped on the Ile Saint-Louis. Opposite the Hôtel des Cignognes there was a bistro surrounded by piles of wood and sacks of coal. Torrence, his cheeks hollow with fatigue, was drinking a coffee when the Superintendent joined him.

'How did the night go?'

'Like all night watches . . . Nothing happened, except that I know that the time that everyone turns out his lights . . . There must be someone ill, on the fourth floor, right-hand side, as there was a light in the window until six o'clock in the morning . . .

'Your friend Ricain didn't go out . . . Some of the guests came back . . . A taxi for a couple of travellers . . . A dog attached itself to me and followed me about most of the night . . . That's about it . . .'

'You can go home and sleep . . .'

'And my report?'

'You can do it tomorrow.'

He went into the hotel, where he had known the manager for thirty years. It was a modest establishment which seldom took in anybody apart from regulars, almost all of them from eastern France, since the owner was from Alsace.

'Is my guest awake?'

'He rang just ten minutes ago to ask for a cup of coffee to be sent up and some croissants . . . They've just been taken in to him . . .'

'What did he eat yesterday evening?'

'Nothing . . . He must have gone to sleep right away as when we knocked on his door at around seven o'clock there was no answer . . . What is he? . . . An important witness? . . . A suspect? . . .'

There was no lift. Maigret climbed the four flights on foot, reached the landing breathing hard, and paused for a moment before knocking on number 43.

'Who is it?'

'Maigret.'

'Come in.'

Pushing aside the tray on the blanket, Francis emerged from the bed, his skinny chest bare, his face covered in a bluish beard, his eyes feverish. He still had a croissant in one hand.

'Excuse my not getting up, but I haven't any pyjamas . . .'

'Did you sleep well?'

'Like a log . . . I slept so soundly that my head is still heavy . . . What's the time?'

'A quarter-past eight . . .'

The room, small and ill-furnished, gave on to the courtyard and the roofs. Through the half-open window could be heard voices from the neighbouring houses, cries of children from a school playground.

89

'Have you found out anything?'

'I had dinner at the Vieux-Pressoir.

Ricain was watching him narrowly, already on the defensive, and one could sense that he felt the whole world thought he was a liar.

'Were they there?'

'The Carus' were . . .'

'What did he have to say?'

'He swears you're some kind of genius.'

'I presume Nora took the trouble to point out that I'm actually an imbecile?'

'More or less . . . She certainly likes you less than he does.

'And she liked Sophie even less!'

'Maki was there too.'

'Drunk?'

'Towards the end, only, he became a little unsteady.'

'He's all right.'

'He's sure you will be somebody one day, too.'

'Which means that I am nobody . . .'

He didn't finish his croissant. Maigret's arrival seemed to have killed his appetite.

'What do they think happened? That I killed Sophie?'

'To tell the truth, nobody thinks you're guilty, However, some of them imagine that the police think differently, and everyone asked me whether I had arrested you.'

'What did you say?'

'The truth.'

'Namely?'

'That you're free.'

'Do you really think that's the truth? What am I doing here? You may as well admit it, you had a man on duty all night outside the hotel . . .'

'Did you see him?'

'No, but I know how it goes . . . And now, what are you planning to do with me? . . .'

Maigret was asking himself exactly the same question. He

didn't want to let Ricain wander freely about Paris, and on the other hand he did not have sufficient grounds to arrest him.

'First of all I am going to ask you to come with me to the Quai des Orfèvres.'

'Again?'

'I may have several questions to put to you . . . Between now and then the frogmen of the River Police may have found your revolver . . .'

'What difference does it make whether they find it or not?'

'You have a razor and some soap . . . There is a shower at the end of the corridor . . . I will be waiting for you downstairs, or outside . . .'

A new day was beginning, as clear, as balmy as the day before and the day before that, but it was too early yet to know what it would bring.

François Ricain intrigued the Superintendent and the opinions he had gathered the day before did nothing to make him less fascinating.

By any standards, he was a youth out of the ordinary, and Carus had been impressed by his possibilities. But then didn't Carus become carried away every time he was confronted with an artist, only to let him drop a few months or a few weeks later?

Maigret resolved to go and see him in his office, where the producer had given him an enigmatic rendezvous. He had something to say to him, something he did not want to talk about in front of Nora. She had sensed it, and the Superintendent wondered whether Carus would be in the Rue de Bassano that morning, or whether his mistress would prevent him from going.

So far, he had only touched the periphery of a circle of which there are thousands, tens of thousands, in Paris, composed of friends, relations, colleagues, lovers and mistresses, regular customers at a café or restaurant, little groups which form, cling together for a while and disperse to form into other more or less homogeneous little groups.

What was the name of the photographer who had been married twice, had children by both wives, and had just given another to a new mistress?

He was still confusing the names, the places corresponding to each of them. The fact was, Sophie's murder had been committed by someone intimately acquainted with the household—or with the young girl herself. Otherwise, she would not have opened the door.

Unless someone had a key?

He was pacing to and fro, as Torrence had done all night, but he had the good fortune to be walking in the sun. The street was teeming with housewives who turned round to look at this figure who was walking up and down, hands behind his back, like a schoolmaster supervising a school break.

Yes, he had plenty of questions to put to Francis . . . And, no doubt, he was about to be faced once again with a moody animal, in turns bridling and calming down, suspicious, impatient, suddenly giving a roar . . .

'I'm ready . . .'

Maigret pointed to the bistro with the sacks of coal.

'Don't you want a drink?'

'No, thank you.'

A pity, as Maigret would have been most agreeable to starting off this spring day with a glass of white wine.

CHAPTER FIVE

IT WAS A BAD PATCH to get through. In nearly all of his cases, Maigret came across this period of suspense, during which, as his colleagues used to whisper, he appeared to be ruminating.

During the first stage, that is to say when he suddenly found himself face to face with a new world, with people he knew nothing about, it was as if he was breathing in the life around him, mechanically, and filling himself with it like a sponge.

He had done this the day before at the Vieux-Pressoir, his memory registering, without his realizing it, the smallest details of the atmosphere, the gestures, the facial quirks of each person.

If he had not felt himself flagging, he would have gone on afterwards to the Club Zéro which some members of the circle frequented.

At present he had absorbed a quantity of impressions, a whole jumble of images, of phrases that had been uttered, of words of varying importance, of surprised looks, but he did not yet know what to do with them all.

His close acquaintances knew that it was best not to ask him questions nor to give him inquiring looks, as he would quickly turn nasty.

As he expected, a note, on his desk, asked him to call Camus, the magistrate.

'Hallo! . . . Maigret here . . .'

He had seldom worked with this magistrate, whom he classed neither among the outright meddlers, nor among the ones who prudently leave the police time to get on with their work.

'I asked you to ring as I had a call from the Public Prosecutor's Office . . . He is impatient to know where the inquiry has got to . . .'

The Superintendent almost growled:

'Nowhere.'

Which was true. A crime does not pose a problem of algebra. It involves human beings, unknown the day before, who were just passers-by among the rest. And now, all of a sudden, each one of their gestures, their words, takes on an importance, and their very existence is examined with a fine toothcomb.

'The inquiry is going ahead,' he said instead. 'It's likely that we'll have the murder weapon in our hands within an hour or two. The frogmen are scouring the bottom of the Seine for it.'

'What have you done with the husband?'

'He's here, in the icebox.'

He corrected himself, as it was an expression which could only mean anything to the detectives in his squad. When they didn't know what to do with a witness, but still wanted to keep him on a string, or when they had a suspect who was not being co-operative they put him in the '*glacière*'.

They would tell them, as they showed them into the long glass-lined waiting room which ran along one side of the corridor:

'Just wait in here a moment, please . . .'

There were always people in there waiting, nervous women, some weeping and dabbing their eyes with their handkerchiefs, would-be tough customers trying to put on a bold front, some honest citizens who waited patiently, staring at the pale green walls, wondering whether their existence had been forgotten.

An hour or two in the *glacière* was often enough to make people talkative. Witnesses determined to say nothing became more amenable.

Sometimes they were 'forgotten' for more than half the day, and they would keep watching the door, half rising to their

94

eet every time the attendant came over, hoping it was their turn at last.

They could see the Inspectors going off at noon, and would take their courage in both hands to go and ask Joseph:

'Are you sure the Superintendent knows that I am here?'

'He's still in conference.'

For want of a better solution, Maigret had put Ricain in the *glacière*.

He translated, for the magistrate:

'He's in the waiting-room. I'll be interrogating him again, as soon as I have more information.'

'What is your impression? Guilty?'

Another question which the magistrate would not have asked if he had worked longer with Maigret.

'I have no impressions.'

It was true. He was waiting as long as possible before forming an opinion. And he still had not started 'forming'. He was keeping his mind free until evidence of fact imposed itself or until his prisoner broke down.

'Do you think it will be a long business?'

'I hope not.'

'Have you discarded the possibility of a simple sordid crime?'

As though all crimes weren't sordid! They didn't speak the same language, they didn't have the same concept of a human being at the Law Courts as they did at Police Headquarters.

It was difficult to accept that an unknown man, in quest of money, could have presented himself at the Rue Saint-Charles after ten o'clock at night, and that Sophie Ricain, already in her night-dress, would have let him into the studio without being suspicious.

Either her killer had a key, or else it was somebody she knew and trusted. Especially if the murderer had had to open the drawer in the chest in her presence and take out the revolver.

'Kindly keep me informed . . . Don't leave me too long

without news . . . The Prosecutor's Office is getting impatient . . .'

All right! The Prosecutor's Office is always impatient. Gentlemen who live comfortably in their offices and who only see crime in terms of legal texts and statistics. A telephone call from the Minister's offices makes them tremble in their shoes.

'How is it that nobody has been arrested yet?'

The Prosecutor himself was under pressure from the impatience of the newspapers. What they like is a really good crime which brings in a spectacular new angle every day. If the reader is kept in suspense too long, he forgets about the case. And some nice front page headlines are gone to waste.

'Certainly, Monsieur le Juge . . . Yes, Monsieur le Juge . . . I'll call you, Monsieur le Juge . . .'

He winked at Janvier.

'Go and take a look in the corridor every so often to see how he's reacting . . . He's the kind that'll either have a nervous breakdown or else will come and beat on my door . . .'

In spite of it all he went through his mail and attended the morning conference, where he saw his colleagues and where they discussed without emotion several of the cases that were in hand.

'Anything new, Maigret?'

'Nothing new, Monsieur le Directeur.'

Here, they didn't insist. One was among professionals.

When the Superintendent returned to his office, just before ten o'clock, the River Police were asking for him.

'Have you found the weapon?'

'It so happens that the current is rather weak these days and the Seine was dragged at this point last autumn. My men found the weapon almost immediately, at about ten yards from the left bank, a 6.35 Belgian-made automatic. There were still five bullets left.'

'Will you send it round to Gastinne-Renette?'

And, to Janvier:

96

'Will you see to it? He's got the bullet already.'

'Right, chief.'

Maigret was on the point of ringing up the Rue de Bassano, decided not to announce himself, and set off for the main staircase, taking care not to look towards the waiting-room.

His departure could not have escaped the notice of Ricain, who must have wondered where he was going. He ran into Lapointe on his way in and instead of taking a taxi, as he intended, had himself driven to the building where Carus had his offices.

He paused to read the copper name-plates in the entrance arch, noting that there was a film company on almost every floor. The company he was concerned with was called Carrosoc and its reception suite was on the first floor.

'Shall I come with you?'

'I'd prefer you to.'

Not only was it his way of doing things, but it was recommended in the manual of instructions for officers of the Police Judiciaire.

A somewhat dark entrance hall, with a single window giving on to the courtyard, where a chauffeur could be seen polishing a Rolls-Royce. A red-headed secretary at the telephone switchboard.

'Monsieur Carus please?'

'I don't know if he's in.'

As if he did not have to pass her to reach the other offices!

'What name shall I say? ... Have you an appointment? ...'

'Superintendent Maigret.'

She rose, endeavouring to lead him to the ante-room, to put them, in their turn, in the *glacière*.

'Thank you ... We'll wait here ...'

She was patently displeased by that one. Instead of telephoning her boss, she went through a padded door and disappeared for three or four minutes.

She was not the first person to reappear. Instead it was

Carus in person, in light grey worsted, freshly shaved and imparting a smell of lavender.

He had evidently just come from his barber and no doubt he had had a face massage. He was just the type to take his ease every morning for a good half hour in the articulated chair.

'How are you, my friend?'

He held out a cordial hand to the good friend he had not even known at six o'clock the previous evening.

'Come in, I beg you . . . You, too, young man . . . I presume this is one of your colleagues?'

'Inspector Lapointe . . .'

'You may leave us, mademoiselle . . . I'm not in to anybody and I won't take any calls, unless it's New York.'

He explained, with a smile:

'I hate to be interrupted by the telephone . . .'

There were none the less three of them on his desk. The room was enormous, the walls covered in beige leather to match the armchairs, the thick pile carpet a very soft chestnut colour.

As for the immense Brazilian rosewood desk, it was piled high with enough files to keep a dozen secretaries busy.

'Pray be seated . . . What can I offer you? . . .'

He went over to a low piece of furniture which turned out to be a sizeable bar.

'It's a little early for an apéritif, perhaps, but I happened to observe that you are a connoisseur of beer . . . So am I . . . I have some excellent beer, which I have sent directly from Munich . . .'

He was being even more expansive than the day before, perhaps because he did not have to bother about Nora's reactions.

'Yesterday, you caught me unawares . . . On my way to have dinner, as I often do, at the restaurant kept by my old friend Bob, I was not expecting to meet you . . . I had had two or three whiskies before I got there, and what with the champagne . . . I wasn't drunk . . . I never am . . . Even so,

98

I have only a rather hazy recollection this morning of certain details of our conversation . . . My wife reproached me for talking too much and too enthusiastically . . . Your good health! . . . I hope that's not the impression I gave you?'

'You appear to consider François Ricain as somebody worthwhile, with every chance of becoming one of our leading film directors . . .'

'I must have said that, yes . . . It's in my nature to be open with young people, and I express my enthusiasm very readily . . .'

'You are no longer of the same opinion?'

'Oh yes! Oh yes! With, however, certain nuances . . . I find a tendency, in this young man, towards disorder, towards anarchy . . . At one moment he will show too much self-confidence and at the next he has none at all . . .'

'If I remember your words correctly, in your opinion they were a very devoted couple.'

Carus had settled himself down in one of the armchairs with legs crossed, glass in one hand, cigar in the other.

'Did I say that?'

He suddenly changed his mind and sprang to his feet, put the obstructing glass down on a console table, took several puffs at his cigar, and started pacing the carpet.

'Listen, Superintendent, I was hoping you would come round this morning . . .'

'That's what I gathered.'

'Nora is an exceptional woman . . . Although she never so much as sets foot in my offices, I could describe her as the best business colleague I have . . .'

'You mentioned her gifts as a medium . . .'

He waved a hand as if to erase words written on an invisible blackboard.

'That's what I say in her presence, because it pleases her . . . The truth is that she has got solid common-sense and that she is seldom wrong in her assessment of people . . . Personally I get carried away . . . I trust people too readily . . .'

99

'In effect, she's a sort of safety catch?'

'If you like . . . I've made up my mind quite definitely, when my divorce is through, to make her my wife . . . It's already as if . . .'

He was obviously getting into difficulties, searching for words, while his eyes remained fixed on his cigar ash.

'Well . . . How can I put it? . . . Although Nora's a superior being, she still can't help being jealous . . . That's why yesterday, in her presence, I was obliged to lie to you . . .'

'The bedroom incident?'

'Precisely . . . It didn't happen as I recounted it, of course . . . It is true that Sophie took refuge in the room to go and cry as a result of the cruel words which Nora had spoken about her . . . I don't remember what they were, as we had all been drinking . . . In short, I went up to comfort her . . .'

'Was she your mistress?'

'If you insist on the word . . . She flung herself into my arms, one thing led to another, and we were imprudent, very imprudent . . .'

'Did your wife see it happening?'

'A Superintendent would not have hesitated to corroborate a charge of adultery . . .'

He smiled, with a touch of satisfaction.

'Tell me, Monsieur Carus. I presume pretty girls must pass through your offices every day. Most of them are ready to do anything to land a part.'

'That is correct.'

'I believe I am right in thinking that you have been known to take advantage of this circumstance.'

'I make no secret of it . . .'

'Even from Nora?'

'Let me explain . . . If I take advantage, as you put it, on a pretty girl now and then, Nora doesn't let it upset her too much on condition that there is no future . . . It's part of the job . . . All men do the same, unless they don't have the opportunity . . . Even you yourself, Superintendent . . .'

Maigret looked at him stonily, unsmiling.

'Excuse me, if I have shocked you . . . Where was I ? . . . I am not unaware that you have questioned some of my friends and that you will continue to do so . . . I prefer to be quite straight with you . . . You have heard the way Nora talks about Sophie . . .

'I would prefer you did not form an impression of the girl from those words . . .

'She wasn't ambitious, on the contrary, and nor was she the girl to sleep with just anybody . . .

'She had been drawn to Ricain on an impulse when she was still very young, and it was fatal, as he has a kind of magnetism . . . Women are impressed by men who are tortured, ambitious, bitter, violent . . .'

'Is that your picture of him?'

'And yours?'

'I don't know yet.'

'In short, he married her . . . She put her trust in him . . . She followed him about like a well-trained small dog, keeping her mouth shut when he didn't want her to talk, taking up as little space as possible so as not to get in his way, and accepting the precarious life he led.'

'Was she unhappy?'

'She suffered, but she took care not to let it be seen . . . Well, while he needed her, her passive presence, there were moments when he became irritated with her, complaining that she was a dead weight, an obstacle to his career, accusing her of being a dumb animal . . .'

'Did she tell you this?'

'I had already guessed it, from remarks made in my presence . . .'

'Did you become her confidant?'

'If you like to put it that way . . . In spite of myself, I assure you . . . She felt herself lost in a world too hard for her, and she had nobody to turn to . . .'

'At what period did you become her lover?'

'Another word I dislike . . . It was mostly pity, tenderness which I felt for her . . . My intention was to help her . . .'

'To make a career in the cinema?'

'I'm going to surprise you, but it was my idea and she resisted it . . . She was not a striking beauty, one of those women who make heads turn in the street like Nora . . .

'I have a pretty good instinct for the public's tastes . . . If I hadn't, I wouldn't be doing the job I do . . . With her some-what ordinary face, and her small, rather fragile body, Sophie was exactly the image of the young girl as most people imagine her to be . . .

'Parents would have been able to recognize their daughter, young people their cousin or their best friend . . . Do you see what I mean? . . .'

'Did you have plans to launch her?'

'Let's say I was thinking about it . . .'

'Did you tell her about it?'

'Not in so many words. I sounded her out discreetly . . .

'Where did your meetings take place?'

'That is an unpleasant question, but I am obliged to answer it, am I not?'

'Especially since I would find out for myself.'

'Well, I've rented a furnished studio, quite chic, quite comfortable, in a new block of flats in the Rue François-Premier . . . To be exact it's the big block on the corner of the Avenue Georges V . . . I only have three hundred yards to walk from here . . .'

'One second. This studio, was it exclusively intended for your rendezvous with Sophie, or was it for the other ones as well?'

'In theory, it was for Sophie . . . It was difficult for us to find privacy here and I couldn't go to her house either.'

'You never went there when her husband was away?'

'Once or twice . . .'

'Recently?'

'The last time was a fortnight ago . . . She hadn't tele-

phoned me as she usually did . . . I didn't see her in the Rue
François-Premier either . . . I called her at home and she told
me she wasn't feeling well . . .'

'Was she ill?'

'Depressed . . . Francis was becoming more and more
nervy . . . Sometimes he was even violent . . . She was at the
end of her endurance and wanted to go away, anywhere, work
as a sales-girl in the first store she came across . . .'

'Did you advise her to do nothing?'

'I gave her the address of one of my lawyers to consult about
the possibility of a divorce . . . It would have been better
for both of them . . .'

'Had she made up her mind?'

'She was hesitating . . . She felt sorry for Francis . . . She
felt it her duty to stay with him, until he became a success . . .'

'Did she talk to him about it?'

'Certainly not . . .'

'How can you be so sure?'

'Because he would have reacted violently . . .'

'I would like to ask you a question, Monsieur Carus.
Think carefully before answering, as I won't hide from you
the fact that it is important. You knew that, about a year
ago, Sophie was pregnant.'

He flushed scarlet all of a sudden, nervously stubbed out his
cigar in the glass ash-tray.

'Yes, I knew . . .' he muttered, sitting down again. 'But I
can tell you right away, that I can swear by all that's dear to
me in this world, that the child was not mine . . . I noticed
that she was upset, preoccupied . . . I mentioned it to her . . .
She admitted that she was expecting a child and that Francis
would be furious . . .'

'Why?'

'Because it would be another burden, another obstacle to
his career . . . He was on the bread line . . . With a child . . .
In short, she was sure he would never forgive her and she
asked me for the address of a midwife or a compliant doctor .. '

'Did you oblige her?'

'I am bound to admit that I transgressed the law . . .'

'It's a bit late now to pretend anything else.'

'I did her that small service . . .'

'Francis knew nothing about it?'

'No . . . He's too wrapped up in himself to notice what is going on around him, even when it concerns his wife . . .'

He rose hesitantly and, no doubt to restore his composure, went to fetch some fresh bottles from the bar.

* * *

Everyone called him Monsieur Gaston, with a respectful familiarity, for he was a conscientious and worthy man, aware of the responsibilities which weigh upon the shoulders of the porter of a great hotel. He had spotted Maigret before the latter had entered the revolving doors, and had puckered his brows while there quickly flashed through his mind the faces of the hotel guests liable to have earned him this visit from the police.

'Wait here for a moment, Lapointe . . .'

He waited himself for an old lady to check the time of arrival of an aeroplane from Buenos Aires before discreetly shaking Monsieur Gaston's hand.

'Don't worry. Nothing unpleasant.'

'When I see you coming, I can't help wondering . . .'

'If I am not mistaken, Monsieur Carus has a suite here, on the fourth floor?'

'That's right . . . With Madame Carus . . .'

'Is she registered in that name?'

'Well, it's the name we give her here . . .'

A whisper of a smile sufficed to make Monsieur Gaston's meaning clear.

'Is she upstairs?'

A glance at the key-board.

'I don't know why I look . . . A habit . . . At this hour she'll certainly be having her breakfast . . .'

'Monsieur Carus has been away this week, hasn't he?'

'Wednesday and Thursday . . .'

'Did he go alone?'

'His chauffeur took him to Orly around five o'clock . . . I think he had to take the plane to Frankfurt . . .'

'When did he come back?'

'Yesterday afternoon, from London . . .'

'Although you aren't here at night yourself, perhaps you have a way of finding out if Madame Carus went out on Wednesday evening and at what time she came home?'

'That's easy . . .'

He leafed through the pages of a big register bound in black.

'When they come home in the evening, the guests usually stop for a moment to tell my colleague on the night-shift what time they want to be called and what they will have for breakfast.

'Madame Carus never fails . . . The times they come in aren't noted down, but according to the order of the names on the page, it's possible to fix an approximate time . . .

'Wait now . . . There are only a dozen names for Wednesday, before hers . . . Miss Trevor . . . An early bedder, an old lady who always comes home before ten o'clock . . . the Maxwells . . . At first glance, I would say she came back before midnight, say between ten o'clock and midnight . . . At any rate, before the theatres finished . . . I'll ask the night porter this evening to confirm it . . .'

'Thank you. Would you announce me?'

'Do you want to see her? . . . Do you know her? . . .'

'I had coffee yesterday evening with her and her husband. Let us say it's a courtesy visit.'

'Put me through to 403, please . . . Hallo? . . . Madame Carus? . . . The hall porter here . . . Superintendent Maigret is asking if he can come up . . . Yes . . . Right . . . I'll tell him . . .'

And, to Maigret:

'She asks you to wait ten minutes . . .'

Was it to finish that fearful and elaborate ritual of making herself up, or was it to telephone the Rue de Bassano?

The Superintendent rejoined Lapointe, and the two of them wandered in silence from show-case to show-case, admiring the stones exhibited by the leading Parisian jewellers, as well as the fur coats and the underwear.

'Aren't you thirsty?'

'No, thank you . . .'

They had the unpleasant sensation of being followed by pairs of eyes, and it was a relief when the ten minutes were up and they went into one of the lifts.

'Fourth floor.'

Nora, who came and let them in, was wearing a pale green satin dressing-gown matching her eyes, and her hair seemed more discoloured than the day before, almost white.

The sitting-room was enormous, with light coming in from two bay windows, one of which opened on to a balcony.

'I wasn't expecting your visit and you caught me as I was getting up . . .'

'I hope we are not interrupting your breakfast?'

The tray was not in the room, but probably next door.

'It's not my husband you want to see? . . . He left for the office a long time ago . . .'

'It's you I would like to put a few questions to as I am passing by. Of course, there's no obligation to answer. First of all, a question I am putting, as a matter of routine, to everybody who knew Sophie Ricain. Don't read anything into it. Where were you on Wednesday night?'

Without flinching, she sat down in a white armchair and asked:

'At what time?'

'Where did you have dinner?'

'Just a moment . . . Wednesday? . . . Yesterday, you were with us . . . On Thursday I dined alone at Fouquet's, not in the first floor dining-room, which is where I go when I'm

with Carus, but on the ground floor, at a small table . . .
Wednesday . . . On Wednesday, I didn't have any dinner,
that's all there is to it . . .

'I should tell you that apart from a light breakfast I normally only have one meal a day . . . If I have lunch, I don't
dine . . . So, if I dine it's because I didn't eat lunch . . . On
Wednesday we lunched at the Berkeley with friends . . .

'In the afternoon I went to a fitting, just round the corner
from here . . . Then, I had a drink at Jean's in the Rue
Marbeuf . . . It must have been around nine o'clock when I
came in . . .'

'Did you go straight up to your suite?'

'That's right . . . I read until one o'clock in the morning,
as I can't get to sleep early . . . Before that I looked at
television . . .'

There was a set in the corner of the room.

'Don't ask me what programme it was. All I know is that
there were young singers, boys and girls . . . Do you want me
to call the floor waiter? . . . True, it's not the same . . . But
tonight you can question the night waiter . . .

'Did you order anything?'

'A quarter of a bottle of champagne . . .'

'At what time?'

'I don't know . . . Shortly before preparing to go to bed . . .
Do you suspect me of going to the Rue Saint-Charles and
murdering that wretched Sophie?'

'I don't suspect anybody. I am only doing my duty, and
in the process trying to be as unobtrusive as possible. Yesterday
evening you referred to Sophie Ricain in terms which implied
a lack of warmth between the two of you.'

'I made no effort to hide it . . .'

'There was talk of an evening here, when you found her
in your husband's arms . . .'

'I oughtn't to have brought it up . . . It was just to show
you that she would throw herself at any man that came along,
and that she wasn't the little white lamb or the timid little

107

devoted slave of Francis that certain people have doubtless described . . .'

'Who have you in mind?'

'I don't know . . . Men tend to let themselves be taken in by that sort of act . . . Among most of the people we mix with I probably pass as a cold, ambitious, calculating woman . . . Go on, say it! . . .'

'Nobody has spoken to me in such terms . . .'

'I'm sure that's what they think . . . Even a person like Bob, who ought to know better . . . Little Sophie, on the other hand, all sweet and submissive, becomes the misunderstood girl in love . . . You can think what you like . . . I'm telling you the truth . . .'

'Was Carus her lover?'

'Who says so?'

'You told me yourself that you had surprised them . . .'

'I said she had thrown herself into his arms, that she was snivelling to get sympathy, but I never claimed Carus was her lover . . .'

'All the others were, weren't they? Isn't that what I'm meant to understand?'

'Question them . . . We'll see if they dare to deny it . . .'

'And Ricain?'

'You put me in an awkward position . . . It's not up to me to pass final judgement on people we mix with and who are not necessarily friends . . . Did I say Francis knew what was going on? . . . It's possible . . . I don't remember . . . I am in the habit of speaking my mind, in the heat of the moment . . .

'Carus was flattered by the boy, and insisted that he had a fantastic future before him . . . Personally, I regard him as a little con-man posing as an artist . . . You can take your pick . . .'

Maigret rose, pulling his pipe from his pocket.

'That's all I wanted to ask you. Ah! Just one small question. Sophie had started to have a child, a year ago now.'

'I know . . .'

108

'Did she tell you about it?'

'She was two or three months pregnant, I forget which . . . Francis didn't want a child, because of his career . . . So, she asked me if I knew an address . . . She had heard about Switzerland, but was hesitating to make the journey . . .'

'Were you able to help her?'

'I told her I knew no one . . . I was not keen for Carus and myself to become involved in that sort of thing . . .'

'How did it end?'

'Well, no doubt, from her point of view, since she made no further mention of it and she didn't have a child . . .'

'Thank you . . .'

'Haven't you been to Carus' office?'

Maigret answered the question with another:

'Hasn't he telephoned?'

He was making sure, in this way, that once she was on her own the young woman would ring the Rue de Bassano.

'Thank you, Gaston . . .' he said, as he passed the hall porter.

Out on the pavement he took a deep breath.

'If it ends up with a general confrontation of witnesses, it should be quite an exciting event.'

As though to wash out his mouth, he went and drank a glass of white wine in the first bar he passed. He had been wanting one all morning, ever since the events of the Rue Saint-Louis-en-l'Ile, and Carus' beer had not removed the urge.

'To the Quai, Lapointe, my boy. I'm curious to see what sort of a state our Francis is in.'

He was not in the *glacière*, where there was only an old lady to be seen together with a very young man with a broken nose. In his office he found Janvier who gestured towards Ricain, fuming in a chair.

'I had to let him in here, chief. He was making so much noise in the corridor, demanding the attendant to let him in to see the Director, threatening to tell all the newspapers . . .'

'I'm within my rights . . .!' stormed the youth. 'I've had enough of being treated like an imbecile or a criminal . . . My wife has been killed and it's me who's being watched, as if I was trying to escape . . . I'm not left one moment's peace and . . .'

'Do you wish for a lawyer?'

Francis looked him in the eyes, hesitantly, his pupils dilated with hatred.

'You . . . you . . .'

His anger was preventing him from finding words.

'You give yourself paternal airs . . . You must love yourself for being so kind, so patient, so understanding . . . I thought so too . . . Now I see that everything they say about you is just hot air.'

He was becoming incoherent, his words came tumbling on top of one another, his delivery getting faster and faster.

'How much do you pay them, the newspapermen, to flatter you? . . . What a damn fool I was . . . When I saw your name in the wallet I thought I was saved, that I had found someone at last who would understand . . .

'I called you . . . For without my telephone call you wouldn't have found me . . . With your money, I'd have been able . . . When I think I didn't even take the price of a meal . . .

'And what's the result? You shut me up in a crummy hotel bedroom . . . With a detective standing guard on the pavement . . .

'Then you put me into your rat-trap and every now and then your men come and take a peek at me through the glass . . . I totted up at least twelve who gave themselves this little treat . . .

'All this, because my wife was killed in my absence and the police are powerless to protect citizens . . . Because the next thing is, instead of looking for the real culprit, they have to seize on the obvious suspect, the husband who was unfortunate enough to take fright . . .'

Maigret was puffing slowly at his pipe, facing Francis, in full spate now, standing in the middle of the room raising his clenched fists.

'Have you finished?'

He put the question in a calm voice, without any trace of impatience, or irony.

'Do you still want to call a lawyer?'

'I am quite capable of defending myself . . . And when the time comes and you realize your mistake and let me go, you'll have to . . .'

'You're free to go.'

'What do you mean . . .?'

His fury was abating all of a sudden, and he stood there, his arms dangling, staring in disbelief at the Superintendent.

'You've been free all along, as you know perfectly well. If I provided you with a roof over your head last night it's because you had no money and you did not, or so I presume, want to sleep in the studio in the Rue Saint-Charles.'

Maigret had pulled his wallet from his pocket, the same wallet that Francis had stolen from him on the platform of the bus. He took out two ten franc notes.

'Here is something to buy a snack and get back to the Rue de Grenelle. One of your friends will lend you a little money to tide you over. I should inform you that I have had a telegram sent to your wife's parents in Concarneau, and that the father arrives in Paris at six o'clock this evening. I don't know whether he will get in touch with you. I didn't speak to him on the telephone myself, but it seems he wants to take his daughter's body back to Brittany.'

Ricain no longer spoke of leaving. He was trying to understand.

'Of course, you're the husband, and it's up to you to decide.'

'What do you advise me to do?'

'Funerals are expensive. I don't suppose you will often have time to visit the cemetery. So if the family are very anxious . . .'

'I'll have to think about it . . .'

Maigret had opened the door of his cupboard, where he always kept a bottle of brandy and some glasses, a precaution which had often proved useful.

He filled a single glass, and offered it to the young man.

'Drink that.'

'What about you?'

'No thank you.'

Francis drank the brandy down in one gulp.

'Why are you giving me alcohol? . . .'

'To steady you up.'

'I suppose I'll be followed?'

'Not even that! On condition you let me know where I can get in touch with you. Are you planning to return to the Rue Saint-Charles?'

'Where else could I go?'

'One of my inspectors is there at the moment. By the way, yesterday evening the telephone went twice in the studio. The inspector picked up the receiver and both times nobody answered.'

'It couldn't have been me, because . . .'

'I'm not asking if it was you. Somebody called the studio. Somebody who hadn't read the newspapers. What I am wondering is whether this man or this woman was expecting to hear your voice or your wife's.'

'I have no idea . . .'

'Hasn't it ever happened to you that you picked up the receiver and only heard breathing?'

'What are you driving at?'

'Suppose they thought you were out, and wanted to talk to Sophie?'

'That again? What have they been telling you, all the people you were questioning yesterday evening and this morning? What scraps of scandal are you trying to . . . to . . .'

'One question, Francis.'

The latter started, surprised to hear himself addressed in this way.

'What did you do, about a year and a half ago, when you found out that Sophie was pregnant?'

'She's never been pregnant . . .'

'Has the medical report arrived, Janvier?'

'Here it is chief . . . Delaplanque has just sent it through . . .'

Maigret ran his eye over it.

'There! You can see for yourself that I'm not making allegations, and that I am simply referring to medical facts.'

Ricain was looking savagely at him once more.

'And what's all this about, for God's sake? Anyone would think you had sworn to drive me out of my mind . . . First you accuse me of killing my wife, then . . .'

'I have never accused you.'

'It's just as if . . . You insinuate . . . Then, to calm me down . . .'

He seized the glass which had contained the brandy, and dashed it violently to the floor.

'I ought to get to know your tricks better . . .! A fine film that would make . . . But the Préfecture would take care to stop it . . . So, Sophie was pregnant a year ago? . . . And, of course, as we had no children, I presume we took ourselves off to an abortionist . . . Is that right? . . . So that's the new charge that's been dreamed up for me, because you couldn't make the other one stick!'

'I never pretended you were aware of what was happening. I asked if your wife mentioned it to you. In fact she went to someone else.'

'Because it had to do with someone besides me, the husband?'

'She wanted to spare you the worry, perhaps a battle with your conscience. She imagined a child would be a handicap at this point in your career.'

'And so?'

'She confided in one of your friends.'

'But who, for God's sake?'

'Carus.'

'What? You want me to believe that Carus . . .'

'He told me so this morning. Nora confirmed it half an hour later, with just one variation. According to her, Sophie was not alone when she spoke of being a mother. You were both there.'

'She was lying . . .'

'Quite possibly.'

'Do you believe her?'

'For the time being, I believe nobody.'

'Me included.'

'You included, Francis. But even so, you're free to go.'

And Maigret lit his pipe, sat at his desk, and began thumbing through some papers.

CHAPTER SIX

RICAIN HAD DEPARTED hesitantly, awkwardly, suspicious like a bird that sees its cage open, and Janvier had shot an inquiring glance at his boss. Was he really being let loose, without any kind of watch being put on him?

Pretending not to understand the mute question, Maigret went on thumbing through his papers, finally got up and went and stood at the window.

He was morose. Janvier had returned to the Inspectors' room where he was exchanging views in undertones with Lapointe when the Superintendent came in. Instinctively the two men separated, but it was pointless. Maigret seemed not to have seen them.

He was wandering to and fro between offices as if he did not know what to do with his heavy body, pausing by a typewriter, a telephone or an empty chair, moving pieces of paper about for no particular reason.

Finally he grunted

'Tell my wife I won't be home for dinner.'

He didn't call her himself, which was significant. Nobody dared to speak to him, far less ask questions. In the Inspectors' room, everybody was in a state of suspense. He sensed it, and with a shrug he returned to his office and picked up his hat.

He said nothing, neither where he was going nor when he would be back, left no instructions, as if all of a sudden he had lost interest in the case.

On the big dusty staircase he emptied his pipe, tapping it against his heel, then crossed the courtyard and nodded vaguely in the direction of the porter, and set off in the direction of the Place Dauphine.

Perhaps it wasn't really where he wanted to go. His mind was elsewhere, in the area which was not familiar to him, the Boulevard de Grenelle, the Rue Saint-Charles, the Avenue de La-Motte-Picquet.

He could see the sombre outline of the Métro Aérien which cut a diagonal in the sky, thought he could hear the muted rumble of carriages . . . The padded, somewhat syrupy atmosphere of the Vieux-Pressoir, the liveliness of Rose who never stopped wiping her hands on her apron, the wax-like face of the former stuntman, with its ironical smile . . .

Maki, huge and gentle in his corner, his eyes growing darker and more bleary as he drank . . . Gérard Dramin, with his ascetic face, ceaselessly correcting his script . . . Carus who took so much trouble to be friendly with everyone, and Nora, artificial from dyed hair to fingertips . . .

One would have said his feet were carrying him, without his knowledge, by force of habit, to the Brasserie Dauphine and he greeted the proprietor, sniffed the restaurant's warm smell, went over to his corner where he had sat on the bench thousands of times before.

'There's *andouillette*, Superintendent.'

'With mashed potatoes?'

'And to start with?'

'Anything. A carafe of Sancerre.'

His colleague from Records was eating in another corner with someone from the Ministry of the Interior whom Maigret knew only by sight. The other customers were nearly all regulars, barristers who would not stop long before going across the square to plead their cases, a magistrate, an inspector from the Gambling Squad.

The proprietor realized, too, that it was not the moment to start a conversation, and Maigret ate slowly, with concentration, as if it was an important act.

Half an hour later he was walking round the Law Courts,

his hands behind his back, with slow strides, like a lonely man exercising his dog, then he was back once more on the great staircase, and finally pushing open his office door.

A note from Gastinne-Renette was waiting for him. It was not the final report. The gun found in the Seine was indeed the one which had fired the bullet in the Rue Saint-Charles.

He shrugged his shoulders again, for he knew it in advance. At moments he felt himself submerged beneath these secondary questions, these reports, these telephone calls, these routine activities.

Joseph, the ancient attendant, knocked on his door and came in, as usual, without waiting for an answer.

'There's a gentleman to see you . . .'

Maigret put out a hand, glanced at the form:

'Show him in.'

The man was wearing black, which emphasized his ruddy complexion and the shock of grey hair standing out on his head.

'Sit down, Monsieur Le Gal. Let me offer my condolences . . .'

The man had had time for weeping on the train, and it appeared that he had had a few drinks to give himself courage. His eyes were hazy, and his words came with difficulty.

'What have they done with her . . .? I didn't want to go round to her place, in case I met that man, as I think I would strangle him with my bare hands . . .'

How many times had Maigret witnessed this same reaction from families?

'In any case, Monsieur Le Gal, the body is no longer in the Rue Saint-Charles. It's in the Police Pathological Department . . .'

'Where's that?'

'Near the Austerlitz bridge, on the river. I'll have you driven over, as it's necessary for you to make an official identification of your daughter.'

'Did she suffer?'

He was clenching his fists, but it was not convincing. It was

117

as though his momentum had evaporated on the way, his rage as well, so that he was merely repeating words he no longer believed in, with an empty head.

'I hope you have arrested him?'

'There is no proof against her husband.'

'But, Superintendent, from the day she first spoke to me about this man, I predicted it would all end badly . . .'

'Did she bring him to see you?'

'I never saw him . . . I only know him from a bad photograph . . . She didn't want to introduce him to us . . . The moment she met him the family no longer meant anything to her . . .

'All she wanted was to get married as quickly as possible . . . She had even drawn up the letter of consent which I had to sign . . . Her mother wanted to stop me . . . In the end I gave in, so now I hold myself partly responsible for what happened . . .'

Wasn't there always this side of things in every case, at once sordid and moving?

'Was she your only child?'

'Fortunately we have a son of fifteen . . .'

In fact, Sophie had vanished from their lives a long time before.

'Could I take the body back to Concarneau?'

'As far as we are concerned the formalities have been completed.'

He had said 'formalities'.

'You mean they've . . . I mean there was a . . .'

'A post-mortem, yes. As for transport, I advise you to get in touch with an undertaker's who will see to the arrangement.

'And him?'

'I've spoken to him. He has no objection to her being buried in Concarneau.'

'I hope he isn't thinking of coming? . . . Because if he does, I won't be answerable for what happens . . . There are people in our part of the world who have less self-control than I have . . .'

'I know. I'll see to it he stays in Paris.'

'It's him, isn't it?'

'I assure you I do not know.'

'Who else would have killed her? She only saw through his eyes. He had literally hypnotized her. Since her marriage she hasn't written three times and she didn't even take the trouble to send us a New Year card . . .

'I found out her new address through the newspapers . . . I thought she was still in the little hotel in Montmartre where they lived after their marriage . . . A funny sort of wedding, with no relations, no friends! . . . Do *you* think that's a promising start?'

Maigret heard him out, nodding sympathetically, then closed the door behind his visitor, whose breath reeked of alcohol.

And Ricain's father? Wouldn't he be making an appearance in his turn? The Superintendent was expecting him. He had sent one detective to Orly, another to the Raphael to photograph the page in the registry which the hall porter had shown him.

'There are two reporters, Superintendent . . .'

'Put them on to Janvier.'

The latter came in a moment later.

'What do I tell them?'

'Anything. That we're going ahead with our inquiries.'

'They thought they would find Ricain here and they brought a photographer along with them.'

'Let them look. Let them go and knock on the door of the Rue Saint-Charles if they like.'

He was laboriously following a train of thought, or rather of several different trains of contradictory thoughts. Had he been right to free Francis, in the overwrought state he was in?

He would not get far with the twenty francs which the Superintendent had given him. He would be forced to start his begging rounds again, knocking on doors, calling on friends.

'Well, it's not my fault if . . .'

Anybody would have thought Maigret had an uneasy conscience, that he had something with which to reproach himself. He kept on returning to the starting point of the affair, the very start, namely on the platform of the bus.

He could see in his mind's eye the woman with the blank face whose shopping bag bumped against his legs. A chicken some butter, eggs, leeks, some leafy celery. He had wondered why she was doing her shopping so far afield.

A young man was smoking a pipe that was too short and too heavy. His blond hair was as pale as Nora's dyed hair.

At the time, he still had not met Carus' mistress, who passed herself off, at the Raphael and elsewhere, as his wife.

For a moment he had lost his balance and somebody had neatly extracted his wallet from his pocket.

Somehow he would have liked to dissect that instant of time, which seemed to him to be the most important one of all. The unknown man leaving the moving bus, in the Rue du Temple, and hurrying away, zig-zagging among the house-wives, towards the narrow streets of the Marais . . .

His face was clear in the Superintendent's memory. He was certain he would recognize him, because the thief had turned round . . .

Why had he turned round? And why, on discovering Maigret's identity from the contents of the wallet, had he put it in a brown envelope and sent it back?

At the time, the time of the theft, he thought he was being followed . . . He was convinced that he would be accused of his wife's murder and that they would come and shut him up . . . He had given a curious reason for not wanting to let himself be arrested . . . Claustrophobia.

It was the first time, in the thirty years of his career, that he had heard a suspect give this as a reason for flight. On reflection, however, Maigret was forced to concede that sometimes it was perhaps the case. He didn't take the underground himself, except when there was no other means of transport, because he felt suffocated in it.

And what was the source of this mania, in his office, for jumping to his feet every few seconds and standing by the window?

Sometimes people, especially people from the Public Prosecutor's Office, criticized him for doing the Inspectors' jobs for them, for going and interrogating witnesses on the spot instead of summoning them to him, for returning to the scene of the crime without any concrete reason, even for taking over watches himself, in sunshine and rain alike.

He liked his office, but he could never stay there for two hours at a stretch without feeling an urge to escape. In the course of a case he would have liked to be everywhere at the same time.

Bob Mandille must be having his siesta at this time, for the Vieux-Pressoir shut late at night. Did Rose take a siesta as well? What would she have told him if they had sat down together at a table in the deserted restaurant?

They all had different opinions about Ricain and Sophie. Some of them, like Carus, didn't think twice, after an interval of a few hours, about expressing contradicting views.

What was Sophie? One of those teenagers who throw themselves at every man's head? An ambitious girl who had believed that Francis would launch her on a film star's way of life?

She used to meet the producer in a *garçonnière* in the Rue François-Premier. If Carus was telling the truth, that is.

They had talked about Ricain's jealousy, and how he virtually never left his wife. On the other hand, he did not hesitate to borrow money from her lover.

Did he know? Did he close his eyes?

'Show him in . . .'

He had expected it. It was the father, Ricain's, this time, a large, powerful man, with a youthful look despite his iron grey hair, which he wore in a crew cut.

'I hesitated to come . . .'

'Sit down, Monsieur Ricain.'

'Is he here?'

'No. He was this morning, but he's gone.'

The man had strongly etched features, pale eyes, a reflective expression.

'I would have come earlier, but I was on driver's duty on the Ventimiglia-Paris express . . .'

'When did you last see Francis?'

Surprised, he echoed:

'Francis?'

'That's what most of his friends call him.'

'At home we called him François . . . Wait now . . . He came to see me just before Christmas . . .'

'Had you remained on good terms?'

'I saw so little of him.'

'And his wife?'

'He introduced her to me several days before the marriage.'

'How old was he when his mother died?'

'Fifteen . . . He was a good lad, but he was already beginning to be difficult and he couldn't stand being corrected . . . It was no use trying to stop him doing what he wanted . . . I wanted him to go into the railways . . . Not necessarily as a worker . . . He would have got a good desk job . . .'

'Why did he come and see you before Christmas?'

'To ask for money, of course . . . He never came for anything else . . . He had no proper job . . . He scribbled a bit and said one day he'd be famous.

'I did my best . . . But I couldn't keep him . . . Sometimes I was away three days on end . . . It wasn't much fun for him coming back to an empty place and getting his own meals . . . What do you think yourself, Superintendent?'

'I don't know.'

The man showed surprise. That a senior functionary of the police should have no definite opinion was beyond his understanding.

'Don't you think he's guilty?'

'Up till now there's nothing to prove it, any more than there's anything to prove the contrary.'

'Do you think this woman has been good for him? . . . She didn't even take the trouble to put on a dress when he introduced us; she came in slacks, with shoes that were more like clogs . . . She hadn't even combed her hair . . . It's true one sees others like that in the streets . . .'

There was a longish pause while Monsieur Ricain shot hesitant glances at the Superintendent. Finally he pulled a worn wallet from his pocket and took several hundred franc notes from it.

'It would be better if I don't go and see him myself . . . If he wants to meet me, he knows where I live . . . I suppose he still has no money . . . He might need some to get himself a good lawyer . . .'

A pause. A question.

'Have you any children, Superintendent?'

'Unfortunately not.'

'He mustn't feel abandoned . . . Whatever he's done, if he's done anything wrong, he isn't responsible . . . Tell him that's what I think . . . Tell him he can come to the house any time he wants . . . I don't insist . . . I understand . . .'

Moved, Maigret looked at the banknotes that a broad, calloused hand with square-ended fingernails was pushing across the desk.

'Well . . .' sighed the father, as he rose, crushing his hat in his hands. 'If I understand you right, I can still hope he's innocent . . . Mind you, I'm sure of it . . . The papers can say what they like, I cannot bring myself to believe that he's done such a thing . . .'

The Superintendent accompanied him to the door, shook the hand that was hesitantly offered.

'Can I keep on hoping?'

'One must never despair.'

Alone once again, he was on the point of telephoning

123

Doctor Pardon. He would have liked to chat, to put various questions to him. Pardon was no psychiatrist, certainly. Nor was he a professional psychologist.

But in his career as general practitioner he had seen all kinds and often his advice had reinforced Maigret in his opinions.

At that time Pardon would be in his surgery, with a score of patients lined up in the waiting-room. Their monthly dinner was not due to take place until the following week.

It was curious: suddenly, for no precise reason, he had a painful sensation of loneliness.

He was no more than an element in the complicated machinery of Justice, and he had at his disposal specialists, inspectors, the telephone, the telegraph, all kinds of desirable services: above him there were the Public Prosecutor, the magistrate and, in the last resort, the judges and juries of the Assize Courts.

Why, from that point on, did he feel responsible? It seemed to him that it was on himself that there depended the fate of a human being, he still did not know which, the man or woman who had taken the revolver from the drawer in the white-painted chest and fired it at Sophie.

A detail had struck him, from the outset, that he had not yet managed to explain. It is rare in the course of a dispute, or in a moment of emotion, for a person to aim at the head.

The reflex action, even in self-defence, is to shoot at the chest, and only professionals shoot at the stomach, knowing that victims seldom recover.

From a distance of around a yard, the murderer had aimed at the head . . . To make it look like suicide?

No, because he had left the weapon in the studio . . . At least, if Ricain was to be believed . . .

The couple came home, at about ten o'clock . . . He needed money . . . Francis left his wife behind in the Rue Saint-Charles, which was unusual for him, while he set off in search of Carus or another friend who might be able to lend him two thousand francs . . .

Why wait until that night if the money had to be handed over next morning?

He went back to the Vieux-Pressoir, half-opened the door to see whether the producer had arrived . . .

At that time Carus was already in Frankfurt, a fact they were just cross-checking at Orly. He hadn't mentioned his journey to Bob or any other member of the little band . . .

Nora, on the other hand, was in Paris . . . Not in her suite at the Raphael, as she had claimed that morning, as the hall porter's register contradicted her story . . .

Why had she lied? Did Carus know she was absent from the hotel? Hadn't he telephoned her, on arriving at Frankfurt?

The telephone rang.

'Hallo . . . Doctor Delaplanque . . . Shall I put him through? . . .'

'Please do . . . Hallo!'

'Maigret? Sorry to disturb you, but there's something that's been bothering me since this morning . . . I didn't mention it in my report because it's rather vague . . . In the course of the autopsy, I came across faint marks on the wrists of the deceased, as if someone had grasped them with some force . . . You couldn't call them bruises, properly speaking . . .'

'I'm listening.'

'That's all . . . While I can't positively say there was a struggle, I wouldn't be surprised if there was . . . I picture the aggressor seizing the victim by the wrists and pushing her . . . She might have fallen against the divan, recovered, and it would have been just before she was upright again that the shot was fired . . . That would explain why the bullet was taken from the wall nearly four feet from the floor, whereas if the young girl had been standing upright . . .'

'I follow . . . Are the marks very light?'

'There's one more pronounced than the others . . . It could be a thumb, but I can't say anything for sure. That's why I can't record it officially . . . You may be able to make something of it . . .'

'The way things are at the moment I'm ready to try and make something of everything that comes along. Thank you, Doctor.'

Janvier was standing, silent, in the doorway.

*   *   *

He had returned to the area on his own this time, with an obstinate set to his face, as if it was a matter to be settled between the Boulevard de Grenelle and himself. He had walked along the banks of the Seine, and paused forty yards upstream from the Bir-Hakeim bridge, at the spot where the revolver had been thrown in and fished out of the river, then set off in the direction of the big new block in the Boulevard de Grenelle.

Eventually he had gone in and rapped on the glass-fronted porter's lodge. The girl inside was young and alluring, and she had a small well-lighted sitting-room.

After showing her his medallion he asked:

'Is it your job to collect the rents?'

'Yes, Superintendent.'

'You know François Ricain, I presume?'

'They live on the courtyard and they seldom pass by here . . . I mean seldom *used* to pass by here . . . But she . . . I knew them, of course, but it wasn't very nice always having to demand money from them . . . In January they asked for a month to pay, then on the fifteenth of February they asked for another delay . . . The landlord had decided to turn them out if they hadn't paid the two outstanding amounts by the fifteenth of March . . .'

'And they didn't?'

'That was the day before yesterday, the fifteenth . . . The Wednesday . . .'

'Weren't you concerned when you didn't see them?'

'I didn't expect them to pay . . . In the morning he didn't

126

come for his mail and I said to myself he didn't want to face me . . . Anyway they didn't have many letters . . . Mostly prospectuses and magazines he subscribed to . . . In the afternoon I went and knocked on their door and nobody answered . . .

'On the Thursday, I knocked again and as there still was no answer, I asked a tenant whether she had heard anything . . . It even occurred to me that they might have done a moonlight flit . . . It would be easy for them because of the entrance in the Rue Saint-Charles, which is always open . . .'

'What do you think of Ricain?'

'I didn't pay much attention to him . . . Every so often the tenants complained that they had been making a row or had guests in till the early hours, but there are others in the building who don't exactly creep about on tip-toe either, especially the young ones . . . He looked like some sort of artist . . .'

'And she?'

'What do you want me to say? They were living a hand to mouth existence . . . It's not much of a life . . . Is it certain she didn't kill herself? . . .'

He was learning nothing new, nor really seeking to learn anything. He was prowling, taking in the streets round about, the houses, the open windows, the interiors of the shops.

At seven o'clock he pushed open the door of the Vieux-Pressoir and he was almost disappointed not to see Fernande perched on her bar-stool.

Bob Mandille was reading the evening paper at one of the tables, while the waiter was finishing off laying the tables, arranging a glass vase bearing a rose on each of the check table-cloths.

'Hallo! . . . The Superintendent . . .'

Bob rose, and came over to shake hands with Maigret.

'Well? What have you found out? . . . The newspapers aren't too happy . . . They say you're being all mysterious and keeping them at arm's length . . .'

'Simply because we have nothing to tell them.'

'Is it true you have released Francis?'

'He was never detained and he is free to come and go. Who's been talking to you about it?'

'Huguet the photographer, who lives in the same building on the fourth floor. That's the one who's had two wives already, and given a child to a third girl . . . He saw Francis in the courtyard as he was coming back home . . . I'm surprised he hasn't been in to see me . . . Tell me, has he got any money? . . .'

'I gave him twenty francs for a bite to eat and a bus fare . . .'

'In that case it won't be long now before he's round here . . . Unless he's called on his newspaper and by a miracle there was some spare cash in the till . . . It does happen sometimes . . .'

'You didn't see Nora on Wednesday evening?'

'No, she didn't come in . . . Besides, I can't remember ever seeing her without Carus . . . He was on his travels . . .'

'In Germany, yes. She went out alone. I wonder where she could have gone.'

'Didn't she say?'

'She claims she went back to the Raphael around nine o'clock.'

'Isn't it true?'

'The hall porter's register says it was more like eleven.'

'Strange . . .'

Bob's face wore his thin, ironical smile, which made a sort of crack in the fixed mask.

'Does it amuse you?'

'You must admit that Carus would not have let the opportunity slip! . . . He took advantage of every occasion without any inhibitions . . . It would be funny if Nora, for her part . . . But somehow I can't believe it of her . . .'

'Because she's in love with him?'

'No. Because she is too intelligent and too level-headed. She would not risk losing everything, just when she was so

128

near to achieving her objective, for the sake of an adventure, even with the most attractive man in the world.'

'Perhaps she wasn't so near to achieving her objective as you think.'

'What do you mean?'

'Carus used to meet Sophie regularly in an apartment in the Rue François-Premier specially rented for the purpose.'

'Was it as serious as that?'

'So he claims. He even claims she was star material and that she would soon have become one.'

'Are you serious? Carus, who . . . But she was just a chit of a girl, the kind you find thirteen to the dozen . . . You've only got to walk down the Champs-Elysées and you can pick up enough like her to cover all the screens in the world . . .'

'Nora knew about their liaison.'

'Then I don't understand anything any more . . . It's true, if I were to believe all I heard every time a customer poured his heart out to me, I would have ulcers . . . Go and tell my wife about it . . . She'd be upset if you didn't pop in to pass the time of day . . . She's got a soft spot for you . . . How about a drink? . . .'

'Presently . . .'

The kitchen was bigger, more modern than he had imagined. As he expected, Rose wiped her hand before offering it to him.

'So, you've decided to let him go?'

'Are you surprised?'

'I don't know any more . . . Everybody who comes in here has a version of his own . . . For some, Francis did it out of jealousy . . . For others, it's a lover she wanted to get rid of · . . And for others still, a woman was after her revenge . . .'

'Nora?'

'Who told you that?'

'Carus was having a serious affair with Sophie . . . Nora knew about it . . . He was planning to launch her . . .'

'Is that true, or are you just making it up to get me talking?'

'It's true. Does it surprise you?'

'Me . . . It's a good while now since I stopped being surprised by things . . . If you were in this business like I am . . .'

The idea never occurred to her that one acquires a certain experience of human beings in the P.J.

'Only, my fine Superintendent, if it's Nora who did it you'll have trouble proving it . . . She's sharp enough to outwit the lot of you . . .

'Are you eating here? I've got duck à l'orange . . . Before that I can offer you two or three dozen scallops just in from La Rochelle . . . They're from my mother . . . Ah, yes . . . She's turned seventy-five and she goes every morning to the market . . .'

Huguet, the photographer, arrived with his companion. He was a pink youth with innocent face and jovial expression, and he looked as if he was proud to be seen with a woman seven months pregnant.

'Do you know each other? . . . Superintendent Maigret . . . Jacques Huguet . . . His friend . . .'

'Jocelyne . . .' Huguet put in, as if it was important or as if he had pleasure in pronouncing this poetic name.

And, with exaggerated attentiveness, almost as though he were making fun of her:

'What will you have to drink, my darling?'

He smothered her with little attentions, enveloped her with warm and tender glances, as if to say to the others:

'As you can see, I am in love and I am not ashamed . . . We have made love . . . We are expecting a child . . . We are happy . . . And it makes no difference to us if you find us ridiculous.'

'What will you have, my children?'

'A fruit juice for Jocelyne . . . A port for me . . .'

'And what about you, Monsieur Maigret?'

'A glass of beer.'

'Hasn't Francis come yet?'

'Have you a date with him here?'

'No, but it strikes me he would probably like to see his

130

friends again . . . If only to show them that he's free, and that you couldn't keep him inside . . . He's like that . . .'

'Did you have the impression that we intended to keep him inside?'

'I don't know . . . It's difficult to tell what the police are going to do . . .'

'Do you think he killed his wife?'

'It makes so little difference whether it was him or someone else! . . . She's dead, isn't she? . . . If Francis killed her, it's because he had good reasons . . .'

'What reasons, in your opinion?'

'I don't know . . . He'd got fed up with her, perhaps? Or else she made scenes? . . . Or perhaps she was deceiving him? . . . One must let people lead the lives they want, mustn't we, my sweetheart? . . .'

Some customers came in, not regulars, and hesitated to go to a table.

'Three?'

It was a middle-aged couple and a young girl.

'This way . . .'

This was Bob's big moment: the menu, the whispered advice, the praise for the Charentes wine, for the *chaudrée* . . .

Occasionally he addressed a wink to his companions who had remained at the bar.

It was then that Ricain came in, stopped in his tracks on seeing the Superintendent together with Huguet and the pregnant girl.

'So there you are . . .!' cried the photographer. 'Well, what happened? . . . We thought you were in the darkest depths of some prison . . .'

Francis forced a smile.

'As you see, I'm here . . . Good-evening, Jocelyne . . . Have you come for me, Superintendent?'

'For the time being, for the duck *à l'orange* . . .'

'What will you have?' Bob came over to ask after passing on the order to the waiter.

'Is that port? . . .'

He hesitated.

'No . . . a Scotch . . . Unless my credit note is too long . . .'

'Today I'll let you have credit . . .'

'And tomorrow?'

'That depends on the Superintendent.'

Maigret was a little put out by the tone of the conversation, but he supposed this was a special brand of humour peculiar to the gang.

'Did you go to the newspaper?' he asked Ricain.

'Yes . . . How did you know? . . .'

'Because you needed money . . .'

'I just managed to get an advance of a hundred francs against what they owe me . . .'

'And Carus?'

'I didn't call on him . . .'

'But you were looking for him everywhere on Wednesday evening, then nearly all night as well.'

'It's not Wednesday any more . . .'

'By the way,' the photographer put in, 'I've seen Carus . . . I went to the studio and he was giving some girl I don't know a screen test . . . He even asked me to take some pictures . . .'

Maigret wondered whether he had had some taken of Sophie as well.

'He's dining here . . . At least, that was his intention at three o'clock this afternoon, but with him you never know . . . Especially with Nora . . . By the way, I ran into Nora too . . .'

'Today?'

'Two or three days ago . . . In a place I never expected to see her . . . A small night club in Saint-Germain-des-Prés, where you see nothing but teenagers . . .'

'When was this?' asked Maigret, suddenly attentive.

'Wait now . . . It's Saturday . . . Friday . . . Thursday . . . No, on Thursday I was at the first night of the ballet . . . It was Wednesday . . . I was looking for pictures to illustrate an article on teenagers . . . I had been told about this club . . .'

'What time was that?'

'Around ten o'clock . . . Yes, I must have arrived at ten o'clock . . . Jocelyne was with me . . . What do you think, sweetheart? . . . It was ten o'clock, wasn't it . . .? A crummy place, but picturesque, with all the boys wearing hair down to their collars . . .'

'Did she see you?'

'I don't think so . . . She was in a corner, with a beefy character who certainly wasn't a teenager . . . I suspect he was the proprietor, and they looked as if they were talking seriously about something . . .'

'Did she stay long?'

'I fought my way into the two or three rooms where almost everybody was dancing . . . Well, if you can call that dancing . . . They were doing their best, glued together . . .

'I saw her once or twice again, between the heads and the shoulders . . . She was still deep in conversation . . . The character had pulled a pencil from his pocket and was writing figures on a piece of paper . . .

'It's funny when I think about it . . . She's already not a very real person in daily life . . . But there, in that abracadabra atmosphere, it would have been worth a photograph . . .'

'Didn't you take one?'

'I'm not that daft! . . . I don't want trouble with Papa Carus . . . I rely on him for a good half of my meal ticket . . .'

They heard Maigret order:

'Another beer, Bob . . .'

His voice, his manner, were no longer quite the same.

'Could you keep me the place I had yesterday?'

'Aren't you going to eat with us?' asked the photographer in surprise.

'Another time.'

He needed to be alone, to reflect. Once again, by chance, the ideas that he had carefully placed in order had been thrown into the melting pot, and nothing held together any more.

Francis was covertly watching him, anxious. Bob, too, was aware that a change had come over him.

'Anyone would think you were surprised to learn that Nora would go to a place like that . . .'

But the Superintendent had turned to Huguet:

'What's the club called?'

'Do you want to make a study of beatniks, too? . . . Wait . . . it's not a very original name . . . It must date from the time it was just a bistro for tramps . . . The Ace of Spades . . . Yes . . . On the left as you go up . . .'

Maigret emptied his glass.

'Keep my corner,'' he repeated.

A few moments later, a taxi was taking him to the other side of the river.

The place, by day, was a livid colour. There were only three hirsute customers to be seen and a girl in a man's jacket and trousers smoking a small cigar. A character in a cardigan hustled in from the second room and took up his place behind the bar, a suspicious look in his eye.

'What's it to be?'

'A beer,' said Maigret mechanically.

'And after that?'

'Nothing.'

'No questions?'

'What do you mean?'

'That I wasn't born yesterday and that if Superintendent Maigret comes in here, it isn't because he's thirsty. So, I'm waiting for the commercial.'

With bantering air, the man poured himself a short drink.

'Somebody came in to see you on Wednesday evening . . .'

'Hundreds of somebodies, if I may make so bold as to correct you.'

'I'm referring to a woman, with whom you spent a long time in conversation.'

'Half of the people were women and I was in conversation, as you put it, with quite a lot of them.'

'Nora.'

'Now we're talking. Well . . . ?'

'What was she doing here?'

'What she comes to do here once a month on average.'

'That's to say?'

'Look at the books.'

'Because . . . ?'

Astounded, Maigret guessed the truth before the man told him.

'Because she's the boss, that's why, Superintendent! . . . She doesn't shout about it . . . I'm not even sure Papa Carus is in the picture . . . Everyone has the right to do what they like with their money, haven't they? . . .

'I didn't say anything, mind . . . You tell me a story and I don't say yes or no . . . Even if you ask me if she owns any other night clubs of the same sort . . .'

Maigret looked at him, questioningly, and the man flickered his eyelids affirmatively.

'There are some people who know which way the wind blows . . .' he concluded lightly. 'It's not always the ones who think themselves clever who make the best investments . . . With three clubs like this, for just one year, I'd retire to the Riviera . . .

'So, with a dozen, and some of them in the Pigalle area and one on the Champs-Elysées . . .'

CHAPTER SEVEN

WHEN MAIGRET RETURNED to the Vieux-Pressoir, they had placed three tables end to end and started their dinner all together. On seeing him Carus rose to his feet and came over, check table-napkin in hand.

'I trust you will give us the pleasure of joining us . . .?'

'Please don't be offended if I prefer to eat alone in my corner.'

'Are you afraid to have dinner with somebody you will be forced to arrest sooner or later?'

He looked him in the eyes.

'There's every chance, isn't there, that poor Sophie's murderer is among us this evening? . . . Well! . . . As you wish . . . But we shall ask you at least to have a glass of armagnac with us . . .'

Bob had shown him to his table, in the corner by the revolving-door, and he had ordered the scallops and duck *à l'orange* that Rose had recommended.

He could see them side-view, in two rows. It was obvious, from first glance, that Carus was the dominant figure. His manner, his bearing, his gestures, his voice, his look, all were those of somebody conscious of his weight and his import.

Ricain had taken a place opposite him unwillingly, it seemed, and only joined half-heartedly in the conversation. As for Dramin, he was with a young girl whom Maigret had not yet met, a rather dim creature with scarcely any make-up, soberly dressed, and whom Bob later described as a film-cutter.

Maki ate a lot, drank neat spirits, looked at his companions in turn and replied to their questions with grunts.

It was Huguet, the photographer, who talked back to the producer most of the time. He seemed to be in top form and kept gazing with proprietorial satisfaction at the belly of the placid Jocelyne.

It was not possible, from a distance, to follow the conversation. But from odds and ends of phrases, from exclamations and facial expressions, Maigret managed more or less to follow the sense.

'We'll soon see whose turn it is next . . .' the facetious photographer had said, or words to that effect.

And his eyes turned for a moment in Maigret's direction.

'He's watching us . . . He's peeling off our skins . . . Now that he's got all he can from Francis, he'll turn on someone else . . . If you go on making such a sour face, Dramin, he'll pick on you . . .'

Several lone diners, watching from a distance, envied their merriment. Carus had ordered champagne and there were two bottles cooling in silver buckets. Bob came over to pour out in person.

Ricain was drinking heavily. It was he who was drinking the most, and not once did he smile at the photographer's cracks, not all of which were in the best of taste.

'Look natural, Francis . . . Don't forget that the eye of God is fastened upon you . . .'

Maigret was the butt of his humour. Were they funnier on other evenings when they got together?

Carus was doing his best to help Huguet ease the tension. As for Nora, she turned her cold eyes on each of them in turn.

Beneath it all, the dinner was a gloomy affair and nobody was behaving quite naturally, perhaps partly because they all sensed the Superintendent's presence.

'I bet you'll turn out a film one day that our good friend Carus will produce . . . All dramas end that way . . .'

'Shut up, will you?'

'I'm sorry . . . I didn't know you . . .'

It was worse when silence fell around the table. In reality

137

there was no friendship between them. They hadn't chosen one another. Each one of them had a vested interest in being present.

Weren't they all dependent on Carus? Above all Nora, who extracted from him the wherewithal to buy her night-clubs. She had no guarantee that he would marry her one day, and she preferred to take precautions.

Did he suspect anything? Did he imagine that he was loved for himself?

It was unlikely. He was a realist. He needed a companion, and for the time being she filled the bill well enough. He could not have been averse to her appearance being striking enough to attract attention wherever they went together.

'That's Carus and his friend . . . Nora . . . She's quite a number . . .'

Why not? He had none the less become Sophie's lover, and was planning to make a star of her.

This presupposed that he would get rid of Nora . . . He had had others before her . . . He would have others after . . .

Dramin lived in a world of unfinished scripts to which Carus had the power to give life . . . So long as he believed in his talent . . .

Francis was in the same boat, with the difference that he was less humble, less patient, that he readily adopted an aggressive attitude, especially when he had had a few drinks . . .

As for Maki, he kept his thoughts to himself . . . His sculpture did not sell, yet . . . While he was waiting for the dealers to show an interest, he painted scenery, good or bad, for Carus and anybody else, content when he did not have to pay for his dinner, eating twice as much on such occasions and ordering the most expensive items on the menu . . .

The photographer, now . . . Maigret found it less easy to read his character in his face . . . At first sight he didn't seem to matter . . . In nearly all groups which get together frequently, one finds this sort of simpleton character, with big, frank eyes, who plays the role of buffoon . . . His transparent

honesty entitled him to put both feet in the trough, and every
now and then to utter an unwelcome truth which somebody
else would not have been able to get away with . . .

His very job indicated someone of little importance . . .
They laughed at him and his ever-pregnant women . . .

Rose, wiping her hands, came over to make sure that everyone was all right and, without sitting down, accepted a glass
of champagne.

Every now and then Bob came over and stood beside
Maigret.

'They are doing their best . . .' he whispered knowingly.

Sophie was missing. Everyone felt it. How did Sophie
behave on these occasions?

Sulkily, no doubt, or shyly, but with the knowledge, however, that she was the one the rich man of the group, Carus,
was interested in. Had she not met him, in all probability, that
same afternoon in the flat in the Rue François-Premier?

'Patience, my turtle dove . . . I'll look after you . . .'

'But Nora . . . ?'

'It won't be for very much longer . . . I'm preparing the
ground . . . Cost what it may . . .'

'Francis?'

'To start with he will be annoyed that you have succeeded
before him, and that you're making a lot of money . . . He'll
get down to work . . . I will give him a film to direct . . . Then,
one day, when the time is ripe, you can ask for a divorce . . .'

Was this the way it happened? Carus needed them, too.
It was through launching young people that he made most of
his money. To be thus surrounded by a sort of court at the
Vieux-Pressoir gave him more of a sense of importance than
dining with financiers who were richer and more influential
than himself.

A wink to Bob, who brought two fresh bottles to the big
table. Ricain, exasperated by the photographer's witticisms,
answered him curtly. One could see the moment approaching
when, tried beyond endurance, he would jump to his feet and

stalk out. He didn't yet dare to do so, but he was straining at the leash.

True, one of them had probably killed Sophie, and Maigret studied the faces, while the heat made the blood rise to his head.

Carus was in Frankfurt on Wednesday evening, of that they had confirmation from Orly. Nora was talking figures between ten and eleven o'clock in the overcharged atmosphere of the Ace of Spades.

Maki? . . . But why would Maki want to kill her? . . . He had slept with Sophie, by chance, because she expected it, or so it appeared, of all their friends. It was a way of reassuring herself, of proving she had some charms, that she wasn't just any other girl hooked on the cinema.

Huguet? . . . He already had three women . . . It seemed to be a mania, like giving them children . . . It was a wonder he managed to feed all his different broods . . .

As for Francis . . .

Again Maigret went over Ricain's movements in his mind . . . The return to the Rue Saint-Charles, around ten o'clock . . . The pressing need of money . . . He had hoped to find Carus at the Vieux-Pressoir, but Carus was not there . . . Bob had jibbed at the amount . . .

He left Sophie at home . . .

Why, when he usually took his wife everywhere with him?

'No!' cried the photographer in a loud voice. 'Not here, Jocelyne . . . It's not time to sleep . . .'

And he explained that since she had been pregnant she had taken to dropping off to sleep, anywhere, any time.

'There are some who demand gherkins, some who devour pig's trotters, or *tête de veau* . . . She sleeps . . . Not only does she sleep, but she snores . . .'

Maigret attached no importance to the incident, and went on trying to reconstruct Ricain's comings and goings up to the moment when the latter had stolen his wallet, in the Rue du Temple, on the platform of the bus.

Ricain, who had not kept a centime for himself . . . Ricain, who had telephoned to tell him . . .

He filled his pipe, lit it. Anybody might have thought that he, too, was dozing off in his corner over his coffee.

'Won't you come and have one for the road with us, Superintendent?'

Carus again . . . Maigret decided to accept, and sit with them for a moment . . .

'Well,' laughed Huguet, 'who are you going to arrest? . . . It's impressive enough to know you're there, watching all our expressions . . . Every now and then I even begin to feel guilty myself . . .'

Ricain looked so ill that nobody was surprised when he suddenly got to his feet and headed for the lavatory.

'There should be a drinking licence, like a driving licence . . . ' said Maki dreamily.

The sculptor would certainly have got one at the drop of a hat, for he had drained glass after glass and the only effect was to make his eyes shine, and his face turn brick red.

'It's the same with him every time . . .'

'Your health, Monsieur Maigret . . .' Carus was saying, holding up his glass. 'I was going to say, to the success of your inquiry, as we are all in a hurry for you to find out the truth . . .'

'All except one!' the photographer corrected him.

'Except one, perhaps . . . Unless it isn't one of us . . .'

When Francis returned his eyelids were red and his face had lost its composure. Without being asked Bob brought a glass of water.

'Is that better?'

'I can't take alcohol . . .'

He was avoiding Maigret's eyes.

'I think I'm going home to bed . . .'

'Won't you wait for us!'

'You forget I haven't had much sleep these past three days . . .'

He looked younger, in his physical disarray. He called to mind an overgrown schoolboy ashamed of being made ill by his first cigar.

'Good-night . . .'

They watched Carus get up, follow him over to the door, speak to him in a low voice. Then the producer sat at the table which Maigret had occupied, pushed away the coffee cup and filled in the blank portions of a cheque while Francis waited, eyes averted.

'I couldn't leave him in the lurch . . . If I had been in Paris on Wednesday, perhaps nothing would have happened . . . I would have had dinner here . . . He would have asked me for his rent money and he wouldn't have had to leave Sophie . . .'

Maigret started, repeated the phrase over to himself in his mind, looked at them each in turn.

'If you will excuse me, I will leave you now.'

He needed to be out of doors, as he was beginning to suffocate. Perhaps he had drunk too much, too? In any case, he did not finish the enormous glass of armagnac.

Without any precise aim, and with his hands in his pockets, he wandered along the pavements where several windows remained lit. It was couples, in the main, who stopped to stare at the washing machines and television sets. Young couples dreaming, making calculations.

'A hundred francs a month, Louis . . .'

'Plus two hundred and fifty on the car . . .'

Francis and Sophie must have walked like this, arm-in-arm, in this area.

Did they dream of washing machine and television set?

A car they had, the battered old Triumph which Ricain had abandoned somewhere during the course of that famous Wednesday night. Had he gone back to fetch it?

With the cheque he had just received he had enough to pay his rent . . . Was he intending to live by himself in the studio where his wife had been murdered?

Maigret crossed the boulevard. An old man was sleeping on a bench. The big new building towered in front of him, with about half of its windows lit.

The other tenants were at the cinema, or else they were lingering on, as they were at the Vieux-Pressoir, at restaurant tables.

The air remained balmy, but some large clouds would shortly be passing in front of the full moon.

Maigret turned the angle of the Rue Saint-Charles, and went into the courtyard. There was a light on in a small window with frosted glass beside Ricain's door, the window of the bathroom with the hip bath.

Other doors, other windows, also lit, both on the studio side and in the main block . . .

The courtyard was deserted, silent, the dustbins in place, a cat was making its way stealthily against the wall . . .

Now and then a window would shut, and a light would go out. Early bedders. Then, on the fourth floor, a window lit up. It was a little like the stars which suddenly begin to shine brightly or disappear in the sky.

He thought he could make out, behind the blind, the voluminous silhouette of Jocelyne, and the outline of the photographer's dishevelled hair.

Then his eye travelled from the fourth floor to the ground floor.

'At about ten o'clock . . .'

He knew the time-table of that night by heart. The Huguets had dined at the Vieux-Pressoir and as they had been alone at table the meal must have been brief. What time had they come home?

As for Ricain and Sophie, they had opened the studio door and switched on the lights somewhere near ten o'clock. Then, almost immediately afterwards, Francis had gone out . . .

Maigret could still see the human shapes, high up, coming and going . . . Then there was only one, the photographer's . . . The man opened the window, looked at the sky for a moment . . . Just as he was about to go off, his eye lit upon the courtyard . . . He must have seen the lighted studio window and, in the middle of the empty space, Maigret's silhouette etched in the moonlight . . .

The Superintendent emptied his pipe against his heel, and went into the building. Coming from the courtyard, he did not have to pass in front of the porter's lodge. He went into the lift, pushed the button for the fourth floor, and a moment later found himself back once again among corridors.

When he knocked on the door, it was as if Huguet was waiting for him, for he opened up at once.

'It's you . . .!' he said, with a curious smile. 'My wife is getting ready for bed . . . Will you come in, or would you rather I came out with you . . .?'

'Perhaps it would be better if we went downstairs?'

'One moment . . . I'll tell her and get my cigarettes . . .'

An untidy sitting-room was half visible, with the dress Jocelyne had been wearing that evening, thrown on to an armchair.

'No . . . No . . . I promise I'll be back in a moment . . .'

Then he lowered his voice. She was whispering. The bed-room door remained ajar.

'Are you sure?'

'Don't worry . . . See you in a moment . . .'

He never wore a hat. He didn't take a coat.

'Let's go . . .'

The lift had not moved. They took it.

'Which side? . . . The street or the courtyard? . . .'

'The courtyard.'

They reached it, walked side by side in the dark. When Huguet raised his head, he saw his wife looking out of the window, and signalled her to go back in.

There was still a light in Ricain's bathroom. Was his stomach turning over again?

'Have you guessed?' asked the photographer finally, after a cough.

'I'm just wondering.'

'It's not a pleasant situation, you know . . . Ever since it happened, I've been trying to be smart . . . Just now, at dinner, I spent the most disagreeable night of my life . . .'

'It was quite obvious.'

'Have you got a match? . . .'

Maigret handed him his box, and began slowly to fill one of the two pipes he had in his pocket.

CHAPTER EIGHT

'DID RICAIN AND HIS WIFE have dinner at the Vieux-Pressoir on Wednesday evening?'

'No . . . The fact is, they only ate there when they happened to be in funds, or when they could find someone to invite them . . . They looked by at about half-past eight . . . Only Francis went in . . . Often, in the evenings, he only half-opened the door . . . If Carus was there, he would go on in, with Sophie following, and sit at his table . . .'

'Who did he speak to, on Wednesday?'

'When I saw him, he only exchanged two words with Bob . . . He asked: "Is Carus there?"'

'And when he was told no, he left . . .'

'He didn't try to borrow money?'

'Not then . . .'

'If he was counting on Carus to invite him to dinner, does it mean they hadn't eaten?'

'They must have gone for a snack to a self-service place in the Avenue de La-Motte-Picquet. They often used to go there.'

'Did you and your wife stay long?'

'We left the Vieux-Pressoir at about nine . . . We took the air for about a quarter of an hour . . . We went home and Jocelyne undressed immediately . . . Since she's been pregnant she's always tired . . .'

'So I heard . . .'

The photographer looked puzzled.

'You talked about it at dinner. It seems she even snores.'

'Both my others did, as well . . . I think all women snore

146

when they are a few months pregnant . . . I said that to tease her . . .'

They were talking in low voices, in the silence unbroken but for the sound of cars in the Boulevard de Grenelle, on the far side of the building. The Rue Saint-Charles, beyond the open gate, was empty and, at long intervals, only, there would come into view the silhouette of a man going by, or a girl tripping past on her high heels.

'What did you do?'

'I put her to bed and went to say good-night to my children . . .'

It was a fact that his first two wives lived in the same block, one with two children, the other with one.

'Do you do that every night?'

'Nearly every night. Unless I get home too late . . .'

'Are you welcome?'

'Why not? . . . They don't hold anything against me . . . They know me . . . They know that I cannot act otherwise.'

'In other words, one day or other, you will leave Jocelyne for somebody else?'

'If it comes to the point . . . You know, for myself, I don't attach any importance to it . . . I adore children . . . the greatest man in history was Abraham . . .'

It was hard not to smile, especially when, this time, he was talking seriously. Beneath the over-contrived jokes, there really was a core of sincerity.

'I stayed with Nicole for a moment . . . Nicole, that's the second one . . . Sometimes we have a little reunion for old times' sake . . .'

'Does Jocelyne know?'

'It doesn't bother her . . . If I wasn't made like that, she wouldn't be with me . . .'

'Did you make love?'

'No . . . I thought about it . . . The child started to talk in its sleep and I tip-toed out . . .'

'What time was this?'

147

'I didn't look at my watch . . . I went back home . . . I changed the film in one of my cameras, as I had to take some pictures early next morning . . . Then I went to the window and opened it . . .

'I open it every night, wide at first, to get rid of the cigarette smoke, then half, because, winter or summer, I can't sleep shut in . . .'

'Then?'

'I smoked a last cigarette . . . There was a moon, like tonight . . . I saw a couple crossing the courtyard and I recognized Francis and his wife . . . They were not holding hands, as they usually did, and they were having an animated conversation . . .'

'Didn't you hear anything?'

'Just one thing which Sophie said in a piercing voice, which made me think she was in a furious temper.'

'Did she often get into one?'

'No . . . She said: "*Don't act the innocent . . . You knew perfectly well . . .*"'

'Did he answer?'

'No. He seized her by the arm and dragged her towards the door . . .'

'You still don't know what time this was?'

'Yes, I do . . . I heard the church clock strike ten. A light went on in the bathroom window . . . I lit another cigarette . . .'

'Were you curious?'

'I just wasn't sleepy, that's all . . . I poured myself out a glass of calvados . . .'

'Were you in the living room?'

'Yes . . . The bedroom door was open and I had put out the lights so Jocelyne could sleep . . .'

'How long did all this take?'

'The time it took me to finish the cigarette I had lit in my first wife's place, then the one I lit by the window . . . A little over five minutes? . . . Less than ten, in any case . . .'

'Did you hear anything?'

'No . . . I saw Francis leave, and move quickly towards the gate . . . He always kept his car in the Rue Saint-Charles . . . After a while the motor coughed, then, a few moments later, it started . . .'

'When did you go down?'

'A quarter of an hour later . . .'

'Why?'

'I told you . . . I wasn't sleepy . . . I wanted a chat . . .'

'Just a chat?'

'Perhaps a bit more . . .'

'Had you previously had relations with Sophie?'

'You want to know if I slept with her . . . Once . . . Francis was drunk and as there was nothing left in the house he had gone out to fetch a bottle from a bistro that was still open . . .'

'Was she willing?'

'It seemed perfectly natural to her . . .'

'And afterwards?'

'Afterwards, nothing . . . Ricain came back without the bottle as they had refused to sell him one . . . We put him to bed . . . The next few days there was no question of anything more happening . . .'

'Let's go back to Wednesday evening . . . You went down . . .'

'I went to the door . . . I knocked . . . And so as not to scare Sophie, I whispered: "It's Jacques . . ." '

'Nobody answered?'

'No . . . There wasn't a sound inside . . .'

'Didn't this strike you as odd?'

'I told myself she had had a row with Francis and didn't want to see anybody . . . I assumed she was on her bed, in a rage, or in tears . . .'

'Did you go on trying?'

'I knocked two or three times, then I went upstairs again to my place . . .'

'Did you go back to the window?'

149

'When I had got into my pyjamas, I looked down into the courtyard . . . It was empty . . . The light was still on in Ricains' bathroom . . . I climbed into bed and went to sleep . . .'

'Go on . . .'

'I got up at eight, made myself some coffee while Jocelyne was still sleeping . . . I opened the window wide and I noticed that the light was still on in Francis's bathroom . . .'

'Didn't it strike you as funny?'

'Not really . . . These things happen . . . I went to the studio, where I worked until one o'clock, then I had a bite to eat with a friend. I had a date at the Ritz with an American film star who kept me cooling my heels for an hour, and then hardly gave me enough time to take pictures of him . . . What with one thing and another, it was four o'clock before I got back . . .'

'Hadn't your wife gone out?'

'To do her shopping, yes . . . After breakfast, she had gone back to bed . . . She was asleep . . .'

He was aware of the comic side to this leitmotiv.

'Was there still . . .'

'A light on, yes . . .'

'Did you go down and knock on the door?'

'No . . . I telephoned . . . Nobody answered . . . Ricain could have gone back, slept, gone out with his wife, forgetting to turn out the light . . .'

'Did that happen sometimes?'

'It happens to everybody . . . Let's see . . . Jocelyne and I went to a cinema in the Champs-Elysées . . .'

Maigret only just stopped himself from asking:

'Did she fall asleep?'

The cat came and rubbed itself against his trouser leg and looked at him as if demanding to be stroked. But when Maigret bent down, it jumped away and miaowed at him from a few feet further on.

'Who does he belong to?'

'I don't know . . . Everybody . . . People throw him scraps of meat from the window and he lives out in the open . . .'

'What time did you come back on the Thursday evening?'

'Around ten-thirty . . . After the cinema, we had a drink in a *brasserie* and I met up with a chum . . .'

'The light?'

'Obviously . . . But there was nothing surprising about that, as the Ricains could well have been back . . . Even so, I rang . . . I admit I was a bit worried when I didn't get an answer . . .'

'Only a bit?'

'Well, I didn't suspect the truth . . . If one were to imagine a murder every time somebody forgets to switch off the light . . .'

'In short . . .'

'Look! . . . He hasn't put out his light now, either . . . I don't think he can be working . . .'

'Next morning?'

'Of course I rang again, and twice more during the day, until I learned from the newspaper that Sophie was dead . . . I was at Joinville, in the studios, taking stills for a film being made . . .'

'Did someone answer?'

'Yes . . . A voice I don't know . . . I decided to say nothing and hung up after waiting a few moments . . .'

'You didn't try to get hold of Ricain?'

Huguet said nothing. Then he shrugged his shoulders and put on his comic face again.

'Look, I don't work at the Quai des Orfèvres!'

Maigret, who was staring idly at the light diffused by the frosted glass, suddenly started towards the studio door. Thinking he understood, the photographer went after him.

'While we were busy chatting . . .'

If Francis wasn't working, if he wasn't sleeping, if the light was still on, that night . . .

He hammered violently on the door.

'Open up! . . . Maigret here . . .'

He was making so much noise that a neighbour appeared at the door in pyjamas. He looked at the two men in astonishment.

'Now what's happening? Can't one get a moment's peace? . . .'

'Run to the concierge . . . Ask her if she has a pass-key . . .'

'She hasn't . . .'

'How do you know?'

'Because I already asked her, one evening when I had forgotten my key . . . I had to call a locksmith . . .'

For a man who made himself out to be simple, Huguet did not lose his head. Wrapping his handkerchief round his fist, he delivered a punch at the frosted glass, which splintered into fragments.

'We must act fast . . .' he panted, as he looked in.

Maigret looked, too. Fully dressed, Ricain was seated in the bath which was too small for him to lie in. Water was flowing from the tap. The bath was overflowing and the water was pink.

'Have you got a strong screwdriver, a jack, anything heavy?'

'In my car . . . Wait . . .'

The neighbour went off to put on a dressing-gown, and emerged followed by a barrage of questions from his wife. He went out of the main door, and there was the sound of a car boot being opened.

As the woman appeared in turn, Maigret shouted:

'Call a doctor . . . The nearest one . . .'

'What's happening? . . . Isn't it enough that . . .?'

She went off, grumbling, while her husband came back with a tyre-lever. He was taller, broader and heavier than the Superintendent.

'Let me do it . . . As long as I don't have to worry about damage . . .'

The wood resisted at first, then cracked. Another two heaves, one lower, then higher up, and the door suddenly yielded, while the man had to stop himself from falling in.

The rest was confusion. Other neighbours had heard the noise, and there were soon several of them in the narrow entrance. Maigret had pulled Francis out of the bath and dragged him over to the divan bed. He remembered the drawer in the chest, and its assortment of contents.

He found some string. With the aid of a large blue pencil he improvised a tourniquet. He had scarcely finished it when a young doctor pushed him to one side. He lived in the building and had hastily pulled on a pair of trousers.

'How long ago?'

'We've just found him . . .'

'Telephone for an ambulance . . .'

'Is there any chance of . . .?'

'For God's sake, don't ask me questions! . . .'

The ambulance pulled up in the courtyard five minutes later. Maigret climbed in front beside the driver. At the hospital, he had to wait in the corridor while the acting house surgeon performed a blood transfusion.

He was surprised to see Huguet arrive.

'Will he pull through?'

'They don't know yet.'

'Do you think he really meant to commit suicide?'

It was apparent that he had his doubts. Maigret likewise. Cornered, Francis had had to make a theatrical gesture.

'Why do you think he would have done a thing like that?'

The Superintendent took the question in the wrong sense.

'Because he considered himself too intelligent.'

Naturally the photographer did not understand and stared at him with some bewilderment.

It was not Sophie's death that Maigret had in mind at that precise moment. It was an event much less serious, but perhaps of greater consequence for Ricain's future: the theft of his wallet.

CHAPTER NINE

HE HAD SLEPT until ten o'clock, but he had not been able to have his breakfast by the open window as he had been promising himself, because of a downpour of fine rain.

Before going to the bathroom, which had no window, frosted or otherwise, giving on to the courtyard, he rang the hospital and had the greatest difficulty in getting through to the doctor on duty.

'Ricain? . . . What is it? . . . An emergency? . . . We had eight emergencies last night and if I had to remember all their names . . . Good . . . Blood transfusion . . . Attempted suicide . . . Hum! . . . If the artery had been cut he wouldn't be here, or else we'd have laid him out in the basement . . . He's all right, yes . . . He hasn't opened his mouth . . . No . . . Not one word . . . There's a cop outside his door . . . Obviously you know all about that . . .'

At eleven o'clock Maigret was in his office. His feet were hurting him once more, since he had decided to put his new shoes on again, as he had to break them in sometime.

Seated opposite Lapointe and Janvier, he began mechanically arranging his pipes in order of size, chose one, the longest, and filled it carefully.

'As I was saying, he is too intelligent. Sometimes it's as dangerous as being too stupid. An intelligence not applied in conjunction with a certain force of character. It doesn't matter! I know what I want to say, even if I can't find the words to express it.'

'Besides, it isn't my concern. The doctors and psychiatrists will take care of all that.

'I'm almost sure he was an idealist, an idealist incapable of living up to his ideal. Do you see what I mean?'

Not too clearly, perhaps. Maigret had seldom been so prolix and so confused all at once.

'He would have liked, above all, to be exceptional in all things. To succeed very fast, as he was burning with impatience, but all the while remaining pure . . .'

He was losing heart, his words lagging behind his thoughts.

'The best and the worst. He must have hated Carus, because he needed him. That didn't stop him from accepting the dinners the producer stood him and he didn't think twice about touching him for a loan.

'He was ashamed of himself. He was angry with himself.

'He was not so naive that he didn't realize that Sophie hadn't turned into the wife he thought he could see in her. But he needed her, too. He even took advantage, when all's said and done, of her affair with Carus.

'He will refuse to admit it. He can't admit it.

'And that's just the reason he shot his wife. They were already quarreling, on Wednesday evening, as they came into the courtyard. What it was about doesn't matter. She must have been exasperated, watching his two-faced game, and probably spat out the truth in his face.

'I wouldn't be surprised if she called him a pimp. Perhaps the drawer was partly open. At any rate, he could not tolerate hearing a truth of that sort being voiced.

'He shot her. Then he stopped in his tracks, frightened by what he had just done, and by the consequences.

'I'm convinced that from this moment he made up his mind that he would not allow himself to be convicted, and while he roamed the streets, his brain began to work, to concoct a complicated plan.

'So complicated in fact, it almost worked.

'He goes back to the Vieux-Pressoir. He asks for Carus. He needs two thousand francs right away, and he knows Bob isn't the man to lend him a sum like that.

'He has thrown the weapon into the Seine, so as to get round the question of fingerprints.

'He shows his face several times at the Club Zéro—"Hasn't Carus got here yet?"—he drinks, walks about ceaselessly adding little touches to his plan.

'True, he hasn't enough money to leave the country, but even if he had, it wouldn't be of any use to him, because sooner or later he would be extradited.

'He must get back to the Rue Saint-Charles, make a pretence of discovering the body, and alert the police.

'And so he thinks of me.

'He's about to pull a trick on me that no normal person would have even dreamed of. The details begin to fall into place. His wanderings are starting to pay dividends.

'He watches me, from early morning, at the door of my house. If I don't take the bus, no doubt he has some alternative solution.

'He steals my wallet. He rings me up, plays his part in such a way as to take suspicion away from himself.

'And that's just it—he overdoes it! He gives me the menu of Sophie's non-existent dinner at the Vieux-Pressoir. He lacks stability, simple common-sense. He can invent an extravagant story and make it plausible, but he doesn't think of the simplest and most mundane details.'

'Do you think his case will ever get to the courts, chief?' asked Lapointe.

'That depends on the psychiatrists.'

'What would you decide yourself?'

'The courts.'

And, as his two colleagues showed surprise at such a definite reply, so uncharacteristic of what they knew of the Superintendent, Maigret observed:

'He would be too unhappy to be thought mad, or even only partially responsible. In the dock, on the other hand, he will be able to play the role of the exceptional being, a sort of hero.'

He shrugged, smiled sadly, went over to the window and gazed at the rain.

Epalinges, November 11, 1966

MAIGRET AND THE NAHOUR CASE

*

*Translated from
the French by*
ALASTAIR HAMILTON

CHAPTER ONE

HE HAD BEEN SEIZED by the shoulder and was struggling. He even tried to deal a punch, with the humiliating feeling that his arm would not do what he wanted, but lay inert and stiff.

'Who is it?' he shouted, vaguely realizing the inadequacy of the question.

Did he really make a sound?

'Jules! . . . Telephone . . .'

He had heard a menacing noise in his sleep, but he had not thought for a minute that it was the telephone ringing, that he was lying in bed, that he was having a nightmare which he had already forgotten, and that his wife was shaking him.

He automatically put out his hand to pick up the receiver as he opened his eyes and sat up. Madame Maigret was also sitting up in the warm bed, and the bedside lamp next to her gave out a soft, intimate light.

'Hello . . .'

He repeated, as he had in his dream:

'Who is it?'

'Maigret? . . . Pardon speaking . . .'

The Superintendent could just see the time on the alarm clock on his wife's night-table. It was half past one. They had left the Pardons soon after eleven, after their monthly dinner which had consisted of a tasty shoulder of mutton.

'Yes . . . I'm listening . . .'

'I'm sorry to wake you up so early . . . Something has just happened here which seems quite serious to me: it's up your street . . .'

The Maigrets and the Pardons had been friends and had dined together once a month for almost ten years, and yet it had never occurred to the two men to be on Christian name terms.

'I'm listening, Pardon . . . Go on . . .'

The voice at the other end of the line sounded anxious, embarrassed.

'I think it would be better if you came to see me . . . You'd understand the situation better . . .'

'I hope there hasn't been an accident?'

A pause.

'No . . . Not exactly, but I'm worried . . .'

'Is your wife all right? . . .'

'Yes . . . She's making us some coffee . . .'

Madame Maigret was trying to make out what was going on from her husband's answers, and looked at him questioningly.

'I'll be there at once . . .'

He hung up, uneasily. He was wide awake by now, but he looked anxious. It was the first time that Doctor Pardon had called him like this, and the Superintendent knew him well enough to know that it must be serious.

'What's going on?'

'I don't know . . . Pardon needs me . . .'

'Why didn't he come and see you?'

'There seems to be a reason for me to go there . . .'

'He was in a very good mood when we saw him . . . So was his wife. We talked about his daughter and son-in-law, and the cruise they were going to make to the Balearic Islands next summer . . .'

Was Maigret listening?

He dressed uneasily, trying to figure out, in spite of himself, why the doctor had telephoned.

'I'll make you some coffee . . .'

'No point . . . Madame Pardon is already making some . . .'

'I'll call a taxi, shall I? . . .'

'Either you won't find one in this weather, or else it'll take half an hour to get here . . .'

It was January 14, Friday, January 14, and the temperature in Paris had been twelve degrees below zero all day. The snow, which had fallen abundantly on the previous days, had frozen so hard that it was impossible to sweep it away, and, in spite of the salt strewn on the pavements, there were still some patches of sheer ice on which the passers-by would slip.

'Put on your heavy scarf . . .'

A thick woollen scarf which she had knitted for him and which he hardly ever had a chance to wear.

'Don't forget your galoshes . . . Can't I come with you ? . . .'

'Why should you ?'

She didn't like seeing him go out alone that night. On their way back from the Pardons', as they were walking along cautiously, watching the pavement in front of them, Maigret had fallen heavily at the corner of the Rue du Chemin-Vert, and he had remained seated on the ground for some time, dazed and ashamed of himself.

'Did you hurt yourself?'

'No . . . I was just surprised . . .'

He had not allowed her to help him up or to hold him by the arm.

'There's no point in our both falling . . .'

She followed him to the door, kissed him and murmured: 'Be careful . . .'

Then she left the door ajar until he got to the ground floor. Maigret avoided the Rue du Chemin-Vert, where he had fallen so recently, and preferred to make a slight detour along the Boulevard Richard-Lenoir to the Boulevard Voltaire, where the Pardons lived.

He walked slowly, and he couldn't hear any footsteps besides his own. There was neither a taxi nor a car in sight. Paris seemed empty and he could only remember having seen it like that, congealed with cold, two or three times in his life.

In the Boulevard Voltaire, however, the throttled engine of

a lorry was running near the Place de la République, and Maigret could see the dark silhouettes of men throwing shovelfuls of salt onto the pavement.

The light was on in two windows of the Pardons' flat, the only lighted windows in the row of houses. Maigret could just make out a dark shadow behind the curtains, and when he got to the door, it opened before he had time to ring.

'I'm sorry, Maigret . . .'

Doctor Pardon was wearing the same navy blue jacket he had worn at dinner.

'I'm in such a tricky situation that I really don't know what to do . . .'

In the lift the Superintendent noticed that his face looked strained.

'Haven't you been to bed?'

And the doctor started to explain awkwardly:

'I wasn't sleepy when you left, so I decided to fill in the files I was behind-hand with . . .'

In other words, in spite of his work, he had not wanted to postpone the traditional dinner.

Strangely enough the Maigrets had stayed later than usual. The main topic of conversation had been holidays, and Pardon had observed that his patients were increasingly tired when they returned home, particularly after organized tours.

They went through the waiting-room where a single lamp was lit, and instead of going into the drawing-room they went into Pardon's office.

Madame Pardon arrived soon after with a tray, two cups, a coffee-pot and some sugar.

'Please forgive me for appearing like this . . . I didn't bother to dress . . . Anyhow, I won't stay a moment, because it's my husband who wants to speak to you . . .'

She was wearing a pale blue dressing-gown over her night-dress and her feet were bare in her slippers.

'He didn't want to bother you . . . I insisted, and if I'm wrong I'm sorry . . .'

She poured out the coffee and went to the door.

'Since I won't be asleep before you're ready you must call me if you need anything . . . Are you hungry, Maigret?"

'I had too good a dinner to be hungry . . .'

'How about you?'

'No thanks . . .'

A door was open and gave into the little room where the doctor examined his patients. In the middle of the room stood a high surgical couch covered with a sheet stained with blood, and Maigret noticed some large patches of blood on the green linoleum.

'Sit down . . . Drink your coffee first . . .'

He pointed to a heap of papers and cards on the desk.

'You see . . . People don't realize that we have a bureau-crat's job to do besides consultations and visits . . . Since we frequently get urgent calls we put it off and then, one fine day, we're submerged by it . . . I thought I could spend two or three hours at it : . .'

Pardon started his rounds at eight in the morning, before consulting patients in his surgery at ten o'clock. The Picpus quarter is not a rich one. It is full of poor people and there were frequently anything up to fifteen patients in the waiting-room. Few of the monthly dinners ended without a call which would keep Pardon out for an hour or more.

'I was engrossed in these papers . . . My wife was asleep . . . I didn't hear a sound until the front door bell suddenly rang and made me jump . . . When I went to the door I saw a couple on the landing who looked rather odd to me . . .'

'Why?'

'First of all because I knew neither the man nor the woman, and usually my patients are the only people who call on me in the middle of the night, or rather only the ones who haven't got a telephone . . .'

'I see . . .'

'Then I didn't think they were in my district. The woman was wearing a sealskin coat and hat . . . It so happened that my wife was looking through a fashion magazine two days ago, and suddenly said to me:

' "If you ever give me a coat, don't give me a mink but a sealskin . . . Mink has become so common, but seal . . ."

'I didn't listen to anything else, but I remembered that when I was standing at the door, looking at them in amazement.

'The man was also wearing clothes which one doesn't usually see in the Boulevard Voltaire.

'He was the one who asked, in a slight foreign accent:

' "Doctor Pardon?"

' "That's me, yes."

' "This lady has just been injured and I wondered whether you could see her."

' "How did you get my address?"

' "An elderly lady walking down the Boulevard Voltaire gave it to us . . . I suppose she's a patient of yours . . ."

'They came into my office. The woman was very pale. She seemed about to faint and looked at me with large, expressionless eyes, clutching her chest with both her hands.

' "I think you should hurry, Doctor . . ." said the man taking off his gloves.

' "What sort of a wound is it?"

'He turned to the woman, who had very fair hair and must have been under thirty.

' "You'd better take off your coat . . ."

'Without a word she took off her fur-coat, and I saw that the back of her straw-coloured dress was soaked in blood down to the waist.

'Look, there's a blood-stain on the carpet, next to my desk, where she stood unsteadily.

'I made her go into the surgery and offered to help her take off her dress. Without even saying a word, she shook her head and undressed on her own.

'The man didn't follow us, but the door between the two rooms was open and he continued to talk to me, or rather to answer me. I had put my white coat on and washed my hands. The woman lay motionless on her stomach, without a groan.'

'What time was it?' asked Maigret, who had just lit his first pipe since the telephone call.

'I looked at the clock when the bell rang. It said ten past one. It all happened very quickly, far more quickly than it takes to tell you the story.

'In fact I was already washing the wound and staunching the blood when I realized what was happening. At first sight the wound was not too deep. It was in the back, on the right-hand side: a wound about six inches long, with the blood still flowing.

'As I worked I asked the man who was out of sight, in my office:

' "Tell me what happened . . ."

' "I was walking along the Boulevard Voltaire, about a hundred yards away from here, and this lady was in front of me . . ."

' "You're not going to say she slipped?"

' "No . . . I was rather surprised to see her alone in the street at that time of night and I walked slowly so that she shouldn't think I was trying to pick her up . . . That was when I heard a car . . ." '

Pardon stopped to drink his coffee and pour a second cup.

'Do you want some?'

'I'd love some . . .'

Maigret was still sleepy, his eye-lids were stinging, and he felt he was starting a cold. Ten of his detectives were in bed with 'flu, and that had complicated his work in the last few days.

'I'm repeating our conversation as accurately as possible but I can't swear to every word . . . I discovered that the wound was deeper between the third and fourth ribs and as I was disinfecting it something fell to the ground, without my immediately noticing it.'

'A bullet?'

'Wait a minute . . . The man in the next room went on:

' "When the car drew level with this lady, it slowed down, nearly to a standstill, and I saw an arm stretch out of the door . . ." '

Maigret interrupted:

'The front door or the back door?'

'He didn't say, and it didn't occur to me to ask him . . . Don't forget that I was performing a surgical operation . . . I occasionally have to do this, in emergencies, but it isn't something I specialize in and I found the whole business rather strange . . . What surprised me most was the silence of the patient . . .

'The man continued:

' "I heard an explosion and I saw this lady stagger, try to catch hold of the wall of a house, and then bend her knees and slowly sink into the snow . . .

' "The car had driven away and had turned right, into a street which I didn't know . . .

' "I rushed forward . . . I saw that she wasn't dead and she helped herself up by clinging on to me . . .

' "I asked her if she was wounded and she nodded."

' "She didn't talk to you?"

' "No . . . I didn't know what to do . . . I looked round for help . . . An old woman went past and I asked her where I could find a doctor . . . She pointed to your house and gave me your name . . ." '

Pardon stopped talking and looked at Maigret like a truant child. It was the Superintendent who asked:

'Didn't it occur to the man to take her to a hospital?'

'I said the same thing. I said we were very close to the Pitié and not far from the Hôpital Saint-Antoine. He just muttered:

' "I didn't know that." '

'I suppose he didn't know that the local police station was a hundred yards away either?'

'I don't suppose so . . . I was embarrassed . . . I know I

had no right to attend to a wound caused by a fire-arm without
alerting the police immediately . . . But on the other hand I
had already started . . . I told them:

' "I'm just giving first-aid treatment, and when I've finished
I'll call an ambulance . . ."

'I put on a temporary dressing.

' "Don't wear those blood-stained clothes: I'll give you a
bath-robe . . ."

'She shook her head and a few minutes later she put on
her clothes and joined the man in my office.

'I said to both of them:

' "Sit down . . . I'll be with you in a minute . . ."

'I wanted to take off my rubber gloves, my stained coat,
and stop the bottles I'd been using. I went on talking:

' "You must both give me your name and address . . . If
you prefer a private clinic to a hospital, say so, and I'll see
to it . . ." '

Maigret had already understood.

'How long did you leave them alone for?'

'I can't be sure . . . I remember picking up the bullet which
had fallen while I was dressing the wound, and throwing
away the blood-stained cotton wool and bandages . . . Two
or three minutes? . . . As I was talking I went to the door and
saw that my office was empty . . .

'First I rushed into the hall, and then onto the landing . . .
Not hearing either the lift or steps on the stairs I came back
to my office and looked out of the window, but I couldn't see
the pavement at the foot of the building.

'It was then that I clearly heard a car drive off . . . I could
swear that it sounded like a powerful car, a sports model . . .
By the time I'd opened the window the Boulevard Voltaire
was empty except for a salt lorry near the Place de la
République and one solitary figure far off in the other
direction . . .'

Apart from his closest collaborators, like Lucas, Janvier,
Torrence, and, more recently, young Lapointe, of whom

167

Maigret was very fond, Doctor Pardon was the Superintendent's only friend.

There was only a year's difference in their ages and each day both men inspected the diseases of men and society, so that their attitude was fairly similar.

They could chat for hours after their monthly dinners in the Boulevard Richard-Lenoir and the Boulevard Voltaire without noticing the time, and the experiences which they described were almost identical.

Was it the mutual respect which they felt which stopped them ever calling each other by their Christian names? On this night, in the tranquillity and silence of the doctor's office, they were not as relaxed as they had been a few hours earlier, maybe because they were facing each other on a professional level for the first time in their life.

Intimidated, the doctor was talking faster than usual and he was obviously in a hurry to prove his good faith, just as though he were being interrogated by the Public Prosecutor. On his side, Maigret restrained himself from asking too many questions, only asking ones which he considered indispensable after a moment's hesitation.

'Look, Pardon, at the beginning you said that neither the man nor the woman seemed from this district.'

The doctor tried to explain.

'Most of my patients are shopkeepers, workmen, and poor people. I'm not a society doctor, or a specialist, but a doctor who lugs his case up five or six floors twenty times a day. There are some well-to-do, middle-class blocks of flats in this street, but I've never seen people in the street who look anything like the couple I've just seen.

'Although the woman didn't say a word, I have a feeling she's a foreigner . . . She looks very Nordic, with a milky complexion, fair hair which one rarely sees in Paris unless it's dyed, and hers wasn't . . . Judging from her breasts I'd say that she'd had one or more children and that she'd suckled them . . .'

'Any special peculiarities?'

'No . . . Just a minute . . . A scar about an inch long running from the left eye towards the ear . . . I noticed that because it looks like a wrinkle, which is quite attractive on a very young face . . .'

'Do you think she remained silent voluntarily?'

'I'd swear to it . . . Just as I would have sworn, when I saw them on the landing, and then in my office, that they knew each other intimately . . . I may be wrong . . . But I believe that there's a sort of aura around couples who are deeply in love, and that even when they aren't looking at each other, when they aren't touching each other, one can feel a tie between them . . .'

'Tell me about him.'

'I saw less of him than of her, and he never took off his overcoat, made of a soft, supple material . . .'

'Did he wear a hat?'

'No. He was bare-headed. Brown hair, fine features, a sun-burnt skin, dark eyes . . . I'd say he was twenty-five or six, and judging from his voice, his movements, and his clothes, I would say that he'd been brought up with a certain amount of money . . . A handsome boy, gentle-looking, rather melancholy . . . Probably Spanish or South American . . .

'What shall I do now? Since I don't know their name I can't fill in their medical card . . . Well, it's probably a case of criminal assault . . .'

'Did you believe the man's story?'

'I didn't really think at the time . . . It was only when I saw that my office was empty, and while I waited for you after my telephone call, that his account seemed somehow rather strange . . .'

Maigret examined the bullet attentively.

'Probably shot from a 6.35 . . . A weapon which is only really dangerous at point blank range and is usually inaccurate . . .'

'That would account for the wound . . . The bullet had

169

struck her back at an angle, grazing over several inches of skin before lodging between two ribs . . .'

'How far can the woman go?'

'I can't tell. She may well have taken a sedative before coming, because she didn't react and superficial wounds are often the most painful . . .'

'Look, Pardon,' muttered Maigret, getting up, 'I'll see to them. Send me a statement tomorrow morning, repeating what you've just told me.'

'Shall I be in trouble?'

'You're obliged to help somebody in danger, aren't you?' He lit another pipe before putting on his hat and gloves.

'I'll keep in touch . . .'

Outside the air was icy, and gazing at the snow heaped against the houses, he walked a hundred yards without seeing any bloodstains or signs of a fall. Then, retracing his steps, he crossed the Place Léon Blum and went into the police station on the ground floor of the municipal buildings.

He had known Sergeant Demarie, sitting behind the counter, for years.

'Hello, Demarie . . .'

Surprised to see the chief of the Crime Squad appear like that, Demarie looked rather embarrassed, because he had been reading a comic paper.

'Hello, Louvelle . . .'

Constable Louvelle was making coffee on a paraffin stove.

'Did either of you hear anything an hour or so ago?'

'No, sir . . .'

'Anything like a shot about a hundred yards away . . .'

'Nothing . . .'

'Between one and ten past . . .'

'In what direction?'

'Boulevard Voltaire, Place de la République end.'

'A patrol of two men, Constables Mathis and Bernier, went out just then, at eleven o'clock exactly, and went down the Boulevard Voltaire to the Rue Amelot . . .'

170

'Where are they now?'

The Sergeant glanced at the electric clock.

'Near the Bastille, unless they've got to the Rue de la Roquette . . . They'll both be back at three . . . Shall I try and get hold of them?'

'No . . . Call me a taxi . . . Ring me at the Judicial Police when they get here . . .'

It took two or three calls before they could find a free taxi. Maigret telephoned his flat.

'Don't worry If I'm not back till dawn . . . I'm at the local police station . . . A cab's coming for me . . . No, no! . . . He's got nothing to do with what's just happened . . . But I've got to see to it right now . . . No, I didn't fall . . . See you later . . .'

The taxi passed alongside the salt lorry which was driving at walking pace, and they hardly came across three cars before reaching the Quai des Orfèvres, where the sentry at the gate looked stiff with cold.

Upstairs he found Lucas together with Inspectors Jussieu and Lourtie. The other premises appeared to be empty.

'Good evening, boys . . . To start with ring all the hospitals and private clinics in Paris . . . I want to know whether two people, a man and a woman, appeared after half past one. It's possible that the woman, who is wounded in the back, turned up on her own . . . Here's the description . . .'

He tried to repeat Pardon's words.

'Start with the eastern districts.'

While the three men rushed to the telephones he went into his office, turned on the light and took off his overcoat and his heavy knitted scarf.

He didn't believe the story about the shot from the car in the street. Those were gangster tactics and he'd never seen a gangster with a 6.35. Besides, only one shot was fired and that's rare in an attack from a car.

Like Pardon he was sure that the man and the woman knew each other. Wasn't this proved by the fact that they left without a word, like accomplices, while the doctor was tidying up his surgery?

He went back to the three men who had almost got to the end of their list.

'Nothing?'

'No, chief . . .'

He rang the operator on the Emergency switchboard.

'Did you get any calls at about one in the morning? Did anyone report a shot?'

'Just a minute . . . I'll ask my colleagues . . .'

And, a few seconds later:

'Only a brawl and a knife thrust in a bistro at the Porte d'Italie . . . Requests for ambulances on account of broken arms and legs . . . Now that nearly everybody's got home they're less frequent, but we still get a call about every ten minutes . . .'

He had hardly hung up when Lucas called him.

''Phone for you, chief . . .'

It was Demarie, from the police station in the 12th *Arrondissement*.

'The patrol has just got back . . . Mathis and Bernier didn't see anything irregular and have only reported a few falls on ice patches . . . But Mathis noticed a red Alfa Romeo parked in front of 76 B Boulevard Voltaire, and he even told his mate:

' "That's what we need for our rounds . . ." '

'What time was it?'

'Between five past and ten past one. Mathis automatically stroked the bonnet and noticed that it was still warm.'

In other words the man and the woman had just gone into the building where they'd rung at the doctor's door at ten past one.

How had they got Pardon's address? When he was asked, Mathis said that he hadn't noticed an old woman in the whole street.

Where had the couple come from? Why had they parked

almost in front of the police station in the Boulevard Voltaire?

It was too late to warn the radio cars, because the red car had had time to reach its destination, wherever that might be.

Maigret muttered something, knitting his brows and taking short puffs at his pipe, and Lucas tried to make out what he was saying.

'. . . foreigners . . . Spanish-looking . . . the woman didn't say anything . . . because she can't speak French? . . . Nordic looking . . . but why the Boulevard Voltaire and why Pardon?'

That was what vexed him most. If the couple lived in Paris it was almost certainly in a smart district and there are doctors in nearly every street in town . . . If the shot had been fired in a building, why not call a doctor instead of carting the wounded woman through the streets at twelve degrees below zero? . . .

What if they were passing through, in a big hotel? . . . It was unlikely . . . The noise of a shot rarely goes unnoticed . . .

'Why are you looking at me like that?' he asked Lucas brusquely, as though he had only just realized he was standing there.

'I'm waiting for you to tell me what to do.'

'How should I know?'

He grinned at his own attitude.

'It's an unlikely tale, and I don't know where to begin. Apart from the fact that I was woken up by the telephone in the middle of some nightmare . . .'

'Would you like a cup of coffee?'

'I've just had one . . . A Spanish-looking chap and a Nordic-looking woman rang at my friend Pardon's door at ten past one this morning . . .'

As he told the story sulkily he began to realize the weak points.

'The shot wasn't fired in a hotel. Nor in the streets. It must have been a flat or a private house.'

'Do you think they're married?'

'I don't think so, although I can't say why. If they'd called their normal doctor, provided they've got one, he would have had to report to the police . . .'

What intrigued him most was why they chose Pardon, an obscure district doctor. Did they pick his name out of the directory, at random?

'The woman isn't in any hospital or clinic . . . Pardon offered to lend her one of his wife's bath-robes because her clothes were soaked in blood . . . She chose to put them on again . . . Why?'

Lucas opened his mouth, but the Superintendent had already found an answer.

'Because they intended to escape . . . I don't claim that to be a brilliant conclusion, but it makes sense . . .'

'Most of the roads are unfit for traffic . . . Particularly with a wounded passenger in the car . . .'

'I'd thought of that too . . . Call Breuker at Orly . . . If he isn't there get me his idiot assistant, whose name I can never remember . . .'

Breuker, an Alsatian who had never got rid of his accent, was Superintendent at the airport. He wasn't on duty and it was his assistant who replied.

'Assistant-Superintendent Marathieu speaking . . .'

'This is Maigret,' muttered the head of the Crime Squad, irritated by the pretentious voice at the other end of the line.

'What can I do for you, sir?'

'I don't know yet . . . How many foreign departures have you had since two o'clock, or rather since two thirty this morning? . . .'

'Only two . . . One flight to Amsterdam and another to India, via Geneva . . . All departures have been suspended for the last forty minutes because of ice on the runways . . .'

'Are you far from the car park?'

'Not very, but it's not easy to walk outside, again because of the ice . . .'

'Would you be so kind as to see if a red Alfa Romeo is parked there . . .'

174

'Have you got the number?'

'No. There can't be many red Alfa Romeos in your car park at this time of night . . . If you find it, ask the passport inspectors whether they have seen a couple answering to the following description . . .'

He repeated what he had told Lucas and the two others.

'Call me as soon as possible at the Quai des Orfèvres.'

And Maigret, shrugging his shoulders, added as he turned towards Lucas:

'One never knows . . .'

It was an odd investigation and one would have said that the Superintendent wasn't taking it very seriously, that he was doing it rather as one does a crossword puzzle.

'Marathieu must be livid . . .' commented Lucas. 'Imagine sending someone as fussy and conceited as he is splashing about in the snow and doing balancing tricks on the ice!'

It was about twenty minutes before the telephone rang again. Maigret said mockingly:

'Assistant-Superintendent Marathieu speaking . . .'

And they were the first words he heard.

'Well, the red car?'

'There is a red Alfa Romeo in the car park, with a Paris number-plate . . .'

'Is it locked?'

'Yes . . . A couple answering to the description you gave me took the 3.10 flight to Amsterdam . . .'

'Have you got their names?'

'The inspector who checked them can't remember the names . . . He can only remember the passports . . . The man had a Colombian passport and the woman a Dutch one . . . Both passports were full of visas and stamps . . .'

'What time do they arrive in Amsterdam?'

'If there's no delay and the runway is fit for landing they touch down at 4.17.'

It was 4.22. The couple were probably showing their passports and going through customs. At any rate, at this stage

175

in the investigation Maigret could hardly apply directly to the police at the Dutch airport.

'Well, chief? What shall I do?'

'Nothing. Wait to be relieved. As for me, I'm going to bed. Good night, boys . . . Incidentally, will one of you drive me home? . . .'

Half an hour later he was sleeping soundly next to his wife.

CHAPTER TWO

SOME CASES appear dramatic from the start and get straight into the headlines of the newspapers. Others, which seem banal, only get three or four lines on the sixth page before one realizes that a mere news item was really concealing a drama shrouded in mystery.

Maigret was having his breakfast, sitting opposite his wife, near the window. It was half past eight in the morning and it was so dark that all the lights had to be kept on. Since he hadn't slept enough he felt heavy, his mind dull, full of confused ideas.

There was some frost on the corners of the window-panes, and he remembered that when he was a child he used to trace drawings or write his initials in it; he also recalled the curious feeling, both painful and agreeable, when the thin film of frost got under his finger-nails.

After three very cold days it had started snowing again and one could hardly see the houses and shops on the other side of the street.

'You're not too tired?'

'One more cup of coffee and I'll be in fine form.'

In spite of himself he tried to imagine the couple of elegant foreigners who had suddenly appeared, God knows where from, in the local doctor's surgery. Pardon had immediately sensed that they belonged to another world, different to his own, to Maigret's, and to the Picpus district in which they both lived.

The Superintendent had frequently had to deal with people like this, as much at home in London as in New York or Rome, who take an aeroplane as most people take the underground, stay in palaces whatever country they go to, where they find their own friends with their own similar habits, and form a sort of international freemasonry.

Not only a freemasonry of money, but also of a certain sort of life, certain attitudes, even a certain set of morals, different to the morals of the ordinary human being.

Maigret never felt quite at ease with them, and he had difficulty in overcoming an irritation which could be mistaken for jealousy.

'What are you thinking about?'

'Nothing.'

He wasn't aware of thinking. He was in a daze and he started when he heard the telephone ring. It was now a quarter to nine and he was going to get up from the table and put on his overcoat.

'Hello . . .'

'Lucas here.'

Lucas was due to go off duty at nine o'clock.

'I've just had a call from Superintendent Manicle of the 14th *Arrondissement*, chief . . . A man was killed last night in a small private house in the Avenue du Parc-Montsouris . . . A man called Nahour, a Lebanese . . . The charwoman found the body when she started work at eight o'clock.'

'Has Lapointe arrived?'

'I think I can hear him in the corridor . . . Just a minute . . . Yes . . . It's him all right . . .'

'Tell him to come and fetch me by car. Tell Manicle that I'll be there as soon as I can . . . You can go to bed . . .'

Maigret repeated under his breath:

'Nahour . . . Nahour . . .'

Another foreigner. The couple of the night before consisted of a Dutch woman and a Colombian. Now for Nahour and the Near East.

'A new case?' asked his wife.

'A crime, apparently, in the Avenue du Parc-Montsouris.'

178

He wrapped the large scarf round his neck, put on his coat, grabbed his hat.

'Aren't you going to wait for Lapointe?'

'I must get a breath of fresh air.'

So Lapointe found him standing on the pavement. Maigret slipped into the little black car.

'Have you got the right address?'

'Yes, chief. It's the last house before the park, a house in the middle of a garden . . . You can't have had much sleep last night . . .'

The traffic was slow and tiresome. Here and there a car had skidded and stood immobilized in the middle of the road. On the pavements the pedestrians walked cautiously. The Seine was dark green, full of blocks of ice slowly drifting along the surface of the water.

They stopped in front of a villa with part of the ground floor built in glass. The building must have been designed in 1925 or 1930, at a time when houses, which had then been ultra-modern, had sprung up in certain districts of Paris, particularly at Auteuil and Montparnasse.

A policeman on duty saluted the Superintendent and opened an iron gate leading into a small garden in which stood a bare tree.

The two men walked along the path, climbed the four steps to the entrance, and found another policeman in the corridor, who showed them into the studio.

Manicle was there with one of his detectives. He was a small thin man with a moustache whom Maigret had known for over twenty years, and the two men shook hands. The Police Superintendent then pointed to a body lying behind a mahogany desk.

'The charwoman, called Louise Bodin, informed us by telephone at five past eight. She starts work at eight every day. She lives nearby, in the Rue du Saint-Gothard.'

'Who is Nahour?'

'Felix Nahour is forty-two years old, a Lebanese citizen,

with no known profession. He moved into this house six months ago, and he rents it furnished from a painter who has left for the United States . . .'

It was very hot in the room in spite of the huge windows partly covered in frost, as in the Boulevard Richard-Lenoir.

'Were the curtains open when you arrived?'

'No . . . They were drawn . . . As you see, they're thick curtains padded with felt to stop the cold getting in.'

'Has the doctor been here?'

'A local doctor came a moment ago and confirmed that he was dead, which is all too obvious . . . I've informed the medical expert and he should be arriving at any minute, together with the Public Prosecutor . . .'

Maigret turned to Lapointe.

'Ring Moers and tell him to come round at once with his men from the records office . . . No, not from here . . . there may be some fingerprints on the receiver . . . You'll find a bistro or a call-box near here . . .'

He took off his overcoat and his scarf, because, after an almost sleepless night, the heat went to his head and made him dizzy. The room was enormous. The floor was covered in pale blue moquette and the furniture, although dissimilar, was in good taste and of considerable value.

As he went round the Empire desk to look at the dead man more closely the Superintendent saw a photograph in a silver frame near the blotting pad.

It was the portrait of a young woman, with very fair hair and a sad smile, who had a little girl of three next to her, and a baby of about a year old on her knees.

Knitting his brows he seized the frame, and, staring at the picture, he saw a scar about an inch long running from her left eye towards her ear.

'Is that his wife?'

'I suppose so. I've looked her up in our files. She is registered under the name of Evelina Nahour, maiden name Wiemers, born in Amsterdam . . .'

'Is she in the house?'

'No. We knocked at her door. When there was no answer we opened it. The room is a bit untidy, but the bed has not been slept in . . .'

Maigret bent over the crumpled body. He could only see half the face, but as far as he could judge without moving the man, a bullet had gone into his throat, severing the carotid and leaving a vast pool of blood on the carpet.

Nahour was fairly small, plump, and had a short brown moustache. He was going slightly bald. He wore a wedding ring on his left hand, which was carefully manicured, and he had tried to stop the blood flowing with his right hand.

'Do you know who was living in this house?'

'I've only questioned the charwoman briefly, thinking that you would rather do that. I then asked the secretary and the maid to stay upstairs, where one of my men is making sure they don't speak to one another.'

'Where is this Madame Bodin?'

'In the kitchen . . . Shall I call her?'

'Please . . .'

Lapointe had just come in saying:

'I've done it, chief . . . Moers is on his way . . .'

Louise Bodin came in, with a defiant and obstinate expression. Maigret knew that type, the type of most Parisian charwomen, women who have suffered, who have been ill-treated by life, and who hopelessly await an even more unpleasant old age. They then harden, become suspicious, and consider the whole world responsible for their misfortunes.

'Your name is Louise Bodin?'

'Madame Bodin, yes.'

She emphasized the *Madame* which she regarded as her last remnant of feminine dignity. Her dark clothes hung on a thin body and her dark eyes were so intense that they looked almost feverish.

'Are you married?'

'I was . . .'

181

'Is your husband dead?'

'If you really want to know, he's at Fresnes, and that's the best place for him . . .'

Maigret preferred not to ask about the details of her husband's imprisonment.

'Have you been working here long?'

'Five months tomorrow . . .'

'How did you get the job?'

'I answered an advertisement . . . Before that I did an hour here, a morning or an afternoon there . . .'

She laughed unpleasantly, turning to the corpse:

'It's just as well that they put "steady job" in the advertisement!'

'You don't sleep here?'

'Never. I went home at eight in the evening and I came back at eight the next morning . . .'

'Didn't Monsieur Nahour have any profession?'

'He must have done something, since he had a secretary and used to spend hours deep in his papers . . .'

'Who is his secretary?'

'A chap from his country, Monsieur Fouad . . .'

'Where is he now?'

She turned to the Police Superintendent.

'In his room . . .'

She was talking aggresively.

'Don't you like him?'

'Why should I like him?'

'You arrived at eight this morning . . . Did you come straight into this room?'

'First I went to the kitchen to heat some water on the gas stove and to hang up my coat in the cupboard.'

'Then you opened this door? . . .'

'I always start cleaning here . . .'

'What did you do when you saw the body?'

'I telephoned the police station . . .'

'Without telling Monsieur Fouad? . . .'

182

'Without telling anyone . . .'

'Why?'

'Because I don't trust people, and above all not the people living in this house . . .'

'Why don't you trust them?'

'Because they aren't normal . . .'

'What do you mean?'

She shrugged her shoulders and added:

'I know what I mean . . . No one can stop me thinking what I like, can they?'

'While you were waiting for the police did you go and tell the secretary?'

'No. I went to make my coffee in the kitchen. I don't have time to drink it at home in the mornings . . .'

'Did Monsieur Fouad come downstairs?'

'He hardly ever comes down before ten . . .'

'Was he asleep?'

'I tell you I didn't go up.'

'And the maid?'

'She's Madame's maid. She didn't have anything to do with the gentleman. Since Madame stayed in bed until twelve or later, nothing stopped her making the most of it . . .'

'What's her name?'

'Nelly something . . . I heard her surname once or twice, but I can't remember it . . . A Dutch name . . . She's Dutch, like Madame . . .'

'Don't you like her either?'

'Is there anything wrong with that?'

'I see from this photograph that Madame Nahour has two children . . . Are they in the house?'

'They've never set foot in the house . . .'

'Where do they live?'

'Somewhere on the Riviera, with their nurse . . .'

'Did their parents often go and see them?'

'I have no idea. They travelled a great deal, nearly always separately, but I never asked them where they were going . . .'

The van from the records office drew up in front of the garden and Moers came in with his colleagues.

'Did Monsieur Nahour entertain much?'

'What do you mean by entertain?'

'Did he invite friends to lunch or dinner?'

'Not since I've been here. Anyhow, he usually dined in town.'

'And his wife?'

'So did she.'

'Together?'

'I never followed them.'

'Any visitors?'

'Sometimes Monsieur Nahour would see someone in his office . . .'

'A friend?'

'I don't listen at keyholes . . . Usually foreigners, people from his country to whom he spoke in a language which I couldn't understand . . .'

'Was Monsieur Fouad there when these people came?'

'Sometimes he was, sometimes he wasn't.'

'Just a minute, Moers . . . You can't begin before the medical expert gets here . . . Thank you, Madame Bodin . . . Will you please stay in the kitchen and not do any housework until these premises have been examined . . . Where is Madame Nahour's room?'

'Upstairs, on the first floor . . .'

'Monsieur Nahour and his wife shared a room, did they?'

'No. Monsieur Nahour's rooms are on the ground floor on the other side of the corridor . . .'

'Isn't there any dining-room?'

'The studio was used as a dining-room . . .'

'Thank you for your help . . .'

'Don't mention it . . .'

And she went out with dignity.

A moment later Maigret climbed the stairs, covered with a carpet of the same lavender-blue as the floor of the studio.

Manicle and Lapointe followed him. On the first floor landing they found the local detective in plain clothes smoking a cigarette resignedly.

'Which is Madame Nahour's room?'

'This one, just opposite . . .'

The room was spacious, with Louis XVI furniture. Although the bed hadn't been slept in, it was quite untidy. A green dress and some linen lay on the carpet. The doors of the cupboards were wide open and suggested a hurried departure. Several bare hangers, one on the bed and others on the silk-covered armchair, made it look as though some clothes had been grabbed and stuffed into a suitcase.

Maigret casually opened some drawers.

'Will you call the maid, Lapointe?'

This took some time. Several minutes later a young woman, with hair almost as fair as Madame Nahour's, and astonishingly light blue eyes, appeared in the doorway, followed by Lapointe.

She was not wearing an overall, or the usual black dress and white apron, but a tweed suit which fitted very closely.

She looked like the Dutch girls on chocolate boxes, and all she needed was her national bonnet with its two points.

'Come in . . . Sit down . . .'

Her face was blank, as though she didn't understand what was going on or who the people standing in front of her were.

'What's your name?'

She shook her head, but opened her mouth a little and said: 'No understand . . .'

'Can't you speak French?'

She shook her head.

'Only Dutch?'

Maigret was already imagining the complications involved in getting a translator.

'English too.'

'You speak English?'

'Yes . . .'

185

The little English that Maigret spoke was not enough for an interrogation which might prove important.

'Shall I translate, chief?' suggested Lapointe shyly.

The Superintendent looked at him in surprise because the young Inspector had never told him he could speak English.

'Where did you learn it?'

'I've been studying it for a year . . .'

The girl looked at them in turn. When she was asked a question she did not answer at once, but took the time to assimilate what she had been told.

She was not aggressively suspicious, like the charwoman, but displayed a sort of impassiveness which might have been natural or acquired. Was she purposely trying to appear well below average intelligence?

Even in English the sentences seemed to sink in with difficulty and her replies were brief, elementary.

She was called Velthuis, was twenty-four years old, born in Friesland in the north of Holland, and had gone to Amsterdam when she was fifteen.

'Did she enter Madame Nahour's service at once?'

Lapointe translated the question, and in reply simply got the word:

'No.'

'When did she become her maid?'

'Six years ago.'

'How?'

'Through an advertisement in a paper in Amsterdam.'

'Was Madame Nahour already married?'

'Yes.'

'Since when?'

'She doesn't know.'

Maigret had great difficulty in controlling himself, because with these 'Nos' and 'Yeses' the interrogation could last a long time.

'Tell her I don't like being taken for a fool.'

Lapointe translated awkwardly, and the girl looked at the

Superintendent in slight surprise before resuming her expression of total indifference.

Two dark cars drew up by the house and Maigret muttered:

'The Public Prosecutor . . . Stay with her, will you? . . . Try to get as much as you can out of her . . .'

The Deputy, Noiret, was an elderly man, with an old-fashioned grey goatee, who had served in most of the provincial law courts and had finally been appointed in Paris where he was waiting to retire and cautiously avoiding all difficulties.

The medical expert, a certain Collinet, who was leaning over the body, had replaced Doctor Paul with whom Maigret had worked for so many years. Other men had also disappeared as time went by, like the magistrate, Coméliau, whom Maigret could call his intimate enemy and sometimes even missed.

As for the magistrate Cayotte, who was relatively young, he always let the police work for two or three days on a case before having anything to do with it himself.

The doctor had twice changed the position of the body, and his hands were sticky with clotted blood. He looked round for Maigret.

'Of course, I can't tell you anything definite before the post-mortem. The position of the bullet hole makes me think it was a weapon of medium or large calibre, which was fired at a distance of over two yards.

'Since there's no hole the other side the bullet has remained in the body. I can't imagine that it lodged in the throat, where it would not have met with any resistance, so I suppose that, since it was shot upwards, it lodged in the skull . . .'

'You mean to say that the victim could have been standing up, while the murderer was sitting on the other side of the desk?'

'Not necessarily sitting, but he could have fired without raising his arm, from the hip . . .'

It wasn't until the ambulance men lifted the body onto a

stretcher that a 6.35 revolver with a mother-of-pearl handle was revealed lying on the carpet.

The Deputy and the magistrate looked at Maigret to know what he thought.

'I don't suppose the wound could have been caused by this weapon, could it?' the Superintendent asked the medical expert.

'I would say no, for the time being.'

'Will you examine the pistol, Moers?'

Moers took a rag to pick it up, sniff it, and then to take out the magazine.

'A bullet's missing, chief.'

Since the body was being taken away the men from the records office and the photographer could get down to work. The photographer had already taken pictures of the dead man. Everybody was coming and going. Little groups gathered. The Deputy, Noiret, tugged the Superintendent's sleeve.

'What nationality do you think he was?'

'Lebanese . . .'

'Do you think it's a political crime?'

This prospect scared him, because he could remember similar cases which had ended pretty badly for everybody concerned.

'I think I'll be able to tell you quite soon . . .'

'Have you questioned the staff?'

'The charwoman, who isn't very talkative, and I've asked the maid a few questions, who's even less so. Admittedly she can't speak a word of French and Inspector Lapointe's questioning her in English, upstairs . . .'

'Let me know as soon as possible . . .'

He looked for the magistrate so that they could leave together, because the Public Prosecutor only appeared as a formality.

'You don't need me or my men do you?' asked the district Superintendent.

'I don't need you, old boy, but it would be a help if you

could leave me your detectives for a little longer, as well as the policeman at the door.'

'By all means . . .'

The drawing-room gradually grew emptier, and Maigret found himself standing in front of a library consisting of over three hundred volumes. He was surprised to see that they were nearly all scientific works, mainly mathematical, and a whole row of books in French and English were devoted to the theory of probability. Opening the cupboards, under the book-shelves, he found them full of papers, some of which were roneo-typed, containing columns of figures.

'Don't leave before you've seen me, Moers . . . Send the gun to Gastine-Renette to get an expert analysis . . . Incidentally, send this bullet with it . . .'

He took the bullet Pardon had handed him out of his pocket. It was wrapped up in a piece of cotton wool.

'Where did you find that?'

'I'll tell you later . . . I'd like to know urgently whether the bullet was shot from this revolver.'

Lighting his pipe he went up the stairs, glanced into the room where Lapointe was sitting opposite the Dutch girl and taking notes on a pad which he rested on the dressing-table.

'Where's the secretary?' he asked the local detective who was hanging about in the corridor.

'The door at the end.'

'Has he been complaining?'

'He occasionally opens his door and listens. He had a telephone call . . .'

'What did the Superintendent say to him this morning?'

'That his boss had been murdered and that he wasn't to leave his room until further orders . . .'

'Were you there?'

'Yes.'

'Did he look surprised?'

'He's not the sort of man who shows his feelings. You'll see for yourself.'

Maigret knocked at the same time as he turned the door-handle and pushed the door open. The room was tidy and, if the bed had been slept in that night, it had been carefully re-made. Nothing was out of place. There was a small desk in front of the window, a fawn-coloured leather armchair near the desk, and, from the armchair, a man watched the Superintendent come into the room.

It was difficult to tell exactly how old he was. He looked very Arab, his skin was dark, and his face, in spite of its lines, could just as well have been that of a man of forty as of a man of sixty. His hair was thick, pitch-black, without a trace of white.

He did not get up, made no move to greet his visitor, merely looked at him with his smouldering eyes without betraying any feeling in his face.

'I suppose you speak French?'

He nodded.

'I'm Superintendent Maigret, Head of the Crime Squad. I assume you are Monsieur Nahour's secretary?'

Another nod.

'May I ask your full name?'

'Fouad Oueni.'

The voice was hoarse, as though he suffered from chronic laryngitis.

'Are you aware of what happened last night in the studio?'

'No.'

'But you were told that Monsieur Nahour was killed.'

'No more than that.'

'Where were you?'

Not a feature quivered. Maigret had rarely met with so little co-operation as when he had entered this house. The charwoman only answered questions evasively, with hostility. The Dutch maid simply replied in monosyllables.

As for Fouad Oueni, who was wearing a neat black suit, a white shirt and a dark grey tie, he watched and listened to the Superintendent with total indifference, almost with disdain.

'Did you spend the night in this room?'

'After half past one this morning.'

'You mean you came in at half past one this morning?'

'I thought you'd gathered that.'

'Where were you until then?'

'At the Saint-Michel Club.'

'A gambling club?'

The man simply shrugged his shoulders.

'Where exactly is it?'

'Above the Bar des Tilleuls.'

'Did you gamble?'

'No.'

'What did you do?'

'I made a note of the winning numbers.'

Was it irony that gave him that self-satisfied look? Maigret sat on a chair and went on asking questions as though he were unaware of the other man's hostility.

'Was the light on in the studio when you came in?'

'I don't know.'

'Were the curtains drawn?'

'I suppose so. They are drawn every night.'

'You didn't see a light under the door?'

'One can never see a light under that door.'

'Was Monsieur Nahour usually in bed at that hour?'

'That depended.'

'What on?'

'On him.'

'Did he often go out at night?'

'When he wanted to.'

'Where did he go?'

'Wherever he liked.'

'Alone?'

'He left the house alone.'

'By car?'

'He called a taxi.'

'Didn't he drive himself?'

'He didn't like driving. In the day-time I was his chauffeur.'

'What sort of car has he got?'

'A Bentley.'

'Is it in the garage?'

'I'm not sure. I haven't been allowed out of my room.'

'And Madame Nahour?'

'What about her?'

'Did she have a car too?'

'A green Triumph.'

'Did she go out yesterday evening?'

'I never had anything to do with her.'

'What time did you leave the house?'

'Half past ten.'

'Was she here?'

'I don't know.'

'And Monsieur Nahour?'

'I don't know if he was back. He must have dined in town.'

'Do you know where?'

'Probably at the Petit Beyrouth, where he usually dined.'

'Who does the cooking in this house?'

'Nobody and everybody.'

'How about breakfast?'

'I made it for Monsieur Felix.'

'Who is Monsieur Felix?'

'Monsieur Nahour.'

'Why do you call him Monsieur Felix?'

'Because there's Monsieur Maurice, too.'

'Who is Monsieur Maurice?'

'Monsieur Nahour's father.'

'Does he live here?'

'No. In the Lebanon.'

'And then?'

'Monsieur Pierre, Monsieur Felix's brother.'

'Where does he live?'

'In Geneva.'

'Who telephoned you this morning?'

'Nobody telephoned me.'

'But the telephone was heard ringing in your room.'

'I'd asked for Geneva and they rang me back when they had the number.'

'Monsieur Pierre?'

'Yes.'

'Did you tell him what had happened?'

'I told him Monsieur Felix was dead. Monsieur Pierre will be at Orly in a few minutes, because he took the first 'plane.'

'Do you know what he does in Geneva?'

'He's a banker.'

'And Monsieur Maurice Nahour in Beirut?'

'He's a banker.'

'And Monsieur Felix?'

'He had no profession.'

'Have you been working for him long?'

'I wasn't working for him.'

'Didn't you work as his secretary? You just told me you cooked his breakfast and worked as his chauffeur.'

'I helped him.'

'Since when?'

'Eighteen years ago.'

'Did you know him in Beirut?'

'I met him at Law School.'

'In Paris.'

He nodded, impassive and stiff in his armchair, while Maigret was getting impatient.

'Did he have any enemies?'

'Not as far as I know.'

'Did he meddle in politics?'

'Certainly not.'

'So you went out at half past ten without knowing who was in the house. You went to a gambling club on the Boulevard Saint-Michel where you noted the winning numbers but did not gamble yourself. Then you came back at half past one and came up here still without knowing where anybody was.

Is that right? You saw nothing, heard nothing and you didn't expect to be woken up this morning with the news that Monsieur Nahour had been shot.'

'You're the first person to tell me a fire-arm was used.'

'What do you know about Felix Nahour's family?'

'Nothing. It's none of my business.'

'Was it a happy marriage?'

'I don't know.'

'You give me the impression that the husband and the wife didn't see much of each other.'

'I think that's quite common.'

'Why don't the children live in Paris?'

'Maybe they prefer the Riviera?'

'Where did Monsieur Nahour live before he rented this house?'

'All over the place . . . Italy . . . A year in Cuba before the revolution . . . We also had a villa in Deauville . . .'

'Do you often go to the Saint-Michel Club?'

'Two or three times a week.'

'And you never gamble?'

'Rarely.'

'Will you come down with me?'

They went down the stairs, and when he stood up Fouad Oueni looked even thinner than he had looked in his armchair.

'How old are you?'

'I don't know. In the mountains where I was born there was no such thing as a registry office. The age on my passport is fifty-one.'

'Are you older or younger?'

'I don't know.'

In the studio Moers's men were putting away their equipment.

When the van drove off and the two men were alone together, Maigret asked:

'Look round the room and tell me if anything's missing. Or if something's been added.'

Oueni tore himself away from the patch of blood which he was gazing at, opened the right-hand drawer in the desk and said:

'The revolver's gone.'

'What type?'

'A Browning 6.35.'

'With a mother-of-pearl handle?'

'Yes.'

'Why did Felix Nahour use a gun which is usually regarded as likely to belong to a woman?'

'It used to belong to Madame Nahour.'

'How long ago?'

'I don't know.'

'Did he take it away from her?'

'He didn't tell me.'

'Did he have a licence?'

'He never carried this pistol on him.'

Regarding the matter as settled, the Lebanese opened the other drawers which contained some files, and then went towards the book-shelves, and opened the doors below.

'Can you tell me what these lists of figures are?'

Oueni looked at him in astonishment mingled with irony, as though Maigret should have understood on his own.

'They're the winning numbers in the main casinos. The typed lists are sent by agencies to their subscribers. Monsieur Felix got the others from a croupier.'

Maigret was about to ask another question, but Lapointe appeared in the doorway.

'Will you come up a minute, chief?'

'Something new?'

'Not much, but I think you ought to know.'

'I must ask you not to leave the building without my permission, Monsieur Oueni.'

'Can I make myself some coffee?'

Maigret shrugged his shoulders and turned on his heels.

CHAPTER THREE

MAIGRET HAD RARELY felt so much out of his element, so far
from normal life, with that feeling of ill-ease which we have
when we dream that the ground has slipped away from under
our feet.

In the snow-covered streets the few passers-by walked along
trying to keep their balance; the cars, the taxis, the buses
drove slowly, while lorries full of sand or salt drove along the
edge of the pavement at walking pace.

The lights were on in almost every window and snow still
fell from a sky as grey as slate.

He could almost have told what was going on in all these
little compartments where human beings were breathing. In
the course of over thirty years he had learnt to know Paris
quarter by quarter, street by street, and yet here he felt
immersed in a different world where people's reactions were
unpredictable.

How had Felix Nahour been living a few hours earlier?
What exactly was his relationship with his secretary who was
not secretary, with his wife and his two children? Why were
the children on the Riviera, and why? . . .

There were so many whys that he could only take one on
at a time. Nothing was clear. Nothing happened as it happened
in other families, in other homes.

Pardon had felt just as uneasy the night before when a
strange couple had invaded his little office.

The story about a shot fired from a moving car was unlikely,
as was the old woman who pointed out the doctor's house.

Felix Nahour, with his works on mathematics and his lists

of winning and losing numbers in various casinos, did not fit into any category that Maigret knew of, and Fouad Oueni was also from another world.

Everything here seemed false to him, everyone seemed to be lying, and as he went up the stairs Lapointe confirmed his feeling.

'I wonder if this girl is normal, chief. Judging from her answers, when she does answer, and from the way she looks at me, she seems to have the ingenuousness and the mentality of a child of ten, but I wonder if it isn't a trick, or a game.'

As they went into Madame Nahour's room, where Nelly was still sitting on a silk-upholstered chair, Lapointe said:

'By the way, chief, the children are no longer as young as they were when that picture was taken. The girl's now five and the little boy two.'

'Do you know where they live with their nurse?'

'In Mougins, Pension des Palmiers.'

'Since when?'

'As far as I can gather the boy was born in Cannes and has never been to Paris.'

The maid looked at them with her light, transparent blue eyes, appearing not to understand a word they were saying.

'I found more photographs in a drawer she pointed out to me . . . A dozen snaps of the children as babies, then walking, and this one taken on the beach, of Nahour and his wife, far younger, probably at the time when they met . . . Here's a last photograph of Madame Nahour with a friend, near a canal in Amsterdam . . .'

The friend was ugly, with a flat nose and tiny eyes, but nevertheless she had a pleasant open face.

'The only letters in the room are from a girl, in Dutch. They have been written over about seven years and the last one is dated ten days ago.'

'Has Nelly ever been to Holland with her mistress?'

'She says not.'

'Does Madame Nahour go there often?'

'Occasionally . . . On her own, apparently . . . but I'm not quite sure whether Nelly really understands my questions, even in English . . .'

'Get a translator for these letters . . . What does she say about yesterday evening and last night?'

'Nothing. She doesn't know anything. The house isn't that big, and yet nobody seems to know what anybody else does. She thinks Madame Nahour dined in town . . .'

'Alone? Didn't someone pick her up? Didn't she call a taxi?'

'She says she doesn't know . . .'

'Didn't she help Madame Nahour dress?'

'She says that she didn't ring for her . . . She ate in the kitchen as usual, and then she went up to her room, read a Dutch newspaper and went to bed . . . She showed me the newspaper, which is dated the day before yesterday . . .'

'Didn't she hear any steps in the corridor?'

'She didn't take any notice of them . . . Once she's asleep nothing seems to wake her . . .'

'What time does she start work in the morning?'

'No definite time . . .'

Maigret tried vainly to make out what was going on behind the ivory-like forehead of the maid who was smiling at him vaguely.

'Tell her she can go and have breakfast, but that she isn't allowed to leave the house.'

When Lapointe had translated these instructions Nelly got up, curtsied, and walked quietly towards the staircase.

'She's lying, chief . . .'

'How do you know?'

'She says she didn't come into this room last night. This morning the local detective didn't let her out of her room. And yet the first time I asked her what coat her mistress was wearing she didn't hesitate to say:

' "The seal one . . ."'

'Well, the cupboards were closed and in one of them I found a mink coat and in the other a grey astrakhan . . .'

'I would like you to take the car and go to see Doctor Pardon in the Boulevard Voltaire. Show him the photograph on the desk downstairs . . .'

There was a telephone in the room. When it started ringing Maigret picked up the receiver and heard two voices—the medical expert and Oueni.

'Yes,' said Oueni. 'He's still here . . . Wait a minute . . . I'll tell him . . .'

'You needn't do that, Monsieur Oueni,' Maigret interrupted. 'Would you mind hanging up, please.'

So the three telephones, including the secretary's, were on the same line.

'Hello, this is Maigret . . .'

'This is Collinet . . . I've only just started the post-mortem, but I thought you'd like to know the first result immediately . . . It wasn't suicide . . .'

'I never thought it would be . . .'

'Nor did I, but now we're sure . . . Although I'm not an expert on guns I can tell you that the bullet I've found in the skull was fired from a medium or large calibre gun, a 7.32 or 7.45, as I expected. I'd say it was fired at about three of four yards' range and the skull has been split . . .'

'What time did he die?'

'To be sure about that I'd have to know the time of his last meal and analyse his internal organs . . .'

'Roughly?'

'About midnight . . .'

'Thank you, doctor . . .'

Lapointe had gone out and his car could be heard running in the street.

Downstairs two men were talking in a foreign language which the Superintendent finally recognized as Arabic. He went down and found Oueni standing in the corridor talking to someone he had not seen before, and the local detective who was looking on, not daring to interrupt.

The newcomer looked like Felix Nahour, a little older, a

little thinner, and also taller. His dark hair was growing grey at the temples.

'Monsieur Pierre Nahour?'

'Are you from the police?' he asked suspiciously.

'Superintendent Maigret, Head of the Crime Squad . . .'

'What's happened to my brother? Where's the body?'

'He was killed by a bullet in his throat last night and his body has been taken to the Medico-Legal Institute . . .'

'Will I be able to see him?'

'Later.'

'Why not now?'

'Because the post-mortem is being performed . . . Come in, Monsieur Nahour . . .'

He hesitated to let Oueni into the studio, then made up his mind:

'Will you wait in your room?'

Oueni and Nahour looked at each other, and Maigret could see no sign of sympathy in the newcomer's eyes.

When the door was shut, the banker from Geneva asked:

'What's happened?'

The Superintendent pointed to the large blood patch on the carpet, and the other man drew back an instant, as he would have done in front of a body.

'How did that happen?'

'Nobody knows. He apparently dined in town and nobody saw him afterwards.'

'How about Lina?'

'Do you mean Madame Nahour? . . . Her maid claims that she dined out too and that she isn't back yet.'

'Isn't she here?'

'Her bed hasn't been slept in and she's taken her luggage . . .'

Pierre Nahour did not look surprised.

'And Oueni?'

'He says he went to a gambling club in the Boulevard Saint-Michel and noted the winning numbers until one in the morning. When he came back he didn't look to see whether his boss was in and went to bed. He didn't hear anything . . .'

They were sitting opposite each other and the banker had automatically pulled a cigar out of his pocket which he hesitated to light, maybe out of respect for the dead man, although he was no longer there.

'I must ask you certain questions, Monsieur Nahour, and I beg you to forgive my indiscretion. Were you on good terms with your brother?'

'On very good terms, although we did not see each other very frequently.'

'Why not?'

'Because I live in Geneva, and when I travel it's usually to go to the Lebanon . . . As for my brother, he had no reason to come to Geneva . . . It wasn't one of his centres of activity . . .'

'Oueni told me that Pierre Nahour did not carry on any profession . . .'

'Yes and no . . . Look, Monsieur Maigret, before you ask any more questions I think I ought to give you some information which will enable you to understand the situation . . . My father was, and still is, a banker in Beirut . . . To start with he had a very small firm which was mainly intended to finance imports and exports, because all products on their way to the Near East pass through Beirut . . . In Beirut there are more banks in proportion to the population than anywhere else . . .'

He finally made up his mind to light his cigar. His hands were as well-manicured as his brother's and he was also wearing a wedding-ring.

'We are Maronite Christians, which accounts for our Christian names . . . My father's concern expanded over the years, and he now directs one of the most important private banks in the Lebanon . . .

'I studied at the Law School in Paris, and then at the Institute of Comparative Law . . .'

'Before your brother arrived?'

'He's five years younger than I . . . So I was ahead of him
. . . When he arrived I had almost finished my studies . . .'

'Did you settle in Geneva immediately?'

'First I worked with my father, and then we decided to
open a Swiss branch, the Comptoir Libanais, which I direct
. . . It's a fairly small concern with five employees and offices
on the second floor of a building in the Avenue du Rhône . . .'

Now that he was faced with a man who spoke to him at
least with apparent clarity Maigret tried to fit every character
into place.

'Have you got any other brothers?'

'Only a sister, whose husband directs the same sort of bank
as I do, in Istanbul . . .'

'So that your father, your brother-in-law and you control
a large part of the commerce of the Lebanon?'

'Let's say a quarter, or even less, a fifth . . .'

'And your brother Pierre did not go into the family
business?'

'He was the youngest . . . He also started studying law, but
without much enthusiasm, and he spent most of his time in
the *brasseries* near the University . . . He had just discovered
poker, at which he turned out to be very good, and he spent
whole nights playing it . . .'

'Is that when he met Oueni?'

'I'm not saying that Oueni, who isn't a Maronite but a
Moslem, was his evil genius, but I'm not far off thinking so
. . . Oueni was very poor, like most people from the moun-
tains . . . He had to work to pay for his studies . . .'

'So I'm right in understanding, from certain discoveries
which I've made in this office, that your brother was a
professional gambler . . .'

'As far as one can call that a profession. One day we heard
that he'd stopped studying law and was following a course in
mathematics at the Sorbonne . . . His father and he were
at daggers drawn for several years . . .'

'And you?'

'I saw him from time to time . . . To begin with I had to lend him some money . . .'

'Which he paid back?'

'Every penny. You mustn't think that my brother was a failure. The first months, the first two or three years were difficult, but he was soon winning large sums of money and I'm sure he became richer than I was . . .'

'Did he make it up with his father?'

'Quite quickly . . . We Maronites have a very strong family feeling . . .'

'I suppose your brother gambled mainly in casinos?'

'In Deauville, Cannes, Evian, in Enghien in the winter. For one or two years, before Castro, he was technical adviser and, I should imagine, an associate of the casino in Havana . . . He didn't gamble haphazardly but used his mathematical education . . .'

'Are you married, Monsieur Nahour?'

'Married with four children, one of whom is twenty-one and studies at Harvard.'

'When did your brother get married?'

'Just a minute . . . It was in . . . Seven years ago . . .

'Do you know his wife?'

'Of course I've met Lina . . .'

'Did you meet her before her marriage?'

'No . . . We all had the impression that my brother was a confirmed bachelor . . .'

'How did you find out about his marriage?'

'From a letter . . .'

'Do you know where they were married?'

'At Trouville, where Felix had rented a villa . . .'

Pierre Nahour's face had grown slightly darker.

'What sort of a woman is she?'

'I don't know what to say.'

'Why?'

'Because I've only seen her twice.'

'Did your brother take her to Geneva?'

'No. I came to Paris on business and I met them both at the Ritz where they were living at the time.'

'Didn't your brother ever go to the Lebanon with her?'

'No. My father met them a few months later in Evian where he was taking a cure.'

'Did your father approve of the marriage?'

'I can't answer for my father.'

'Did you?'

'It was none of my business.'

It had all become imprecise again, with vague or equivocal replies.

'Do you know where your brother met the woman who was later to be his wife?'

'He never told me, but it was quite easy to guess. The year before, the Miss Europe beauty contest was supposed to take place in Deauville ... Felix was there because there were some very big games at the casino and the bank was losing almost every evening ... A Dutch girl of nineteen won the contest, Lina Wiemers ...'

'Whom your brother married ...'

'About a year later ... Before the marriage they travelled a great deal, the two of them, or rather the three of them, because Felix never moved without Fouad Oueni ...'

They were interrupted by the telephone. Maigret picked up the receiver. Lapointe was on the line.

'I'm calling you from Doctor Pardon's flat, chief ... He recognized the photograph at once ... It is the woman he saw last night ...'

'Will you come back here? Pass by the Quai des Orfèvres on your way and ask Janvier, if he's there, or else Torrence or somebody, to join me in the Avenue du Parc-Montsouris with a car ...'

He hung up.

'I'm sorry, Monsieur Nahour ... I have a more indiscreet question to ask you, and you'll soon know why ... Do you know if your brother and his wife got on well together?'

Pierre Nahour's face suddenly seemed to close.

'I'm afraid I can't tell you anything . . . I never had anything to do with my brother's married life . . .'

'His room was on the ground floor and his wife's on the first floor . . . As far as I can gather from more than reluctant information they did not have their meals together and rarely went out together . . .'

Pierre Nahour did not flinch, but his cheeks turned slightly pinker.

'The staff in this house consists of a charwoman, Fouad Oueni, who plays a pretty mysterious part, and a Dutch maid who can only speak Dutch and English . . .'

'Besides Arabic, my brother spoke French, English, Spanish and Italian, not to mention a little German . . .'

'Oueni cooked breakfast for his master and Nelly Velthuis for her mistress. The same went for lunch, when they lunched here, and they usually dined in town, but separately . . .'

'I wasn't aware of that . . .'

'Where are your children, Monsieur Nahour?'

'But . . . in Geneva, of course, or rather seven miles outside Geneva, where we have our villa . . .'

'Your brother's children live on the Riviera with a governess . . .'

'Felix frequently went to see them, and he spent part of the year in Cannes . . .'

'And his wife?'

'I suppose she went to see them too . . .'

'Had you ever heard that she had one or more lovers?'

'I don't frequent the same set . . .'

'Now, Monsieur Nahour, I shall try and reconstruct what happened last night, or rather what we know about it . . . Before one o'clock in the morning your brother was hit in the throat by a bullet fired from a revolver of fairly large calibre, and we shall know the type and probably the make as soon as the expert sends us his report . . . At that moment he was standing behind his desk . . .

'Well, your brother, like his aggressor, had a gun in his hand, a 6.35 pistol with a mother-of-pearl handle, which was usually in the right-hand drawer of his desk, a drawer which we found half-open . . .

'I have no idea how many people were in the room, but we know your sister-in-law was there . . .'

'How can you know that?'

'Because she was wounded by a bullet fired from a 6.35. Have you ever heard of a certain Doctor Pardon who lives in the Boulevard Voltaire?'

'I don't know the district and I've never heard that name before.'

'Your sister-in-law must have heard of it, or else the man who was with her . . .'

'You mean there was another man in this study?'

'I'm almost sure . . . Before or after the scene that I've just described Madame Nahour quickly piled some linen and clothes into one or more suitcases . . . Shortly after, wearing a sealskin coat, she and her companion got out of a red Alfa Romeo in front of 76 B Boulevard Voltaire and a little later they both rang at Doctor Pardon's door . . .'

'Who was the man?'

'All we know is that he's a Colombian citizen, twenty-five or six years old . . .'

Pierre Nahour did not flinch, had not even quivered.

'Have you any idea who he could be?' asked Maigret, looking him in the eye.

'None,' he said, taking the cigar out of his mouth.

'Your sister-in-law had a wound in her back but it was not fatal. Doctor Pardon dressed it. The Colombian told an absurd story according to which his companion, whom he did not know, was attacked a short distance away from him by one or more individuals who fired from the door of a car . . .'

'Where is she?'

'In all likelihood in Amsterdam . . . While the doctor was

206

washing his hands and taking off his blood-stained coat the couple crept out of his office . . . Some time later they appeared at Orly, where the red car is still parked. A Dutch woman and a Colombian, answering to the description of the doctor's patient and her escort, got on the aeroplane to Amsterdam . . .'

Maigret stood up and emptied his pipe in an ashtray before filling another one, which he pulled out of his pocket.

'I've put my cards on the table, Monsieur Nahour . . . I expect you to be just as frank with me . . . I'm going back to my office in the Quai des Orfèvres . . . One of my detectives is staying in the building to make sure that neither the charwoman, nor Oueni, or Nelly leave without my permission . . .'

'How about me ?'

'I would like you to stay here too, because as soon as the post-mortem is over I shall ask you to identify the body—this is only a formality, but an indispensable formality . . .'

He went over to the bay-window. It was still snowing, more lightly, but the sky was no brighter. Two black cars from the Judicial Police drew up by the pavement and Lapointe got out of one, and Janvier out of the other. They both crossed the garden and the door could be heard opening in the passage.

'When we see each other again, Monsieur Nahour, you may be able to tell me more about the relationship between your sister-in-law and your brother, and perhaps even about her and other men . . .'

Pierre Nahour did not reply.

'You stay here, Lapointe . . . I'm going to the Quai with Janvier . . .'

And Maigret wound his thick scarf round his neck and put on his overcoat.

*　　　*　　　*

It was ten to twelve when Maigret, sunk in his armchair, finally got his call to Amsterdam.

'Keulemans? . . . Hello . . . This is Maigret, from Paris . . .

The Head of the Crime Squad in Amsterdam, Jef Keulemans, was still young, hardly forty, and he looked about ten years younger because of his tall boyish figure, his pink face and his fair hair.

When he had come to work for a time in Paris it was Maigret who had shown him the wheels of the Judicial Police and the two men had become good friends, occasionally seeing each other again at international congresses.

'Very well, thank you, Keulemans . . . My wife too . . . What? . . . The port's covered with ice? . . . Don't worry, Paris is like a skating-rink and it's starting to snow again . . .

'Hello . . . Look, I want to ask you a favour . . . I'm sorry I'm only calling you for that . . . It's official, of course . . . To start with I haven't got time to fill in the documents necessary to go through official channels . . . And then I haven't got enough information . . .

'Last night two people who interest me took a K.L.M. flight which left Orly at about four in the morning . . . A man and a woman . . . They may have pretended not to be together . . . The man has a Colombian passport and is about twenty-five . . . The woman is of Dutch origin, is called Evelina Nahour, maiden name Wiemars, and pays brief visits to Amsterdam, where she spent her late teens . . .

'I suppose they both filled in landing cards which you can find at the airport . . .

'Madame Nahour does not reside in Holland but she has a friend in Amsterdam, Anna Keegel, who writes an address in the Lomanstraat on the back of her letters . . . You know it? . . .

'Good . . . No, don't arrest them . . . But if you see the Nahour woman maybe you could just tell her that her husband is dead and that she is needed for the reading of the will . . . Tell her her brother-in-law is in Paris . . . Don't mention the police . . .

'Nahour has been murdered, yes . . . A bullet in his throat

... What? ... She probably knows, but maybe she doesn't, because I'm ready for every sort of surprise in this case ...

'I don't want her to be antagonized ... If she's still with her companion, don't bother him ... If they've separated I suppose she'll telephone him and tell him about your call ...

'That's good of you, Keulemans ... I'm going home for lunch and I'll expect your call this afternoon ... Thanks ...'

Since he had a line he dialled his own number.

'What have you got for lunch?' he asked when his wife answered the telephone.

'I'd cooked some sauerkraut, but I thought I'd have to heat it up this evening, or tomorrow!'

'I'll be back in half an hour.'

He took one of the pipes standing on his desk and filled it as he walked slowly down the corridor. When he had nearly reached the end he knocked on Superintendent Lardois's door. Lardois was the head of the Gambling Squad: he had joined the Judicial Police at almost the same time as Maigret, and they had been on Christian name terms from the start.

'Good morning, Raoul ...'

'How can you remember me? ... Our offices are twenty yards apart and you don't even look in once a year ...'

'I could say the same about you ...'

Nevertheless they saw each other in an official capacity every morning at the report session in the Chief of the Judicial Police's office.

'You may think I'm naive, but I don't know anything about gambling ... To start with, are there such things as professional gamblers?'

'Casino managers are, since they are really playing against the guests ... When they're holding a double bank they sometimes go halves with a gambling expert, and sometimes with a group ... So much for the professionals who've got an establishment of their own ...

'Other people, not many of them, live off gambling alone for a certain amount of time, either because they're exceptionally lucky or because they have large financial means and are particularly good at it . . .'

'Can one gamble scientifically?'

'Apparently. A few players are able to make highly complicated calculations of probability between the deal and the choice of a card . . .'

'Have you heard of a certain Felix Nahour?'

'All the croupiers in France and elsewhere know him . . . He belongs to the second category, although he used to run an open bank in Havana together with an American group . . .'

'Was he honest?'

'If he wasn't he'd have been a marked man some time ago and he wouldn't be allowed in to any casino . . . It's only in the small casinos that you get seedy-looking cheats who all get caught sooner or later . . .'

'What do you know about Nahour?'

'First, that he's got a very pretty wife, a Miss something whom I've seen several times in Cannes and Biarritz . . . Then that he once worked for a group from the Near East . . .'

'A group of gamblers?'

'If you like . . . Let's say gamblers who don't want to, or can't, gamble themselves . . . A professional playing against the bank in Cannes or Deauville, for instance, must have enough millions to continue until his luck is in . . . Otherwise he has to be on an equal footing with the casino, which has almost inexhaustible resources . . .

'Hence the formation of groups which work like financial companies, except that they're more discreet . . .

'For a long time a South American group sent an operator to Deauville every year and the bank often found itself in a very nasty position . . .'

'Does Nahour still have a group behind him?'

'Apparently he can fly with his own wings now, but there's no way of finding out . . .'

'One more question . . . Do you know the Saint-Michel Club?'

Lardois hesitated before replying:

'Yes . . . I've raided it a couple of times . . .'

'Why is it still functioning?'

'Don't tell me Nahour plays there?'

'No, but his factotum-secretary spends part of the night there two or three times a week . . .'

'I turn a blind eye to it for the sake of the general information department . . . Most of the guests are foreign students, Orientals who live in the district . . . It's a good place to keep an eye on them and our colleagues don't miss their chance . . . Has there been a row there?'

'No.'

'Anything else?'

'No.'

'Has Nahour been in trouble?'

'He was murdered last night.'

'At a club?'

'At home.'

'Will you tell me about it?'

'When I know something myself.'

Twenty minutes later Maigret was sitting opposite his wife, eating a tasty Alsatian sauerkraut the likes of which can only be found in two restaurants in Paris. The pickled pork was particularly good and the Superintendent had opened two bottles of Strasbourg beer.

It was still snowing beyond the windows and it was good to be indoors, in the warm, and not to have to walk along the pavements as slippery as the port of Amsterdam.

'Tired?'

'Not particularly.'

After a pause he added, with a slightly bantering look at his wife:

'A detective shouldn't really get married.'

'So as not to have to go home and eat sauerkraut?' she answered smartly.

'No, but because he ought to live in every social sphere, to know about casinos, for instance, international banking, Lebanese Maronites and Moslems, foreign bistros in the Latin Quarter and Saint-Germain, as well as young Colombians. Not to mention the Dutch language, or beauty contests . . .'

'You're getting on all right, aren't you?'

She smiled, because he was gradually looking less worried. 'The rest of the investigation will tell . . .'

When he got up he felt heavy, but it was because he had indulged in too much lunch and beer. It would have been wonderful to lie in bed after an almost sleepless night, to have a short siesta and remain vaguely conscious of Madame Maigret moving round the flat.

'Are you leaving already?'

'Keulemans is calling me from Amsterdam . . .'

She knew him too, because he had dined with them several times. This time Maigret called a taxi and went to wait for it, as usual, on the pavement. Janvier had come back to the office.

'Any calls for me?'

'Only Lapointe. Since there wasn't anything to eat in the refrigerator Nahour's brother asked him if he could have some lunch sent round from a nearby caterer. Lapointe didn't see why he should refuse, and as a reward he was invited to share the meal. The two local detectives went back to the police station. The guard at the door was changed . . . Oh, I forgot! . . . The young maid didn't want to touch the meal and heated up a bowl of chocolate into which she dipped some biscuits . . .'

'Did Nahour and Oueni eat at the same table?'

'Lapointe didn't tell me . . .'

'Go to the Boulevard Saint-Michel . . . There's a place called the Bar des Tilleuls which has a gambling casino disguised as a private club on the first floor . . . The club's shut at the moment, but one has to go through the bar to get there . . .

'Tell the owner that Lardois sent you and that we don't

want to get him into any trouble . . . Just try to find out whether Fouad Oueni went to the club last night, and if he did, at what time he arrived and what time he left . . .

'On your way back pass by a restaurant called the Petit Beyrouth in the Rue des Bernardins. The owner is called Boutros. Felix Nahour was one of his most regular clients. Did he dine there last night? Was he alone? When did he last go there with his wife? Was there a time when the couple seemed inseparable? And so on . . . See what you can get out of him . . .'

Maigret had not had time to read his morning's mail which was piling up on his blotter, next to his pipes. He put out his hand to take a letter, yawned, decided to do it later, and, sliding back into his armchair, he dropped his head and shut his eyes.

When the telephone made him start nobody was shaking him by the shoulder and he didn't have to struggle, but the clock said half past three.

'Superintendent Maigret? . . . Hello . . . This is Superintendent Maigret speaking . . .'

The operator had a strong accent.

'This is Amsterdam . . . Just a minute . . . I'll connect you with Superintendent Keulemans . . .'

Two or three clicks, then came the Dutch detective's gay voice:

'Maigret? . . . Keulemans speaking . . . I wish you'd always give me such easy jobs . . . Of course I found the landing cards at the airport . . . I didn't even have to move . . . They dictated their contents to me on the 'phone . . . The woman is indeed Elina Nahour, maiden name Wiemars, resident in Paris, Avenue du Parc-Montsouris . . . She's younger than you thought . . . She's twenty-seven . . . She was born in Amsterdam, but she left the town with her parents when she was very young, when her father became assistant manager of a cheesemongery in Leeuwarden in Friesland . . .'

'Have you seen her?'

'She's staying with her friend, Anna Keegel. The two women lived together for several years when Lina got her parents' permission to work in Amsterdam at the age of seventeen . . .

'Lina was a telephonist in a travel agency, then a receptionist for a well-known doctor, and finally a model for a dress designer . . . Anna Keegel has always had the same job: secretary in a large brewery—I pointed out its warehouses to you when we sailed down the Amstel together . . .'

'How did Lina Nahour react when you told her about her husband's death?'

'To start with she's in bed and the doctor had just seen her . . .'

'Did she mention her wound to you?'

'No. She said she was very tired.'

'Any trace of her companion?'

'Since the flat only consists of a large room, a kitchen and a bathroom, I would have seen her . . . After a pause, she asked:

' "What did he die of?"

'I said I didn't know, but that she had to be there before they could read the will.'

'What did she say?'

'That she hoped to be well enough to take the 'plane tomorrow morning, although the doctor had said she needed a long rest . . . I left one of my men in the neighbourhood just in case . . . Officially, don't worry . . .'

'And the Colombian?'

'Vicente Alvaredo, twenty-six years old, born in Bogota, is a student, resident in Paris, in the Rue Notre-Dame-des-Champs . . .'

'Did you find him?'

'Easily. Very officially too, because I had the telephone of the flat in the Lomanstraat tapped . . . Lina Nahour picked up the receiver before I had left the street . . . She dialled the Rembrandt Hotel and was connected with Alvaredo . . . I've

got the shorthand report of their conversation in front of me
. . . Shall I read it to you?'

Maigret was only sorry that he couldn't hold the receiver
and fill his pipe at the same time and he looked longingly at
the tempting row on his desk.

'Here it is:

' "Vicente?"

' "Yes. Has the doctor been?"

' "Half an hour ago. He believed what I told him and he
put some stitches in after having cleaned the wound. He's
coming back tomorrow morning. I had another visit, someone
from the police, a very tall and very nice man who told me
my husband had died . . ." '

A pause.

'Note that the young man didn't ask any questions,
Maigret.

' "The solicitor needs me to read the will. I promised to
take the 'plane tomorrow morning."

' "D'you think you'll be able to?"

' "I've only got a temperature of 38 . . . Since the doctor
gave me some pills I've hardly felt any pain."

' "Can I come and see you this afternoon?"

' "Not too early, because I want to sleep. My friend rang
her office to say she'd got 'flu . . . Apparently a third of the
staff's in bed . . . She's taking good care of me . . ."

' "I'll be there at about five . . ." '

Another pause.

'That's all, Maigret. They started talking in English and
then went on in French. Can I do anything else?'

'I'd like to know if she's taking the 'plane and at what time
she gets to Orly, if she does . . . Of course, I'd also like some
news of Alvaredo . . .'

'*Officially!*'

And Keulemans ended the conversation gaily, saying, like
Maigret's colleagues:

'Good-bye, *chief*!'

215

CHAPTER FOUR

IT WAS AN IDLE AFTERNOON in an overheated office, and the six or seven pipes standing on the desk lasted Maigret until he went home. At one point, almost every investigation has what Maigret would call a gap, a point when one has a certain number of elements which must be checked but which cannot yet be put into place.

It is both a peaceful and irritating period, because there is a temptation to form theories and to draw conclusions which often turn out to be false.

If Maigret had followed his inclination, if he had not repeated to himself that it was not a Superintendent's job to rush off in every direction like a hunting dog, he would have seen to the whole thing on his own, as he had done when he was still an Inspector.

For example, he envied Keulemans's having seen Lina Nahour and her unattractive friend in the flat in Amsterdam where the two girls had once lived together.

At the same time he would have liked to spend all day, in Lapointe's stead, in the house in the Avenue du Parc-Montsouris, nosing about, sniffing in the corners, opening drawers at random, watching Fouad Oueni, Pierre Nahour, the baffling Nelly who was maybe not as infantile as she was trying to make believe.

He did not follow any preconceived plan. He went straight ahead, haphazardly, trying, above all, not to make up his mind.

He smiled when there was a knock at the door and he saw Pardon's maid come in.

'Good afternoon, Monsieur Maigret . . .'

Because, for her, he was not the Superintendent of the Judicial Police, but the guest who came to dinner every month.

'Here's the statement. The Doctor told me to deliver it to you in person.'

It was typed with two fingers on the doctor's old typewriter and there were crossings-out, letters missing, and words run together.

Had Pardon started writing it the night before, after Maigret had left? Or had he only written a few lines at a time, between patients? The Superintendent simply looked over it, smiled even more at the care which his friend had taken not to omit a single detail, as though it were a medical report.

He soon frowned again, however, because he was told that several journalists were waiting for him in the corridor. He hesitated, and finally muttered:

'Let them in . . .'

There were five of them, and two photographers, and one of the reporters was young Maquille, who was just twenty, but, despite his cherubic face, was one of the keenest men on the Paris press.

'What can you tell us about the Nahour case?'

Ah! So it was already the Nahour case, a headline in every paper.

'Not much, boys, because it's only just started.'

'Do you think Nahour committed suicide?'

'Certainly not. We have proof to the contrary, because the bullet which lodged in the skull after passing through his throat was not shot from the gun found under the body.'

'So he was holding the gun when he was killed?'

'Probably. Since I know what you're going to ask next, let me tell you at once that I have no idea who was in the room just then.'

'And in the house?' asked young Maquille.

'A young Dutch maid, Nelly Velthuis, was asleep on the

first floor in a room fairly far from the studio. Apparently she sleeps deeply and she says she heard nothing . . .'

'Wasn't there a secretary, too?'

They must have questioned the neighbours, or even the local tradesmen.

'Until we receive proof to the contrary the secretary, Fouad Oueni, was in town and came back at half past one in the morning. He did not come into the studio and went straight to bed.'

'And Madame Nahour?'

'She'd left.'

'Before or after the accident?' asked the obstinate Maquille again, always choosing his words well.

'That problem isn't settled yet.'

'But it is a problem?'

'There are always problems.'

'Such as the possibility of a political crime?'

'To the best of our knowledge Felix Nahour had nothing to do with politics.'

'How about his brother in Geneva?'

So they'd got further than the Superintendent thought.

'Wasn't his bank covering up any other activity?'

'You're going too fast for me.'

Nevertheless Maigret decided to check whether Pierre Nahour had arrived in Paris on the morning's flight. So far there was no proof that he had not been in town the day before.

'Had the weapon found under the victim's body been fired?'

And Maigret replied without committing himself:

'It's being examined by the experts and I haven't had a report yet. Now you know about as much as I do, and I want to work. I'll let you know if I hear anything new.'

He was aware that Maquille was going to leave a colleague in the corridor to watch his office and make a note of all his visitors.

'Did . . .?'

'No, boys! I've got a lot to do and I can't spend any more time on you.'

That had gone quite well. He sighed and longed for a cold glass of beer, but didn't dare have one sent up from the Brasserie Dauphine.

'Hello? . . . Lapointe? . . . What's going on down there?'

'The house is just as gloomy as ever. The charwoman is furious about not being able to get on with her work. Nelly's lying on her bed reading an English detective story. As for Pierre Nahour, he hasn't left the studio where he's going through the correspondence and papers in the drawers.'

'Has he made any 'phone calls?'

'Just one, to Beirut, to tell his father. His father's trying to get onto the next flight.'

'Can I speak to Pierre Nahour, please?'

'He's next to me.'

Then came the voice of the banker from Geneva.

'Yes . . .'

'Do you know if your brother had a solicitor in Paris?'

'Felix mentioned one when we last met three years ago, and said that if he died his will was in the hands of Maître Leroy-Beaulieu in the Boulevard Saint-Germain. I happen to know Leroy-Beaulieu very well because I did part of my law studies with him, but we've been out of touch since then.'

'Did your brother tell you what was in his will?'

'No. He only said rather bitterly that, in spite of his father's criticisms, he remained a Nahour.'

'Have you found anything in the papers you're looking at?'

'Mainly bills which show that my sister-in-law had no dealings with the tradesmen, not even with the butcher or the grocer, and left it all to my brother. Then there are almost daily reports from the nurse giving news of the children, which proves that my brother was very fond of them. Invitations, letters from casino managers and croupiers . . .'

'Look, Monsieur Nahour. There is no need for you to stay indoors. You can go wherever you like in Paris, provided you don't leave the city. If you take a room in a hotel . . .'

'I don't intend to. I'll sleep in my brother's room. I may go out, if only to have dinner.'

'May I speak to my Inspector again? . . . Hello . . . Lapointe? . . . I've just given Pierre Nahour permission to go wherever he likes. This does not apply to Oueni and I don't want the maid to leave the house either . . .

'The charwoman can do the shopping and go home, if she likes.

'Towards the end of the afternoon I'll send someone to replace you. See you later . . .'

He went into the detectives' office where about fifteen of them were at work, some typing out reports, others making telephone calls.

'Can anyone speak fairly good English here?'

They looked at each other in silence and Baron raised his hand shyly.

'But I've got a bad accent.'

'Take over from Lapointe between five and six in the Avenue du Parc-Montsouris. He'll give you further instructions . . .'

When he returned to his office a little later Maigret found Janvier in his overcoat; he had brought a blast of icy air from outside into the room.

'I've seen the owner of the Bar des Tilleuls, a large sleepy chap who I suspect is cleverer than he wants to appear. He says he hasn't got anything to do with the club on the first floor, which is run by someone called Pozzi, except that the clients have to pass through the bar . . .

'Every evening, from eight to eleven or twelve, the bar is full, because a great many people come to watch the television.

'It was particularly crowded last night because there was a volley-ball match on the television. He didn't see Oueni arrive, but he saw him leave at about a quarter past one . . .'

'So that Oueni could have arrived at any time before a quarter past one, and just have stayed a few minutes in the club?'

'That's possible. If you don't mind I'll go and question Pozzi this evening, as well as the croupiers, and, if necessary, the clients.'

Maigret would like to have gone himself. He hesitated to admit that he had better go to bed after an almost sleepless night in view of the work he would be faced with the next day.

'How about the restaurant?'

'It's a very small room with such a strong smell of Oriental cooking that it made me dizzy. Boutros is a plump fellow who swings his thick legs as he walks. He apparently didn't know about what had happened last night because when I told him Nahour was dead he started crying.

' "My best customer! . . . My brother! . . ." he exclaimed. "Yes, Inspector, I loved that man like a brother . . . He used to eat here when he was a student and I often let him have credit for weeks on end . . . When he got rich he didn't forget poor Boutros, and when he's in Paris he comes here almost every evening . . .

' "That's his table there, in the corner, you see, near the counter . . ." '

'Did he say anything about Madame Nahour?'

'He's an old fox too, and he watches one out of the corner of his eye . . . He raved on and on about Madame Nahour's beauty, her sweetness, her kindness . . .

' "And she wasn't proud, Inspector! . . . She'd always shake my hand when she arrived and when she left . . ." '

'When did he see her last?'

'He doesn't know . . . He's very vague . . . "Shortly after her marriage she used to come more often with her husband than she has recently, yes . . . They were a handsome couple, very much in love . . . They've always been very much in love . . . No, nothing went wrong, but she had to look after the house and the children . . ." '

'Doesn't he know that the children live on the Riviera?'

'He pretends not to . . .'

Maigret could not suppress a smile. Was everybody lying

in this case? It had started with a lie at Pardon's the night before, what with the incredible story about the shot from a car and the old woman who had pointed out the doctor's house.

'Just a minute!' the Superintendent told Janvier. 'I must make a 'phone call. Wait here . . .'

He had Lapointe on the line again.

'Has the charwoman left?'

'I think I can hear her getting ready.'

'Can I speak to her?'

He had to wait some time before a woman's voice said unpleasantly:

'What do you want now?'

'To ask you a question, Madame Bodin. How long have you been living in the 14th *Arrondissement*?'

'I don't see what that's got to do with it? . . .'

'I can easily find out at the police station, where you must be registered.'

'Three years . . .'

'And where did you live before?'

'Rue Servan, in the 12th . . .'

'Were you ever ill there?'

'My illnesses haven't got anything to do with anybody . . .'

'But you went to Doctor Pardon?'

'He's a good man, he never asks people any questions, he just cures them . . .'

So a little mystery which had been worrying the Superintendent ever since he heard Pardon's story had been cleared up.

'Is that all? Can I do my shopping?'

'Just one more thing . . . You liked Doctor Pardon . . . So you probably sent acquaintances to him? . . .'

'I may have done . . .'

'Try to remember . . . Did you mention him to anyone in the house where you work at present? . . .'

There was a fairly long pause and Maigret could hear the old woman breathing.

222

'I don't know.'

'To Madame Nahour?'

'She was never ill.'

'To Monsieur Oueni? To the maid?'

'I've just told you I don't know! If I can't go and do my shopping, why don't you arrest me? . . .'

Maigret hung up. His pipe had gone out and he told Janvier to call Orly while he filled another.

'Ask the Inspector if the 'plane that arrived soon after eleven is an Air France or a Swissair flight.'

Janvier repeated the question.

'Swissair?' repeated Janvier. 'Just a minute . . .'

'Tell him to connect you with the office that registers the passengers when they arrive . . .'

'Hello . . . Can you . . .'

A few minutes later Maigret was sure about another point. Pierre Nahour had indeed arrived that morning from Geneva on a Metropolitan in which he'd got a seat at the last minute.

'Now, chief?'

'As you see, I'm checking . . . Do you know what time Nahour had dinner last night?'

'At about half past eight . . . He left shortly after half past nine . . . He ate lamb and then a cake with almonds and raisins . . .'

'Go next door and tell Doctor Collinet, who needs to know before he can tell what time he died . . .'

Maigret looked up Maître Leroy-Beaulieu's telephone number, and the name seemed familiar to him. When he was on the line, the solicitor exclaimed:

'What is it this time, my dear Superintendent? I haven't had the pleasure of seeing you or speaking to you for some time . . .'

And since Maigret was searching his memory, the solicitor went on:

'The Montrond case, you remember? . . . That old client of mine whose wife . . .'

'Yes . . . yes . . .'

'What can I do for you?'

'I believe the will of a certain Felix Nahour is in your hands . . .'

'Yes indeed . . . He cancelled the old one and made a new one about two years ago . . .'

'Do you know why he changed his mind?'

There was an embarrassed silence.

'It's an awkward question and I'm in a difficult position . . . Monsieur Nahour never confided in me . . . As far as the will is concerned you realize that I'm bound by professional secrecy . . . If it's of any use, I can only tell you that the reasons were purely personal . . .'

'Felix Nahour was murdered last night in his studio.'

'Ah! The newspapers haven't mentioned it.'

'They will in their next editions.'

'Has the murderer been arrested?'

'So far we can only make some contradictory suppositions. Doesn't it happen fairly frequently—and I assume you can tell me this—that when a husband makes his will, his wife makes hers at the same time?'

'I have known this to happen.'

'Did it in the case of Monsieur and Madame Nahour?'

'I've never seen Madame Nahour and I haven't had any dealings with her. She's a former beauty queen, isn't she?'

'Exactly.'

'When is the funeral taking place?'

'I don't know, because the body is still with the medical expert.'

'We usually wait for the funeral before getting in touch with the people concerned. Do you think it will take long?'

'Possibly.'

'Have you informed the family?'

'The brother, Pierre Nahour, arrived in Paris this morning. And the father, who was still in Beirut at twelve, must have taken the first flight.'

'How about Madame Nahour?'

'We're expecting her tomorrow morning.'

'Look, my dear Superintendent, I shall send out notice on the meeting this evening. Shall we say for tomorrow afternoon?'

'That would suit me.'

'I would like to help you as much as I can, without transgressing our professional rules. All I can tell you is that Madame Nahour, if she knew about the first will, is going to be disagreeably surprised by the second. Is that any use to you?'

'Very much so. Thank you.'

Janvier was back in Maigret's office.

'There's something new,' murmured Maigret ambiguously. 'If I'm right in thinking, Madame Nahour was the main beneficiary of the first will. About two years ago the husband drew up a second one, and I'd be surprised if he leaves his wife more than the legal minimum.'

'Do you think she . . .'

'You forget that I never believe anything before the investigation is over.'

He added with a sceptical smile:

'And even then!'

It was decidedly an afternoon of telephone calls.

'Get me the Pension des Palmiers at Mougins.'

He felt in his pockets and pulled out a piece of paper on which he'd noted the nurse's name.

'See if Mademoiselle Jobe is there.'

He went to stand by the window, because he felt numb after having sat so long in his armchair. The snowflakes were thinning out. The streets had been lit for some time, and in some places they had been lit all day.

There was a traffic jam on the Pont Saint-Michel and three policemen in uniform were trying to sort out the cars and buses with loud blows on their whistles.

'Hello . . . Is that Mademoiselle Jobe? . . . Just a minute,

please . . . I'm connecting you with Superintendent Maigret
. . . No . . . From the Judicial Police in Paris . . .'

Maigret grabbed the receiver and remained standing, one
leg slung over the desk.

'Hello, Mademoiselle Jobe . . . I suppose the two children
are with you? . . . What? . . . You haven't been able to go
out because of the rain and the cold? . . . Don't worry, the
snow has almost stopped traffic in Paris . . .

'Have you heard from Monsieur Nahour? . . . He telephoned you yesterday? . . . At about what time? . . . Ten in
the morning . . . Yes, I see . . . He used to call before your
walk or in the evening . . . Did he have any special reason
for calling you? . . . None in particular . . . He did it two or
three times a week . . .

'And Madame Nahour? . . . Less often? . . . Once? . . .
Anything up to two weeks between one call and another? . . .

'No, Mademoiselle . . . I'm asking you these questions
because Monsieur Nahour was murdered last night . . .
Nobody's been arrested . . . May I ask you how long you've
been working for this family? . . . For five years? . . . Since
the first child was born . . .

'Unfortunately I can't come to Mougins right now . . . I
may have to send instructions to the Judicial Police in Cannes
so that they can take down your statement . . . No, of course
not . . . Don't worry . . . I understand your position perfectly.

'Look, when you entered their service the Nahours travelled
a great deal, didn't they? . . . Yes . . . To Cannes, Deauville,
Evian . . . Most of the time they rented a villa for the season,
or for part of the season . . . Did you go with them? . . .
Frequently? . . . Yes . . . I can hear you . . .

'You lived in the Ritz with them and the little girl . . . Then,
three years later, the boy was born . . . That's what happened,
isn't it? . . . He isn't a sickly child who needs a warmer
climate than Paris, is he? . . . If I'm not mistaken, he's two
years old now . . . And a real little devil . . .

'By all means . . . go ahead . . . I'll stay on the line . . .'

He nodded to Janvier:

'The children are quarrelling in the next room . . . She seems a very nice girl . . . Her answers are clear and she makes them without hesitating . . . Long may it last! . . . Hello . . . Yes . . . So Monsieur Nahour paid more attention to his children than his wife did . . . You sent him a short report on their health and what they did every day . . .

'Did you notice any tension between husband and wife? . . . Hard to tell, I know . . . They each led a life of their own . . . That didn't surprise you? . . . Only to start with? . . . You got used to it . . .

'Did they come and see them together? . . . Hardly ever? . . . I greatly appreciate your assistance . . . I quite understand that you don't know anything else . . . Thank you . . .'

Maigret gave a deep sigh and lit his pipe which had gone out.

'And now comes the worst part . . . I say that out of habit, really, because Cayotte is very agreeable as magistrates go . . .'

He took Pardon's report off his desk and walked slowly towards the examining magistrates' offices in the Palais de Justice. Cayotte had not been given modern offices and his room was straight out of a nineteenth-century novel.

Even the clerk seemed out of a drawing by Forain or Steinlen, and he all but wore linenette sleeves.

Since there was no room on the black wooden shelves files were accumulating on the floor and the lamp hanging over the magistrate's desk had lost its shade.

'Sit down, Maigret . . . Well? . . .'

The Superintendent did not try to cheat. For more than an hour he remained seated on a rickety chair, telling all he knew. When he finally left the smoke from his pipe and the cigarettes, which the magistrate chain-smoked, formed a thick mist round the electric light bulb.

Maigret was at the airport at half past nine in the morning, although the 'plane from Amsterdam was not expected until 9.57. It was Sunday. As he was shaving, Maigret heard radio warnings to motorists, not to drive except when absolutely necessary because the snow crust on the roads had become harder and more slippery than ever.

Lucas had driven him and was waiting for him in the Judicial Police car. There was more bustle at the airport than in all the streets of Paris and the air was hot, an almost human heat which sent the blood to one's head.

After drinking a glass of beer at one of the bars, the Superintendent felt himself growing crimson in the face and regretted having put on the stifling scarf which Madame Maigret had knitted for him and which she insisted he wore.

The loud-speakers announced a delay of about ten minutes for the flight from Copenhagen via Amsterdam, and he strolled round looking at the passport officials who glanced briefly at every traveller, and stamped or did not stamp the passports accordingly.

The day before, at about eight o'clock, Keulemans had telephoned him at the Boulevard Richard-Lenoir just as he was sitting down to dinner after turning on the television.

'Lina Nahour has booked two seats on the flight leaving for Orly at 8.45.'

'Is Alvaredo going with her?'

'No. The second seat is for her friend, Anna Keegel. The young man booked a seat on the flight leaving at 11.22 and arriving in Paris at 12.45.'

'Did they telephone each other again?'

'At about five o'clock. Lina Nahour simply said what time she was leaving and added that her friend was going with her. He said he'd take the next 'plane. When he asked her how she was she said she felt much better and her temperature had dropped to 37.5.'

The flight arrival was announced and Maigret stuck his face to the cold window, gazing after the people moving round the aircraft.

He did not recognize the young woman amongst the passengers, including four children who were the first to

228

disembark, and he started to think that she had changed her mind when he saw a young woman dressed in a seal coat leaning on her companion's arm as she stepped down the gangway.

Anna Keegel, who was small and dark, was wearing a thick woollen coat of a bright green colour.

At the last moment the hostess helped Lina get into the little bus where the other passengers were already standing, and the doors closed.

Having been the last to leave the 'plane the two women were the last to have their passports examined and Maigret, leaning against the barrier, had plenty of time to look at them.

Was Lina Nahour really beautiful? It was a question of taste. She had a light and fresh Nordic complexion, as Pardon had said, a small pointed nose, and pale blue eyes.

That morning her features were strained and one felt that she had considerable difficulty in standing up.

Anna Keegel was ugly in a pleasant way, and even though that was no time for laughter, one felt that she had a sense of humour.

He followed them at a distance to the customs where they waited a few minutes for a green suitcase and another cheaper-looking case, which must have belonged to Anna.

A porter took their luggage and hailed a taxi outside the airport building, while Maigret got into the police car next to Lucas.

'Is that them?'

'Yes. Don't let them give you the slip.'

It wasn't difficult because the taxi driver drove carefully and they took three quarters of an hour to get to the Avenue du Parc-Montsouris.

'Did you think they'd go somewhere else?'

'I didn't think anything. I just wanted to make sure. Park behind the taxi when it stops and wait for me.'

The two women got out and, before going through the garden gate, Lina Nahour looked the house up and down, seemed to hesitate, and finally let her friend lead her in.

Maigret overtook them and arrived at the front door before them.

'Who are you?' asked Lina frowning.

She had a slight accent.

'Superintendent Maigret. I'm investigating your husband's death. May I follow you in . . .'

Although she didn't protest, she looked uneasy and pulled her coat round her. The taxi driver carried the cases to the front door and it was Anna Keegel who opened her bag to pay the fare.

Fat Torrence, who was on day duty, opened the door without saying a word and Lina looked at him also with amazement rather than anxiety.

One felt that she didn't know what to do or where to go, that she hesitated to go up to her room or into the studio.

'Where's the body?' she asked Maigret.

'At the Medico-Legal Institute.'

Was she relieved that it was no longer in the house? She seemed to shiver, but she was so tense that her movements were really reflexes.

She finally put her hand on the door-handle of the studio and, just as she was about to open it, the door was opened from the inside and Pierre Nahour appeared, surprised to find four people in the corridor.

'Hello, Pierre . . .' she said, giving him her hand.

Did the banker from Geneva really hesitate? In all events, he held out his hand too.

'Where did it happen?'

Pierre Nahour stood back to let Lina, her friend and the Superintendent in, while Torrence stayed in the corridor.

'Here . . . Behind the desk . . .'

She hesitantly went a few steps, saw the patch of blood, and turned away.

'How did that happen?'

'Someone shot him.'

'Did he die at once?'

Pierre Nahour remained calm, fairly cold, and watched his sister-in-law with no visible feeling on his face.

'We don't know . . . The charwoman found him when she came to work in the morning . . .'

Seeing her so unsteady, her friend led her to an armchair in which she sat down cautiously, because her back must have been hurting.

She showed that she wanted a cigarette and Anna Keegel lit one and handed it to her.

The silence was rather embarrassing. Even Maigret felt slightly awkward in view of the physical and probably also the mental condition of the young woman, whose nerves must have been strained to breaking point.

'Do you know if he suffered?'

'We don't know,' said Pierre Nahour drily.

'At what time did it . . . did it happen?'

'Probably between midnight and one o'clock . . .'

'Wasn't anyone in the house?'

'Fouad was at the club and Nelly was asleep . . . She says she didn't hear a thing . . .'

'Do I have to go to a meeting at the solicitor's?'

'He rang me, yes . . . Tomorrow afternoon . . . My father arrived last night and is resting in his room at the Hôtel Raspail . . .'

'What shall I do?' she asked, talking to no one in particular.

After a silence still more unpleasant than the previous ones it was her friend who replied in Dutch.

'Do you think? . . .' she asked her in French. 'Yes, maybe that's the best thing . . . I wouldn't have the courage to sleep in this house . . .'

She looked round for Maigret.

'I'm going to a hotel with my friend and my maid . . .'

She didn't even ask his permission, as a suspect would have done, but simply announced her decision.

Then she turned to her brother-in-law again:

'Is Nelly upstairs? Where's Madame Bodin?'

'She hasn't come. Nelly's in her room.'

'I'm going up to get some linen and some clothes . . . Will you come and help me, Anna? . . .'

When they were alone together the two men looked at each other in silence.

'How did your father take it, Monsieur Nahour?'

'Pretty badly . . . My sister went with him and they've both gone to rest in the hotel . . . I insisted that they shouldn't stay here . . .'

'Are you staying?'

'I'd rather . . . Are you starting to get any idea who the murderer could be, Monsieur Maigret?'

'How about you?'

'I don't know . . . Why didn't you question my sister-in-law? . . .'

'I'm waiting for her to settle down in a hotel. For the moment she obviously couldn't bear any more of it . . .'

They were standing up and Pierre Nahour had a hard look on his face.

'I would like to ask you a question,' said the Superintendent gently. 'You've read your brother's letters and you've had a chance to talk to Oueni . . . He doesn't seem prepared to co-operate with us . . . Maybe, with you . . .'

'I tried to get something out of him yesterday evening, but without much success . . .'

'The number of possible suspects seems fairly limited, on one condition . . .'

'Which one?'

'Suppose that your brother, contrary to what you first thought, not only gambled on his own recently, but for a group, as he has been known to do in the past . . .'

'I see what you're driving at, Superintendent, but you are quite wrong . . . My brother was an honest man, like all the Nahours . . . He was scrupulous to the point of fussiness as I realized when I was reading his letters . . .

'It is out of the question that he would have cheated a group of a single penny, and that he was murdered out of vengeance . . .'

'I'm glad to hear you say that . . . I'm sorry that my job forces me to take every possibility into account . . . It may be Oueni's presence in the house that put that idea into my head . . .'

'I don't understand . . .'

'Don't you think Oueni's position is rather equivocal? . . . He's neither a secretary, nor a manservant or chauffeur, and he's not an equal either . . . Hence the possibility that he was watching your brother, representing a group . . .'

Nahour smiled ironically.

'If anyone else were to say that to me I'd say he'd been reading too many thrillers . . . I mentioned the sense of family feeling in the Lebanon . . . Well, the family doesn't stop at one's relatives . . . It sometimes includes old retainers, and friends can sometimes live in the house and be treated as equals . . .'

'Would you have chosen Oueni?'

'No . . . First because I don't like the man, and then because I married young and my wife's enough for me . . . Don't forget that Felix remained a bachelor until he was thirty-five . . . In the family we were all sure that he'd never marry . . .'

'Just a minute, please . . .'

Maigret, who had heard some steps on the stairs, went to open the door. Lina had changed her dress and was now wearing her mink coat. Nelly Velthuis followed her, a distant look in her eyes, carrying a case, and Anna Keegel, carrying more luggage, brought up the rear.

'Could you call me a taxi, Pierre? . . . I shouldn't have let mine go . . .'

She looked at the Superintendent questioningly, and Maigret asked:

'Which hotel are you going to? . . . The Ritz? . . .'

'Oh no! That brings back too many memories . . . Wait a

233

minute, what's the name of that hotel on the corner of the
Rue de Rivoli, near the Place Vendôme . . .'

'The Hôtel du Louvre? . . .'

'That's right . . . We'll go to the Hôtel du Louvre . . .'

'I'll call on you later, because I shall have to ask you a few
questions . . .'

'The taxi's on its way . . .'

It was almost twelve. It was Janvier's turn to go to Orly,
wait for Alvaredo, and follow him.

'Good-bye, Pierre . . . What time is the meeting tomorrow,
and who's the solicitor?'

'Three o'clock, Maître Leroy-Beaulieu in the Boulevard
Saint-Germain . . .'

'No need to write it down,' interrupted Maigret, 'I'll give
you the address at the hotel . . .'

It took some time to get the luggage and the three passengers
into the car. Lina was obviously shivering on the pavement
and looked round as though she did not recognize a setting
which was familiar to her.

Pierre Nahour shut the door again and Maigret thought he
saw a curtain move at a window which must have been
Oueni's.

He said to Lucas as he got in next to him:

'Follow them . . . They're going to the Hôtel du Louvre,
but I'd rather be certain . . . So far I'm not sure that I've
heard one word of truth in this whole case . . .'

The streets were as empty as they were in August, without
the buses full of tourists. The taxi stopped in front of the Hôtel
du Louvre. Lina and her friend went in first, probably to see
whether there were any free rooms. A few seconds later a
porter came for their luggage while the maid looked at the
clock and paid the fare.

'Go and park the car somewhere, and meet me at the bar.
I must give her time to get to her room and make herself
comfortable . . .'

Besides, he was thirsty.

234

CHAPTER FIVE

THE BAR WAS DARK and silent. Two Englishmen sitting on tall stools were moving their lips, but one couldn't hear what they were saying. The walls were covered in oak panels and the brass bracket-lamps only gave out a dim light every four or five yards. In a corner a young woman sat waiting, in front of a pinkish cocktail. In the opposite corner four men occasionally leaned towards each other.

Here too it was Sunday, a hollow day outside reality. Through the cream-coloured curtains one could just see a little dirty snow, black trees, and the head of a passer-by.

'Cloakroom, sir?'

'I'm sorry . . .'

His investigations usually led him to local bistros or noisy bars near the Champs-Elysées, and not to palaces. He took off his coat and sighed with relief as he pulled off his hot scarf.

'A beer . . .' he ordered under his breath to the barman who looked at him as though he were trying to remember where he had seen him before.

'Carlsberg . . . Heineken?'

'Either.'

Good old Lucas was also stopped by the young lady in the cloakroom.

'What will you have?'

'How about you, chief?'

'I ordered a beer.'

'The same for me, then.'

The words *Grill Room* were written up in weakly-lit letters over an open door, through which came a faint noise of plates.

'Are you hungry?'

'Not very . . .'

'Do you know the room numbers?'

'437, 438 and 439. Two bedrooms and a small sitting-room.'

'How about Nelly?'

'She sleeps in one of the rooms. 437 is a large room with two beds for Madame Nahour and her friend . . .'

'I'll be back at once . . .'

In the vast marble corridor Maigret walked towards a door marked *Telephone*.

'Can you give me room 437, please?'

'Just a minute . . .'

'Hello . . . Madame Nahour?'

'Who's speaking?'

'Superintendent Maigret.'

'This is Anne Keegel speaking. Madame Nahour is in the bath.'

'Ask her if she'd rather I came up in about ten minutes or whether she wants to have lunch first.'

He waited for some time. He could hear indistinct voices.

'Hello . . . She isn't hungry because she ate on the 'plane, but she'd rather you didn't come up in less than half an hour.'

Maigret and Lucas went into the grill room a few minutes later. It was as well-upholstered as the bar, with the same wooden panels, the same bracket-lamps, and small lights on the tables. Only three or four of the tables were taken and everybody was whispering, as if in church. The maître d'hotel, the chefs and the waiters came and went in silence, like the priests of some cult.

When he was handed an enormous menu, Maigret shook his head.

'*Assiette anglaise*,' he muttered.

'For me too.'

'Two cold meats,' corrected the maître d'hotel.

'And a beer.'

'I'll send you the wine-waiter.'

'Can you telephone the Quai and tell them we're here? Tell them to try and get in touch with Janvier, who must still be at Orly. Give them the room number.'

Maigret suddenly looked heavy and Lucas, who recognized this symptom, took care not to ask him any unnecessary questions.

The meal was eaten in almost complete silence, under the blasé eye of the maître d'hotel and the waiters.

'Will you have some coffee?'

A man in Turkish national dress served them with affected gestures.

'You'd better come up with me.'

They got to the fourth floor and knocked on door number 437, but it was 438 which opened.

'This way . . .' said Anna Keegel.

She must also have had a bath or a shower, because she had a lock of damp hair.

'Come in . . . I'll tell Lina . . .'

In the small sitting-room everything was soft and gentle, the pale grey walls, the light blue armchairs, the table painted ivory white. Somebody could be heard moving about in the room on the left, probably Nelly Velthuis still unpacking.

They waited for some time, standing up, ill at ease, and finally the two women came in. Maigret was surprised because he expected Lina Nahour to be in bed.

She had just combed her hair and was wearing no make-up. She had on a faded pink velvet dressing-gown.

She looked frail and vulnerable. If she was making an effort, it was not visible and the tension of the morning had disappeared.

She was astonished to see two men instead of one and she looked at Lucas interrogatively.

'One of my detectives,' explained Maigret.

'Sit down, gentlemen . . .'

237

She sat down on the sofa and her friend came and sat next to her.

'I'm sorry to bother you so soon after your arrival, but you do understand that I have some questions to ask, don't you?'

She lit a cigarette and the fingers holding the match trembled slightly.

'You may smoke.'

'Thank you.'

He did not fill his pipe immediately.

'May I ask where you were on Friday night?'

'At what time?'

'I would like you to tell me all you did that evening and that night.'

'I left the house at about eight o'clock.'

'At about the same time as your husband, you mean?'

'I don't know where he was just then.'

'Did you usually go out without telling him where you were going?'

'We were both free to go where we liked.'

'Did you take your car?'

'No. The roads were icy and I didn't want to drive.'

'Did you call a taxi?'

'Yes.'

'From the telephone in your room?'

'Yes, Of course.'

She talked like a little girl reciting her lesson and her innocent eyes reminded the Superintendent of somebody. It was only after several sentences that he thought of the maid, her almost transparent pupils, her childish expression.

He found that Lina behaved in the same way, almost as though one of the two women were copying the other, so similar were their expressions and even the movement of their eyelids.

'Where did you go?'

'To a large restaurant on the Champs-Elysées. The Marignan.'

She had hesitated before saying this last word.

'Do you frequently have dinner at the Marignan?'

'Sometimes.'

'Alone?'

'Usually.'

'Where were you sitting?'

'In the main room.'

Where there were usually about a hundred clients, so it was impossible to check her alibi.

'Did anyone join you?'

'No.'

'Did you have an appointment?'

'I remained alone until the end of the meal.'

'What time was that?'

'I don't know. Maybe ten o'clock.'

'Did you pass through the bar first?'

Another pause, and then she shook her head.

Now the more nervous of the two of them was her friend, Anna Keegel, who looked at Lina and the Superintendent in turn, turning her head at each question.

'Then?'

'I walked along the Champs-Elysées to get some air.'

'In spite of the slippery pavements?'

'The pavements had been cleared. When I was almost level with the Lido I took a taxi and drove back here.'

'You still hadn't seen your husband, who was back around ten?'

'I didn't see him, I went up to my room where Nelly had just finished packing my case.'

'Because you'd decided to go on a journey?'

With complete candour, she replied:

'I'd decided the week before.'

'What was your destination?'

'Why . . . Amsterdam, of course.'

She started talking to Anna Keegel in Dutch. Anna got up, went into the bedroom, and came back a little later with a letter. It was dated January 6, and was not written in French or English.

'You can have it translated. I'm telling Anna to expect me on January 15.'

'Had you booked a seat on the 'plane?'

'No. I had first wanted to go by train. There is a train at 11.12.'

'Were you going to take your maid?'

'There's no room for her in Anna's flat.'

Although Maigret wanted her to swallow the hook completely, he felt a certain admiration for the calm way in which she lied.

'Did you stop on the ground floor on your way out?'

'No. The taxi which Nelly had called was already outside the door.'

'Did you say good-bye to your husband?'

'No. He knew.'

'Did you drive to the Gare du Nord?'

'We arrived late because of the bad road conditions. Since the train had left I went to Orly.'

'Passing by the Boulevard Voltaire?'

She didn't blink. It was Anna Keegel who winced.

'Where's that?'

'I'm sorry to have to tell you that you know as well as I do. How did you get Doctor Pardon's address?'

There was a long silence. She lit another cigarette, stood up, walked a few steps, and sat down again. If she was upset it was not visible. She seemed to be thinking what she should say.

'What do you know?' she asked Maigret in her turn, looking him straight in the eye.

'That you were wounded by your husband in the studio with a bullet from a 6.35 with a mother-of-pearl handle which used to belong to you and which he kept in a drawer in his desk.'

Her elbow on the arm of the chair, she held her chin in her

hand and gazed at the Superintendent with curiosity. She was like a model school-girl listening to her teacher.

'You did not leave the house in a taxi but in the red car of a friend called Vicente Alvaredo. He took you to the Boulevard Voltaire where he told an incredible story about an attack by an unknown motorist . . .

'Doctor Pardon, to whom you didn't say a word, put a temporary dressing on the wound. You returned to his waiting-room and as he was taking off his coat and washing his hands you left the flat without a sound . . .'

'What do you want out of me?'

She was not disconcerted. One could have sworn that she was smiling at him, just like a little girl who had been caught out and who only considers a lie a big sin.

'I want the truth.'

'I'd rather you asked me questions.'

That was clever too, because it meant she could find out exactly what the police knew. Nevertheless Maigret joined in.

'Was this letter really written on January 6? Before you answer, let me tell you that we can check that by analyzing the ink.'

'It was written on January 6.'

'Did your husband know?'

'He must have.'

'Known what?'

'That I was going to leave soon.'

'Why?'

'Because life had been unbearable for some time.'

'How long?'

'Months.'

'Two years?'

'Perhaps.'

'Ever since you met Vicente Alvaredo?'

Anna Keegel was getting increasingly nervous and her foot touched Lina's pink slipper as if by chance.

'That's about right.'

'Did your husband know about your affair?'

'I don't kr ow. Somebody may have seen Vicente and me. We didn't hide.'

'Do you think it normal that a married woman . . .'

'Only just!'

'What do you mean?'

'Felix and I had been living like strangers for years.'

'And yet you had a second child two years ago.'

'Because my husband wanted a son. It's just as well it wasn't another girl.'

'Is your son by him?'

'Definitely. When I met Alvaredo I'd only just got over my confinement and I was beginning to go out.'

'Have you had any other lovers?'

'Believe it or not, he was the first.'

'What were your plans for the evening of the 14th?'

'I don't understand?'

'On the 6th you wrote to your friend that you were arriving in Amsterdam on the 15th.'

Anna Keegel started speaking to her in Dutch, but Lina, sure of herself, shook her head and continued to look at the Superintendent with the same assurance.

Maigret had at last lit his pipe.

'I'll try to explain. Alvaredo wanted me to get a divorce and marry him. I asked him for a week, because I knew it wouldn't be easy. There never has been a divorce in the Nahour family and Felix wanted to keep up appearances.

'We decided that I'd talk to him about it on the 14th and that whatever he said we would leave for Amsterdam immediately.'

'Why Amsterdam?'

She seemed surprised that the Superintendent did not understand.

'Because that's where I spent most of my childhood and my youth. Vicente didn't know Holland. I wanted to show it to him. Once the divorce had been obtained we would have

242

gone to see his parents in Colombia before getting married.'

'Have you got money of your own?'

'No, of course not. But we didn't need the Nahours' money.'

She added with slightly naïve pride:

'The Alvaredos are richer than they are and they own most of the gold mines in Colombia.'

'Good. So you left at about eight without saying anything to your husband. Alvaredo was waiting for you in his Alfa Romeo. Where did you dine?'

'In a little restaurant in the Boulevard du Montparnasse where Vicente eats nearly all his meals since he lives next door.'

'Were you worried about your husband's possible reaction when he knew about your decision?'

'No.'

'Why, because he was against divorce?'

'Because he had no way of keeping me.'

'Did he still love you?'

'I'm not sure that he ever loved me.'

'Why would he have married you?'

'Maybe to be seen around with a pretty, well-dressed woman. It was at Deauville, the year when I was chosen as Miss Europe. We met several times in the halls and corridors of the casino. One evening I found him next to me at a roulette table, he pushed some large rectangular chips towards me and whispered:

' "Play on fourteen." '

'Did fourteen come up?'

'Not the first time, but the third. It came up twice, consecutively, and I'd never seen as much money as when I went to cash my chips that evening at the bank.'

The tables had turned. This time it was her own story which seemed the most plausible, almost obvious.

'He found out the number of my room and he sent me flowers. We dined together several times. He seemed very shy. I felt he wasn't used to talking to women.'

'And yet he was thirty-five years old.'

'I'm not so sure he had known any other woman before me. Then he took me to Biarritz.'

'Without ever asking you for anything?'

'In Biarritz, where he spent most of his nights in the casino, as he had in Deauville, he came into my room at about five o'clock one morning. He usually didn't drink. But that evening I could smell alcohol on his breath.'

'Was he drunk?'

'He'd drunk a glass or two to summon up courage.'

'Is that when it happened?'

'Yes. He didn't stay more than half an hour with me. And in the five months that followed he didn't come to see me more than ten times. Nevertheless he asked me to marry him. I accepted.'

'Because he was rich?'

'Because I liked the life he led, from one hotel to the other, from one casino to the other. We got married in Cannes. We continued to have separate rooms. He wanted it. He was very modest. I think he was rather ashamed of being so fat, because at that period he was fatter than he was in the last few years.'

'Was he tender with you?'

'He treated me like a little girl. He didn't change any of his habits and we were accompanied everywhere by Oueni, with whom he spent more time than with me.'

'How did you get on with Oueni?'

'I don't like him.'

'Why?'

'I don't know. Perhaps because he had too much influence over my husband. And perhaps because he belongs to another race which I don't understand.'

'What was Oueni's attitude towards you?'

'He appeared not to see me. He must despise me profoundly, as he despises all women. One day, when I was bored, I asked to be allowed to have a Dutch girl as a maid. I put

244

an advertisement in the papers in Amsterdam and I chose Nelly because she seemed gay.'

She was smiling now, while her friend, who looked worried, appeared not to approve of the turn the conversation had taken.

'Let's get back to Friday evening. What time did you get back to the house?'

'At about half past eleven.'

'Did you and Alvaredo stay in the restaurant until then?'

'No. We went to his flat to get his case. I helped him pack it. We chatted and had a drink.'

'Once he was here, did he stay in the car?'

'Yes.'

'You went into the studio?'

'No. I went up to my room and changed. I asked Nelly if Felix was downstairs and she answered that she'd heard him come back.'

'Did she also tell you if he was alone or with his secretary?'

'With his secretary.'

'Didn't that upset you in view of the conversation you expected to have?'

'I was used to seeing Oueni there the whole time. I don't know what the time was when I went down. I'd already put my coat on. Nelly followed me with the case which she left in the corridor and we kissed each other.'

'Was going to join you?'

'As soon as I told her to.'

'Did she go up to her room? Without waiting for the result of your encounter?'

'She knew I'd made up my mind and nothing would change it.'

The telephone rang on the little round table. Maigret signalled to Lucas to answer.

'Hello . . . Yes . . . He's here . . . Here he is . . .'

Maigret knew that he would hear Janvier's voice.

'He's arrived, chief . . . He's at home, in the Boulevard . . .

'Boulevard du Montparnasse . . .

'Did you know that already? He lives in a furnished studio on the second floor. I'm in a little bar opposite the building . . .'

'Stay there . . . I'll see you later . . .'

And Lina, looking as natural as ever, asked, as if it were self-evident:

'Has Vicente arrived?'

'Yes. He's at his flat.'

'Why are the police watching him?'

'It's their duty to watch all suspects.'

'Why should he be a suspect? He's never set foot in the house in the Avenue du Parc-Montsouris.'

'That's what you say.'

'Don't you believe me?'

'I never know when you're lying or telling the truth. By the way, how did you get Doctor Pardon's address?'

'Nelly gave it to me. She was told by our charwoman who had lived in the district. I had to have medical aid immediately, as far from the house as possible . . .'

'Very well!' he muttered without conviction, because he was no longer prepared to believe anything. 'You kissed Nelly Velthuis in the corridor where your case was. She went upstairs and you went into the studio. You found your husband there working together with Oueni.'

She nodded.

'Did you mention your departure straight away?'

'Yes. I told him I was going to Amsterdam where my lawyer would write him a letter and settle the divorce.'

'How did he take that?'

'He looked at me for a long time in silence, and then murmured:

' "It's not possible." '

'Did it occur to him to send Oueni out?'

'No.'

'Was Nahour sitting at his desk?'

'Yes.'

246

'Was Oueni sitting opposite him?'

'No. Oueni was standing by his side, holding some papers. I can't remember my exact words. I was a little nervous in spite of it all.'

'Did Alvaredo advise you to carry a gun? Did he give you one?'

'I didn't have a gun. What use would it have been? I told him my decision was final, that nothing would change my mind and I started to walk towards the door. It was then that I heard an explosion and felt a pain, like a burn, in my shoulder.

'I must have turned round, because I can remember Felix standing there holding a pistol. Above all I can remember his eyes wide open as though he had just realized what he had done.'

'What about Oueni?'

'He was standing next to him, motionless.'

'What did you do?'

'I was afraid I was going to faint. I didn't want that to happen in the house, where I would have been at the mercy of the two men. I rushed to the door and found myself standing by the car which Vicente opened for me.'

'Did you hear a second explosion?'

'No. I told Vicente to drive me to the Boulevard Voltaire, to a doctor I knew . . .'

'But you didn't know Doctor Pardon . . .'

'I didn't have time to explain. I felt very ill.'

'Why didn't you go to Alvaredo's flat which was almost next door, and why didn't he call his own doctor?'

'Because I didn't want to cause a scandal. I was in a hurry to be in Holland and I was sure the police wouldn't find out. That was why I didn't say anything at the doctor's in case he should recognize my accent.

'I didn't expect him to ask any questions. I didn't know the bullet had stayed in the wound and I didn't know how deep it was. I just wanted to stop the blood . . .'

'What means of transport did you and Vicente expect to take to Amsterdam?'

'His car. When I left the doctor I felt too weak to spend hours in a car and Vicente thought of the 'plane. I remembered that there was a night flight which I'd taken once before. We had to wait a long time at Orly and we weren't sure whether the 'plane could take off, because of the snow and the ice.

'In Amsterdam Vicente took me in a taxi straight to Anna's flat and I told him to go to a hotel where he was to wait until I felt better. We were going to have separate rooms until the divorce . . .'

'To avoid being sued on grounds of adultery?'

'Precautions were no longer necessary. Felix couldn't refuse a divorce after the shot.'

'So, if I'm right in thinking, it was to your advantage.' She looked at him and couldn't help smiling maliciously. 'Yes,' she admitted.

The strangest thing of all was that it seemed quite likely and Maigret wanted to believe her, so frankly did she appear to answer his questions. As he watched her face, which had remained as child-like as Nelly Velthuis's, Maigret could understand Nahour treating her like a little girl, and he could understand Vicente Alvaredo falling sufficiently in love with her to want to marry her despite her husband and her two children.

It was warm in the comfortable, plush sitting-room and it was easy to be almost engulfed by it. Lucas himself looked like a large cat purring.

'I would like to add one more point, Madame Nahour: there is nobody to confirm your statements. According to you there were three of you in the studio when the first shot was fired.'

'You have Fouad as a witness.'

'Unfortunately for you he pretends that he only returned to the house after one in the morning and it has been established

248

that he left the club in the Boulevard Saint-Michel at about that time.'

'He's lying.'

'He's been seen there.'

'What if he went there after the shot?'

'We'll try and check that.'

'You can question Nelly too.'

'She can't speak French, can she?'

He felt her hesitate, and she answered indirectly:

'She can speak English.'

Suddenly Maigret's massive body seemed to unfold itself. Without a sound he crept up to the door of the adjoining room and opened it suddenly. The maid nearly fell into his arms and had great difficulty in keeping her balance.

'Have you been listening long?'

On the verge of tears, she shook her head. She had changed her suit for a black satin dress and a white apron with embroidered scallops, and she wore a cap on her head.

'Did you understand what we said?'

She said yes, and then no, looking at her mistress for help.

'She understands a little French,' said Lina. 'But whenever she tries to talk, particularly to the local tradesmen, they make fun of her.'

'Come here, Nelly. Don't stay glued to the door. How long have you known that Madame Nahour was leaving for Amsterdam on Friday evening?'

'One week . . .'

'You're not talking to her, but to me.'

She turned to him reluctantly, and still hesitated to look the Superintendent in the face.

'At what time did you pack the case?'

She was obviously translating the answer in her mind.

'Eight o'clock . . .'

'Why did you lie when I questioned you yesterday?'

'I don't know . . . I was frightened . . .'

'What of?'

249

'I don't know.'

'Did someone in the house frighten you?'

She shook her head violently and her cap went askew on her head.

'Did you see Madame Nahour again at about ten? Where?'

'In room.'

'Who brought down the case?'

'I.'

'Where did your mistress go?'

'Studio.'

'Did you hear a shot later?'

'Yes.'

'One or two shots?'

She looked towards Lina again and replied:

'One.'

'Did you come down?'

'No.'

'Why not?'

She shrugged her shoulders, as if to say she didn't know. It was not a case of one of the two women copying the other. Each one had taken certain characteristics from the other, so that the maid was now rather like a muddled answer from Lina.

'Did you hear Oueni go to his room?'

'No.'

'Did you go to sleep at once?'

'Yes.'

'Did you try and find out who was wounded or dead?'

'Saw Madame from window. Heard door and saw Madame and car . . .'

'Thank you. All I hope is that when your statement is recorded tomorrow you don't give us a third version of the facts . . .'

The sentence was obviously too long and too difficult for her and Madame Nahour translated it into Dutch while the girl turned very red and hurried away.

'What I've just said goes for you too, Madame Nahour. I didn't want you to undergo an official interrogation today. Tomorrow I'll ring you and make an appointment. I'll come round in person, or one of my detectives will, to take down your statement.'

'There's a third witness,' she added.

'Alvaredo, I know. I'll see him when I leave here. Since I don't trust the telephone Inspector Lucas will stay in your suite until I relieve him.'

She didn't protest.

'Can I have some food sent up? My friend Anna is always hungry. She's a real Dutch woman. As for me, I'm going to bed.'

'May I go into your room a moment?'

The room was fairly untidy, clothes had been thrown hurriedly onto the bed, and shoes on the carpet. The telephone was plugged into the wall. Maigret unplugged it, brought it into the sitting-room, and then did the same thing to the telephone in Nelly's room.

Nelly, who was putting some linen away into the drawers, looked at him bitterly, as though he had scolded her.

'I'm sorry about these precautions,' he said, as he left the two women.

And Lina replied with a smile:

'It's your job, isn't it?'

*　　　*　　　*

The porter called him a taxi. One could now just distinguish a pale sun behind the clouds, and children were sliding on the snow in the Jardins du Luxembourg. Three or four of them had even brought their toboggans.

He found the bistro where Janvier was waiting for him, seated close to the misty window which he wiped from time to time.

'A beer . . .' he ordered in a tired voice.

The interrogation had completely exhausted him and he

251

still felt the clamminess of the little sitting-room cling to his body.

'Has he been out?'

'No. I suppose he ate on the 'plane. He must be waiting for a 'phone call.'

'He'll have a long wait.'

Maigret could have had the telephone tapped, like his colleague in Amsterdam, but maybe because he belonged to the old school, or more probably because of the way he was brought up, he hesitated to resort to this procedure unless he was dealing with professionals.

'Lucas stayed at the Hôtel du Louvre. Come and see the young man with me. I don't know him yet. By the way, what's he like?'

The beer was refreshing and helped him return to reality. It was good to see a real bar again, with sawdust on the ground and a waiter in a blue apron.

'Very handsome, casually elegant and a rather distant expression . . .'

'Did he try to see whether he was being followed?'

'Not as far as I could tell.'

'Come along.'

They crossed the street and went into a well-to-do building where they took the lift.

'Third floor,' said Janvier. 'I enquired. He's lived in the studio for three years.'

There was no plaque or visiting card on the door which opened a few seconds after Maigret had rung. A very dark young man, rather tall, said extremely politely:

'Come in, gentlemen . . . I was expecting you . . . Superintendent Maigret, I presume?'

He did not hold out his hand but led them into a light sitting-room with modern furniture and pictures, and a balcony window looking onto the street.

'Won't you take your coats off?'

'Just one question, Monsieur Alvaredo. Madame Nahour

252

telephoned you yesterday in Amsterdam to say that her husband was dead. She telephoned again that afternoon to tell you which flight she was taking with her friend. You left Amsterdam this morning and the Dutch papers of last night couldn't have mentioned the case.'

Alvaredo turned casually to the sofa and picked up a Paris paper of the day before.

'There's even a photograph of you on the third page,' he said with a bantering smile.

The two men took off their overcoats.

'Can I give you a drink?'

A variety of bottles and several glasses stood on a low table. Only one glass was off the tray and still held a little amber-coloured liquid.

'Listen to me, Monsieur Alvaredo. Before asking you any further questions I want to tell you that so far in this case I've been constantly confronted with people who take considerable liberties with the truth.'

'Do you mean Lina?'

'She and other people whom I do not have to mention to you. First of all I would like to know when you last set foot in the Nahour's house.'

'If you don't mind my saying so, Superintendent, I don't find your trap very subtle. You must already know that I've never been into that house, either on Friday night or at any other time.'

'Do you know if Monsieur Nahour knew about your affair with his wife?'

'I don't know since I've only seen him a couple of times, in the distance, at a gambling table.'

'Do you know Fouad?'

'Lina has mentioned him, but I've never met him.'

'And yet on Friday evening you did not hide but you waited in a very obvious car just outside the gate.'

'We didn't have to hide any longer since we'd made up our minds and Lina was going to inform her husband.'

253

'Were you worried about the result of this conversation?'

'Why worried? Lina had decided to leave and he couldn't keep her by force.'

He added rather bitterly:

'We're not in the Near East.'

'Did you hear a shot?'

'I heard a muffled sound which I couldn't place at once. A second later the door opened and Lina rushed out onto the pavement, dragging her case. I just had time to open the car. She seemed exhausted. And she told me all about it as we drove off . . .'

'Did you know Doctor Pardon?'

'I'd never heard of him. She gave me his address.'

'Did you still plan to go to Amsterdam by car?'

'I didn't realize how seriously she'd been wounded. She was bleeding profusely. I was very worried . . .'

'Which didn't prevent you from lying to the doctor.'

'I thought it better not to tell him the truth.'

'And to leave his office without a word . . .'

'So that he shouldn't take down our names.'

'Did you know that Nahour kept a weapon in the drawer of his desk?'

'Lina had mentioned it to me.'

'Was she frightened of her husband?'

'He wasn't a man one could be frightened of.'

'How about Oueni?'

'She didn't say much about him.'

'But he played an important part in the house.'

'As far as his master was concerned, maybe, but he had nothing to do with Lina.'

'Are you sure?'

Suddenly the blood rushed to Alvaredo's cheeks and ears, and he replied between his teeth:

'What are you hinting?'

'I'm not hinting anything, except that Fouad, who influenced Nahour, could influence the fate of Madame Nahour indirectly.'

The young man calmed down, embarrassed at having lost his temper.

'You are very passionate, Monsier Alvaredo.'

'I'm in love . . .' he said drily.

'May I ask how long you've been in Paris?'

'Three and a half years.'

'Are you a student?'

'I took a law degree in Bogota. I came here to follow a course at the Institute of Comparative Law . . . I also work as an apprentice for Maître Puget in the Boulevard Raspail, very near here; he is a professor of International Law . . .'

'Are your parents rich?'

He answered rather apologetically:

'They are by Bogota standards.'

'Are you an only child?'

'I've got a younger brother who is at Berkeley in the United States . . .'

'Am I right in thinking your parents are Catholics, like most Colombians?'

'My mother is fairly devout.'

'Are you going to take Madame Nahour to Bogota?'

'I intend to.'

'Don't you expect some trouble with your family if you marry a divorcee?'

'I'm over twenty-one.'

'May I use your telephone?'

Maigret called the Hôtel du Louvre.

'Lucas? . . . You can leave them alone . . . But stay in the hotel . . . I'll have you relieved at the end of the afternoon . . .'

Alvaredo smiled bitterly.

'You left one of your men in Lina's room to stop her telephoning me, didn't you?'

'I'm sorry I have to take these precautions.'

'I suppose your detective will watch me too.'

'I'm afraid so.'

'Can I go and see her?'

'I don't see why not.'

'Did the journey tire her?'

'Not enough for her to lose her presence of mind.'

'She's a child.'

'A very clever child.'

'Won't you have a drink.'

'I'd rather not.'

'Which means you still suspect me?'

'In my profession we suspect everybody.'

On the pavement he sighed, drew a deep breath:

'There we are!'

'Do you think he lied, chief?'

Without answering Maigret went on:

'You can get into your car. That red car will soon be racing towards the Rue de Rivoli. Have a good afternoon . . . Keep in touch with the Quai so that you can be relieved . . .'

'How about you?'

'I'm going back to the Avenue du Parc-Montsouris. Tomorrow we'll have to get a few more men so that the interrogations can be made officially.'

His hands in his pockets he walked to the cab rank at the corner of the Boulevard Saint-Michel, cursing at the knitted scarf which was bundled round his neck and tickled him.

From outside the Nahours' house looked empty. The Superintendent told the driver to wait, crossed the little garden where the snow creaked under his shoes, and pressed the bell.

A sleepy Torrence opened the door yawning.

'Anything new?'

'The father has arrived. He's in the study with his son.'

'What's he like?'

'About seventy-five with very thick white hair, a lined and energetic face.'

The study door opened and Pierre Nahour, recognizing Maigret, said:

'Do you need me, Superintendent?'

'I wanted to see Oueni.'

'He's upstairs.'

'Has your father met him?'

'Not yet. He'll undoubtedly have some questions to ask him later.'

Maigret hung up his overcoat, his scarf and his hat on the coat-stand and went up the stairs. The corridor was dark. He went to Fouad's room, knocked and received an answer in Arabic.

When he opened the door he found Oueni sitting in an armchair. He was not reading. He wasn't doing anything. The face looking at Maigret was expressionless.

'You can come in . . . What did they tell you?'

CHAPTER SIX

IT WAS THE MOST SIMPLE and unsophisticated room in the house. The painter who let the house furnished to the Nahours must have had a young son because Oueni's room looked as though it had belonged to a student. The secretary did not seem to have changed anything and there were no private possessions of his to be seen.

Sitting in his leather armchair, his legs outstretched, looking completely relaxed, the man was dressed as punctiliously as the day before, in a well-cut dark suit. He was closely shaven. His shirt was very white and his nails manicured.

Appearing not to notice his insolent attitude Maigret stood in front of him and looked him straight in the eye, as though he were sizing him up, and both men looked like children trying not to blink.

'You're not very co-operative, Monsieur Oueni.'

There was no sign of anxiety on the secretary's face. It was almost as though he enjoyed flouting Maigret with his smile full of self-assurance and irony.

'Lina . . .'

Fouad emphasized this familiarity.

'I beg your pardon?'

'Madame Nahour, if you'd rather, doesn't quite agree about the way you spent your time on Friday evening. She claims that when she went into the studio at about midnight you were there together with Monsieur Nahour. She says that you were standing next to him, while he was sitting at his desk.'

Maigret awaited an answer which did not come and Fouad went on smiling.

'It's her word against mine, isn't it?' he said in the end.

All through this conversation he spoke with the same calculated slowness, detaching every syllable.

'Do you deny it?'

'I answered your questions yesterday.'

'That doesn't mean you told me the truth.'

His fingers curled up on the arm of the chair as though he thought he had been insulted. Nevertheless he controlled himself and said nothing.

The Superintendent walked to the window and stood for a while in front of it, then, his hands behind his back, his pipe in his mouth, he paced the room.

'You claim to have left the Bar des Tilleuls soon after one in the morning, and the owner has confirmed this . . . On the other hand he does not know when you arrived . . . So far there is nothing to prove that you didn't just come in and out in order to get an alibi.'

'Have you questioned all the members of the club who were in the two gaming rooms that night?'

'You know perfectly well that we haven't had a chance to do that yet and that the club and the bar are shut on Sunday.'

'You have all the time you like. So have I.'

Had he adopted this attitude just to infuriate Maigret? He had the coldness and nerve of a chess player and it was going to be difficult to catch him out.

Stopping in front of him again the Superintendent asked mildly:

'Have you ever been married, Monsieur Oueni?'

And Oueni replied with a sentence which may have been a proverb in his country:

'He who is not satisfied with the pleasures a woman can give him in one night is putting a rope round his neck.'

'That was what happened to Monsieur Nahour, I suppose?'

'His private life is none of my business.'

'Have you had mistresses?'

'I'm not homosexual, if that's what you want to know.'

259

This time his disdain was still more evident.

'I assume that means that you sometimes have affairs with women?'

'If French law is that curious, I can provide names and addresses.'

'It wasn't a woman whom you went to see on Friday night?'

'No. I've already told you.'

Maigret turned towards the window again and gazed vaguely at the Avenue du Parc-Montsouris, covered in snow, where, despite the cold, there were occasional Sunday walkers.

'Have you got a gun, Monsieur Oueni?'

Fouad got up slowly, leaving his armchair almost reluctantly, opened a drawer in the chest of drawers and pulled out a long pistol. It was not an object which could be carried in one's pocket but a training gun with a barrel at least twenty centimetres long and a calibre which did not correspond to the bullet found in Nahour's skull.

'Are you satisfied?'

'No.'

'Have you asked Monsieur Alvaredo the same question?'

It was Maigret's turn not to answer. This interrogation went very slowly, like a game of chess, each man planning his attacks and retreats with care.

The Superintendent's face was serious. He gave long puffs at his pipe, and the tobacco sizzled. They were surrounded by silence; they did not hear a sound from the quilted atmosphere outside.

'You know that Madame Nahour had been trying to get a divorce for almost two years?'

'I told you these questions were none of my business.'

'In view of the intimacy of your relations with Monsieur Nahour it seems likely that he might have mentioned it to you.'

'That's what you say.'

'I'm not saying anything. I'm asking the questions and you're the one who isn't answering.'

'I answer the questions which concern me.'

'Did you also know that Madame Nahour had been planning for over a week to leave for Amsterdam and that this would mean final separation from her husband?'

'Ditto.'

'Do you still claim not to have been in the room when this incident took place?'

Fouad shrugged his shoulders, considering the question superfluous.

'You have known Nahour for about twenty years. You hardly left his side in that time. He became a professional gambler, what one might call a scientific gambler, and you helped him in his calculations.'

Oueni, who did not seem to be listening, had returned to his armchair. Grabbing a chair by its back, Maigret sat astride it less than a yard away from him.

'You arrived in Paris with hardly any money, didn't you? How much did Nahour pay you?'

'I was never paid a salary.'

'Nevertheless you needed money.'

'When I did he gave it to me.'

'Have you got a bank account?'

'No.'

'How much did he give you at a time?'

'Whatever I asked for.'

'Large amounts? Did you save?'

'I've never had anything but my clothes.'

'Were you as able a gambler as he, Monsieur Oueni?'

'It's not for me to say.'

'Did he ever suggest you should replace him at a roulette or baccarat table?'

'Occasionally.'

'Did you win?'

'I lost and I won.'

'Have you kept your winnings?'

'No.'

261

'Was there ever any question of an association between you? For example, he could have given you a percentage of the sums which he won.'

He simply shook his head.

'So you were neither his associate nor his equal, since you were entirely dependent on him. Which means that in spite of everything you had a master-servant relationship. When he got married weren't you afraid that your relationship might become less close?'

'No.'

'Didn't Nahour love his wife?'

'You should have asked him.'

'It's a bit late now. How long have you known that Madame Nahour had a lover?'

'Should I have known?'

If he thought he was making Maigret angry, he was wrong because the Superintendent had rarely been in such control of himself.

'You can't not have known that the relationship between husband and wife, which had never been very intimate, had deteriorated over the last two years. You also knew how insistently Madame Nahour was demanding a divorce. Did you follow her, and who told your master about her affair with Alvaredo?'

A more disdainful smile than before.

'He saw them himself as they were coming out of a restaurant in the Palais-Royal. They didn't hide.'

'Was Nahour in a rage?'

'I have never seen him in a rage.'

'And yet, although he no longer had a sexual relationship with his wife and he knew that she loved someone else, he obliged her to live under the same roof. Wasn't that a form of revenge?'

'Maybe.'

'And wasn't it after this discovery that he separated her from her children by sending them to the Riviera?'

'Unlike you I don't read people's minds, whether they are dead or alive.'

'I am sure that Madame Nahour was not lying when she said you were with her husband on Friday evening, Monsieur Oueni. I am even inclined to think that you knew about her journey and that you knew the date.'

'I can't stop you.'

'Her husband hated her . . .'

'Didn't she hate him?'

'Let's say they both hated each other. She had decided to be free, at all costs . . .'

'At all costs, exactly.'

'Are you accusing Madame Nahour of killing her husband?'

'No.'

'Are you accusing yourself?'

'No.'

'Well?'

With calculated slowness, Oueni said:

'One person is interested in this business.'

'Alvaredo?'

'Where was he?'

'In his car, by the door.'

It was Fouad's turn to lead the interrogation, to ask the questions.

'Do you believe that?'

'Until I have proof to the contrary.'

'He was very much in love, wasn't he?'

Maigret let him talk, curious to see what he was driving at.

'Probably.'

'Very passionate. Didn't you say he'd been Madame Nahour's lover for two years? His parents wouldn't be very pleased to see him arrive with a divorcee and two children. The fact that he takes that risk suggests a great love, doesn't it?'

His eyes suddenly turned cruel, his mouth sarcastic.

'He knew how decisive the evening would be,' he went on, still sitting motionless in the armchair. 'Don't you agree?'

'Yes.'

'Tell me, Monsieur Maigret, in his position and in his state of mind on Friday evening, would you have let your mistress face an obstinate husband alone? Do you really think he waited almost an hour outside without worrying for a moment about what was going on in the house?'

'Did you see him?'

'Don't set me such unsubtle traps. I didn't see anything since I wasn't here. I'm simply showing you that that man's presence in the studio is more plausible than mine.'

Maigret got up, suddenly relaxed, as if he had finally got where he wanted.

'There were at least two people in the room,' he said more lightly. 'Nahour and his wife. That would imply that Madame Nahour was armed with a large revolver which one can hardly hide in a handbag. Nahour would also have to fire first and she would have had to kill him afterwards.'

'Not necessarily. She might have fired first, while her husband held the gun in his hand to defend himself, and it's quite possible that he automatically pressed the trigger as he fell, which would account for the inaccuracy.'

'It doesn't much matter who fired first at the moment. Let us assume you were there. Madame Nahour took a gun out of her bag and you fired in her direction to defend your employer, because you were quite near the drawer with the 6.35.'

'That would suggest that she did not fire at me, as I was armed and could have shot back, but at her husband?'

'Let us assume that you hated the man you call Monsieur Felix . . .'

'Why?'

'For years you've been a sort of poor relation, without really being a relation. You have no special function, but you look after everything, including the boiled eggs in the morning.

You're not paid. You're given small sums, pocket money in fact, when you need it.

'I don't know if the fact that you're of the same race matters or not. But in all events, your position was rather humiliating, and nothing stimulates hatred as much as humiliation.

'You have the chance to take revenge. Nahour shoots at his wife just when she goes to the door, never to come back. You shoot in your turn, not at her, but at him, knowing that she or her lover will be accused, after which you just need an alibi at the Club Saint-Michel.

'We have one way, Monsieur Fouad, of finding out whether that is what happened, within an hour. I shall ring Moers, one of the best technicians at the records office. If he isn't at the Quai he'll be at home. He will bring the equipment necessary for the paraffin test which we performed on Monsieur Nahour, and we will know whether you used a fire-arm.'

Oueni did not flinch. On the contrary his smile became more ironical than ever.

As Maigret went towards the telephone, he stopped him:

'There's no point.'

'Do you admit it?'

'You know as well as I do, Monsieur Maigret, that the test can reveal crusts of powder on the skin up to five days after a shot has been fired.'

'You are remarkably knowledgeable.'

'On Thursday I went to a shooting-range, as I frequently do, in the basement of a gunsmith called Boutelleau and Sons, in the Rue de Rennes.'

'With your pistol?'

'No. I've got another one, exactly like this one, which I leave there, like most of the customers. So it's quite likely that you'll find crusts of powder on my right hand.'

'Why do you practise shooting?'

Maigret was annoyed.

'Because I happen to belong to a tribe which goes armed at every time of the year and which claims to have produced the best shots in the world. Boys use guns after the age of ten.'

Maigret slowly raised his head.

'And what if we don't find any traces of powder on Alvaredo's hand or on Madame Nahour's?'

'Alvaredo came from outdoors where it was twelve degrees below zero. One can assume he was wearing gloves, and probably even fairly thick gloves. Didn't you check that?'

He was trying to be insulting.

'I'm sorry to have to do your job for you. Madame Nahour was getting ready to leave. I suppose she was wearing a coat and she probably put on her gloves.'

'Is that your defence?'

'I didn't think I needed a defence until the examining magistrate accuses me.'

'Please be at the Quai des Orfèvres tomorrow at ten o'clock, where you will be interrogated officially. The magistrate you mention may well want to see you later.'

'And until then?'

'You are not to leave the house and one of my detectives will continue to watch you.'

'I'm very patient, Monsieur Maigret.'

'So am I, Monsieur Oueni.'

Nevertheless Maigret's cheeks were flushed when he left the room, although it may have been because of the heat. In the corridor he gave a friendly nod to Torrence who was reading a magazine and sitting on a straight chair, and knocked on the studio door.

'Come in, Monsieur Maigret.'

The two men stood up. The elder of the two, who was smoking a cigar, came towards the Superintendent and held out a dry and vigorous hand.

'I would rather have met you in different circumstances, Monsieur Maigret.'

'Let me tell you how sorry I am. I didn't want to leave the house before saying that we are doing all we can, the Judicial

Police and the Public Prosecutor, to find out who murdered your son.'

'Have you got any clues?'

'I wouldn't go as far as to say that, but all the characters involved in this case are beginning to reveal their parts.'

'Do you believe Felix shot at that woman?'

'That seems certain, either because he pressed the trigger involuntarily, or because he fired as a reflex after having been hit himself.'

The father and son looked at each other in surprise.

'Do you think that that woman, who made him suffer so much, finally . . .'

'I'm not yet in a position to accuse anybody. Good night, gentlemen.'

'Shall I stay here?' asked Torrence a little later in the corridor.

'Fouad is not to go out. I'd rather have you on the first floor and know about any 'phone calls he makes. I don't yet know who'll be relieving you.'

The taxi driver muttered:

'I thought you were only staying a few minutes!'

'The Hôtel du Louvre.'

'I won't wait for you there. I started work at eleven and I haven't had time for lunch yet.'

Night was falling. The driver must have run the engine occasionally because inside the taxi the air was hot.

Maigret, huddled in the back seat, gazed vaguely at the black and chilly figures sliding past the buildings, and he wasn't really sure how satisfied with himself he was.

*　　　*　　　*

Lucas was dozing, his hands on his stomach, in one of the monumental armchairs in the hall. When he saw, through his drooping lids, the Superintendent coming towards him, he jumped up and asked, rubbing his eyes:

'Everything all right, chief?'

'Yes . . . No . . . Has Alvaredo arrived?'

'Not yet . . . None of the ladies have gone out . . . One of them, the friend, came downstairs and bought some news-papers and magazines at the end of the hall . . .'

Maigret hesitated, then muttered:

'Are you thirsty?'

'I had a glass of beer a quarter of an hour ago . . .'

Maigret went to the bar on his own, left his coat, hat and scarf in the cloakroom, and leant one buttock against a tall stool. There was hardly anybody there except for the barman's assistant who was listening to a football match on the radio.

'A whisky . . .' he ordered.

He needed one before the task he had decided to undertake. Where had he read the maxim: Always attack at the point of least resistance?

He had been thinking about it on the way, in the taxi. Four people knew the truth, or part of the truth about the Nahour case. He had questioned all four of them, some of them twice. They had all lied, at least on one point, if not on several.

Who, of the four, would offer least resistance?

At one moment he had thought of Nelly Velthuis whose ingenuousness cannot have been entirely false, but precisely because she didn't realize the importance of her lies, she might have told him anything.

Alvaredo was really quite nice. He was a passionate man. His love for Lina seemed sincere, and fervent, so that he would not say a word that could injure the young woman.

Maigret had just left Oueni, who was clever enough to foresee and to avoid every trap.

There remained Lina, about whom he hesitated to come to a conclusion. At first sight she was a child struggling amongst grown-ups, without knowing which way to turn.

Starting as a little typist in Amsterdam, she had been attracted by the more glamorous career of a fashion model before thoughtlessly entering a beauty contest.

268

Then the miracle happened, and from one day to the next the girl found herself in a completely strange world.

A rich man, playing for high stakes every night and to whom the staff of the casino bowed low, sent her flowers, and invited her to dinner in the best restaurants without asking for anything in exchange.

He took her to Biarritz, as discreetly as ever, and on the night when he summoned up enough courage to enter her room, he immediately proposed marriage to her.

How could she have understood the psychology of someone like Nahour?

Or still less, of Fouad Oueni, who followed the couple everywhere for no apparent reason?

When she wanted to have a Dutch maid it was as though she had called for help and she had chosen—from a photograph?—the most ingenuous and gayest candidate.

She had had dresses, jewels and furs, but in Deauville, Cannes and Evian, wherever she was taken without being asked her opinion, she was alone, and she occasionally went to Amsterdam to talk openly to Anna Keegel as she had done when the two girls shared the flat in the Lomanstraat.

She had had a child. Was she prepared for motherhood? Was it for fear that the responsibility might be too great for her that Nahour had called in a nurse?

Had she had lovers and affairs since then?

The years went by and her features remained as young, her skin as clear and smooth as ever. But her mind? Had she learnt anything?

Another child, a son, finally satisfied the husband who had only slept with her for a fairly brief period.

She met Alvaredo . . . Her life suddenly took on new colour . . .

Maigret was starting to feel sorry for her, and then told himself:

Nevertheless it's the little girl with innocent eyes who started this whole business . . .

And who had been behaving remarkably coolly ever since Friday evening.

He almost ordered another whisky, decided against it, and took the lift to the fourth floor a few seconds later. Nelly opened the door of the sitting-room.

'Is Madame Nahour asleep?'

'No. She's having tea.'

'Will you tell her I want to see her?'

He found her sitting up in bed, a white silk bed-jacket over her shoulders, reading an English or American magazine. The tea and the slices of cake were on the bed table and Anna Keegel, who must have been lying on the second bed when the Superintendent arrived, ran her hand over her hair and struck an attitude.

'I'd like to talk to you alone, Madame Nahour.'

'Can't Anna stay? I've never hidden anything from her and . . .'

'Let's say that I mind her being here.'

It was almost true. When the door was shut Maigret brought a chair up between the two beds and sat on it clumsily.

'Have you seen Vicente? Is he very worried about me?'

'I told him you were all right, and you did too, on the telephone. I suppose you're expecting him?'

'In half an hour. I told him to come at half past five because I thought I'd sleep longer. What did you think of him?'

'He seems very much in love. It's about him that I'd like to ask you my first question, Madame Nahour. I understand that you're doing all you can to keep him out of this business and to keep his name out of it, since that would make his and your future relationship with his parents more difficult.

'As for me, I shall avoid getting him any publicity as far as I can.

'But one detail worries me. You told me he stayed in his car on Friday evening all the time you were in the house, that is to say about an hour.

'He knew about your decision. He realized that your husband would not hear of a divorce. He could therefore have expected a stormy and dramatic meeting. Why, then, did he leave you alone instead of sharing the responsibility?'

As he spoke she bit her lower lip.

'That's the truth,' she said simply.

'Oueni has a different opinion.'

'What did he tell you?'

'That Alvaredo came into the studio with you, and he added a further detail: that your companion was wearing heavy winter gloves. Oueni also says that when your husband fired it was Alvaredo who pulled a pistol out of his pocket and fired in his turn.'

'Oueni's lying.'

'I am inclined to believe that you first had a violent discussion with your husband while Alvaredo stood discreetly near the door. When Nahour realized that your decision was final he threatened you, after pulling the 6.35 out of the drawer. Thinking he was going to shoot your friend fired first, to protect you, and Nahour pressed the trigger as he fell.'

'That's not what happened.'

'Correct me.'

'I've already told you. To begin with, if Vicente stayed in the car it's because I wanted him to. I even told him I wouldn't come with him if he came into the house.'

'Was your husband sitting at his desk?'

'Yes.'

'And Oueni?'

'Stood on his right.'

'So he was in front of the drawer with the gun.'

'I think so . . .'

'You think so or are you sure?'

'I'm sure.'

'Did Oueni look as though he were going to leave the room?'

'He moved, but he didn't leave.'

'In which direction did he move?'

'Towards the middle of the room.'

'Before you spoke, or after you had started speaking?'

'After.'

'You told me you didn't like him. Why didn't you ask your husband to send him out?'

'Felix would have refused. Besides, by that time I didn't care any more.'

'What was the first thing you said?'

'I said:

' "There you are! I've made up my mind and that's final. I'm leaving . . ." '

'Were you talking French?'

'English. I learnt English when I was very young, but I only learnt French much later.'

'What did your husband say?'

' "With your lover? Is he waiting in the car?" '

'What was Nahour like just then?'

'Very pale, with set features. He got up slowly and I think it was then that he opened the drawer, but I didn't know what he was going to do. I added that I wasn't angry with him, that I thanked him for all he'd done for me, that it was up to him to decide about the children and that my lawyer would get in touch with him . . .'

'Where was Oueni?'

'I didn't pay any attention to him. Not far from me, I suppose. He never makes much noise.'

'Was that when your husband fired?'

'No. Not yet. He repeated what he had often told me, that he would never accept a divorce. I told him he'd have to. Only then did I realize he was holding a gun . . .'

'And then?'

Maigret was leaning slightly towards her, as though to stop her escaping again.

'The two . . .'

She corrected herself:

'The shot was fired.'

272

'No. The two shots, as you were about to say. I'm sure Alvaredo was in the study but he didn't fire.'

'Do you think I did?'

'Not you either. Oueni pulled the gun out of his pocket before or after your husband fired . . .'

'As long as I was in the house there was only one shot, Nelly will confirm it.'

'Nelly lies almost as much as you do, my dear.'

This time it was a menacing Maigret who got up. He had stopped playing.

After putting his chair back in the corner he strode round the room and Lina no longer recognized the man who had seemed almost paternal shortly before.

'At one point, and the sooner the better, you will have to stop lying. Otherwise I'll ring the examining magistrate at once and ask for a warrant for your arrest.'

'Why should Oueni have shot at my husband?'

'Because he loved you.'

'Him? Fouad, love someone?'

'Don't pretend to be innocent, Lina. How long after your first meeting with Nahour did Oueni become your lover?'

'Did he tell you?'

'It doesn't matter. Answer me . . .'

'Several months after my marriage . . . I didn't expect it . . . I'd never seen him with a woman . . . He seemed to despise them . . .'

'Did you decide to excite him?'

'Is that what you think of me?'

'I'm sorry. Besides, it doesn't matter who started it. Until then Nahour had almost owned him. And now he partly escaped him because of you. By becoming your lover he could pay back every humiliation, past and future.'

She had suddenly become almost ugly. Her features faded away and she cried without trying to dry her tears.

'In the hotels and villas where you lived, and you and your husband had separate rooms, it was easy for Oueni to

273

come and see you at night. So in the Avenue du Parc-Montsouris . . .'

'Nothing ever happened there . . .'

She was really upset and she looked at him with poor, imploring eyes.

'I swear it! When it became serious with Alvaredo . . .'

'What do you mean?'

'When I realized that he really loved me and that I loved him, I stopped seeing Fouad.'

'Who agreed to this little break?'

'He tried in every way, once even by force, to resume our affair . . .'

'How long ago?'

'About a year and a half.'

'Did you know that he still loved you?'

'Yes.'

'Weren't you turning the knife in the wound by talking to your husband that evening when he was there?'

'I didn't think of that.'

'If he went near to you at the beginning of the conversation, wasn't he trying to protect you?'

'I didn't think about that. By the end I didn't even know where he was standing.'

'Were the two shots almost simultaneous?'

She didn't answer. She was obviously exhausted and wasn't acting any more.

Her shoulders had sunk into the pillows and her body was curled up under the sheets.

'Why didn't you tell the truth when I first questioned you?'

'About what?'

'About the shot fired by Fouad.'

She answered in a whisper:

'Because I didn't want Vicente to know . . .'

'To know what?'

'About Fouad and me. I was ashamed. I'd had an affair, a long time ago in Cannes, and I told him. But not about

Fouad! If I accuse him he'll say everything at the trial and our marriage will never be possible . . .'

'Wasn't Alvaredo surprised to see Oueni kill your husband?'

They looked straight at each other for several seconds. Maigret's eyes gradually lost their hardness while Lina's blue eyes showed more and more fatigue and resignation.

'He dragged me out and in the car I told him Fouad had always hated my husband . . .'

Her lower lip slightly swollen, she added under her breath: 'Why were you so unkind to me, Monsieur Maigret?'

CHAPTER SEVEN

At eleven o'clock on Monday morning Maigret left one of the offices in the Quai des Orfèvres where he had just officially interrogated his fourth witness.

He had started with Alvaredo, whom he had asked about twenty questions, and Lapointe had taken down the answers and the questions in shorthand. But of all these there had been one of major importance and the young Colombian had taken his time.

'Think well, Monsieur Alvaredo. It's probably the last time that I'll interrogate you because from now on the case will be in the hands of the examining magistrate. Were you in your car or in the house?'

'In the house. Lina opened the door before going into the studio.'

'Was Nahour still alive?'

'Yes.'

'Was anyone else in the room?'

'Fouad Oueni.'

'Where were you standing?'

'By the door.'

'Did Nahour try and make you leave?'

'He pretended not to see me.'

'Where was Fouad Oueni when the shots were fired?'

'About a yard away from Lina, in the middle of the room.'

'That is to say at a certain distance from Nahour?'

'Just over three yards.'

'Who fired first?'

'I think Oueni did, but I'm not sure because the two shots were almost simultaneous.'

Then, while the young Colombian had awaited permission to leave, it had been Anna Keegel's turn in the next-door office, and her interrogation had been fairly brief.

In the third office he had been quite lenient with Nelly Velthuis, who was very surprised.

'How many shots did you hear?'

'I don't know.'

'Could there have been two shots, almost simultaneously?'

'I think so.'

As for Lina, he had made her repeat most of what she had said the day before, but did not mention her affair with Fouad.

It had stopped snowing. The weather was getting damper and the snow was turning to slush. There were the usual draughts in the vast corridor of the Judicial Police building, but the offices were over-heated.

There was a certain effervescence in the whole building because all the detectives, even those who were not in the Crime Squad, had realized that an important operation was going on.

Journalists, with the inevitable Maquille among them, were sitting on the benches and assaulted the Superintendent every time he went into an office.

'In a minute, boys. I'm not ready . . .'

God knows how, probably by questioning the staff at Orly, a morning paper had found out about Lina's short trip to Amsterdam in the company of a mysterious character called Monsieur X. That meant that the case was going to take a sensational turn which Maigret did not like.

He still had to see Oueni.

When the Superintendent had gone home on Sunday evening at about seven, after passing by the Quai, Madame Maigret could see at a glance how he felt.

'Tired?'

'It's not so much tiredness.'

277

'Disheartened?'

'It's a foul job!' he had muttered, as he did every two or three years in cases like this. 'I haven't got the right to close my eyes and ears, and if I don't, I run the risk of ruining the existence of people who don't deserve it.'

She took care not to ask him any questions and after dinner they had watched television in silence.

At the end of the corridor he drew a deep breath and sighed:

'Come on, Lapointe.'

He still had hope. He opened the door of the office in which Oueni was sitting and found him, as usual, deep in the only armchair in the room, his legs stretched out in front of him.

As on the day before, the secretary did not get up, did not even greet the two men whom he looked at in turn with cruel irony.

Maigret remembered Voltaire's 'hideous smile' from his school days, and as he had stood before the bust of the great man, Maigret had never approved of this expression. Since then he had seen many arrogant, aggressive or perfidious smiles, but this was the first time that the word 'hideous' came to mind.

He sat on a chair at a white wooden table covered in brown paper on which stood a typewriter. Lapointe sat at the narrow end of the table and put his pad in front of him.

'Your name and Christian name.'

'Oueni, Fouad, born in Takla, Lebanon.'

'Age.'

'Fifty-one.'

Pulling a foreign resident's card from his pocket he held it out, but did not leave his armchair, so that Lapointe had to get up.

'The French police confirm it . . .' he said ironically.

'Profession?'

'Legal Adviser.'

As he said these two words his voice had become still more bantering.

'It's your police that say it. Read it . . .'

'Were you at any moment on Friday, January 14, between eleven in the evening and one in the morning, in the studio of your employer, Monsieur Felix Nahour, in the Avenue du Parc-Montsouris?'

'No. Please note that Monsieur Nahour was not my employer since I wasn't getting a salary.'

'In what capacity did you follow him to his various houses and in particular to the Avenue du Parc-Montsouris?'

'As a friend.'

'You weren't his secretary?'

'I helped him when he needed my advice.'

'Where were you on Friday evening after eleven?'

'At the Saint-Michel Club, to which I belong.'

'Can you mention the names of a few people who saw you there?'

'I don't know who saw me.'

'How many people would you say were in the two fairly small rooms of the club?'

'Between twenty and thirty, depending on the time.'

'You didn't talk to anybody?'

'No. I wasn't there to talk but to note the winning numbers at roulette.'

'Where were you standing?'

'Behind the players. I was sitting in a corner by the door.'

'What time did you arrive in the Boulevard Saint-Michel?'

'About half past ten.'

'What time did you leave the club?'

'About one in the morning.'

'So you claim that you were surrounded by over thirty people for two and a half hours without anybody noticing you?'

'I didn't say anything like that.'

'But you can't mention a single name.'

'I had no dealings with the other gamblers, who are mainly students.'

'On your way out you went through the bar on the ground floor? Did you talk to anyone?'

'To the owner.'

'What did you say to him?'

'That four had come up over eight times in under an hour.'

'How did you get back to the Avenue du Parc-Montsouris?'

'By car.'

'Monsieur Nahour's Bentley?'

'Yes. I usually drove it and it was at my disposal.'

'Three witnesses claim that you were standing in Monsieur Nahour's studio, on his right, at about midnight.'

'They all have a reason to lie.'

'What did you do when you came back?'

'I went up to my room and went to bed.'

'Without opening the door of the studio?'

'Yes.'

'You've been living off Felix Nahour for twenty years, Oueni, and he's been treating you like a poor relation. You not only acted as a secretary, but also as valet and chauffeur. Weren't you humiliated by this?'

'I was grateful for the confidence he showed in me and it was of my own free will that I did him small favours.'

He continued to look at Maigret defiantly, almost jubilantly. The words that he said could be taken down and used as evidence against him, so he chose them with care. But it was impossible to reproduce on paper his expressions which were a constant defiance.

'Didn't you feel frustrated when Monsieur Nahour got married after having lived alone with you for nearly fifteen years?'

'Our relationship was not in any way governed by passion, if that's what you're implying, and I had no reason for being jealous.'

'Was your employer happily married?'

'He didn't confide in me about his married life.'

'Do you think Madame Nahour was satisfied with the life she was leading with her husband, particularly during the last two years?'

'I never thought about that.'

This time Maigret's face grew heavier, as though it contained a message, and Oueni understood it. Nevertheless, by emphasizing a sort of silent defiance, he sustained his cynical attitude which contrasted with the objectivity of his replies.

'What was your relationship with Madame Nahour?'

'I had nothing whatsoever to do with her.'

Now that the interrogation was official, intended to play a part of capital importance in the future, every word was loaded with dynamite.

'Didn't you try to seduce her?'

'It never occurred to me.'

'Did you ever happen to be alone in a room with her?'

'If you mean a bedroom, the answer is no.'

'Think well.'

'No again.'

'A 7.65 calibre gun has been found in your room. Do you possess another pistol and where is it now?'

'At a gunsmith's in the Rue de Rennes, where I often used to go and practise.'

'When did you last go there?'

'On Thursday.'

'Thursday the 13th, that is to say the day before the murder. Did you then know that Madame Nahour intended to leave her husband the next day?'

'She didn't confide in me.'

'Her maid knew.'

'Nelly and I were not on very good terms.'

'Because you tried to go to bed with her and she rejected you?'

'It was more the other way round.'

'So this shooting session on Thursday was at a convenient

time to explain why you probably have crusts of powder on your fingers. At least two people were present on Friday evening, shortly before or after midnight, in Monsieur Nahour's office. Both of them swear under oath that you were there too.'

'Who are these two people?'

'First Madame Nahour.'

'And what was she doing there?'

'She had come to tell her husband that she was leaving that night and to ask for a divorce.'

'Did she tell you that her husband was prepared to give her a divorce? Was it the first time that she had mentioned it to him? Didn't she know that he would do everything in his power to oppose it?'

'Including shooting at her?'

'Have you proved that he fired intentionally? Finally, have you frequently found that people aim at the throat at two or three yards' range? Did Madame Nahour also tell you why she was suddenly so impatient about the divorce?'

'To marry Vicente Alvaredo who was in the room with her when the shot was fired.'

'One or more shots?'

'There were two shots, almost simultaneously, and it seems to have been the first which hit Nahour in the throat.'

'Which means that the second shot was fired by a dead man?'

'Death was not necessarily instantaneous. Nahour could have pressed the trigger without realizing it, while he was bleeding profusely and staggering to the ground.'

'Who would have fired the first shot?'

'You.'

'Why?'

'Maybe to protect Lina Nahour, maybe out of hatred for your employer.'

'Why not Alvaredo?'

'He apparently has never used a gun in his life and did not

possess one. The investigation will or will not confirm this point.'

'Didn't they run away?'

'They went to Amsterdam as they had planned to do for a week and they returned to Paris as soon as the Dutch police advised them to.'

'On your behalf? And after you had promised that they wouldn't get into trouble? Was Monsieur Alvaredo wearing gloves?'

'He was.'

'Weren't they thick leather gloves which haven't been found?'

'They were found last night at Orly and the laboratory found no trace of powder on them.'

'Wasn't Madame Nahour, who was just about to leave, also wearing gloves?'

'The same test had no result.'

'Are you sure they were the same gloves?'

'The maid has confirmed it.'

'At the beginning you mentioned three witnesses. I suppose the third is Nelly Velthuis?'

'She was leaning over the banisters on the first floor waiting for the end of the conversation and she heard two shots.'

'Did she tell you that on Saturday?'

'That's none of your business.'

'Can you tell me where she spent Sunday?'

'In the Hôtel du Louvre with her mistress and a friend of hers.'

'Didn't these three people receive any calls, apart from you? Because I suppose you went to interrogate them, just as you interrogated me in the Avenue du Parc-Montsouris.'

'Alvaredo went to see them at the end of the afternoon.'

Then Oueni said drily, reversing the rôles:

'That'll do. From now on I'll only talk in the presence of my lawyer.'

'There is, however, one question which I have already asked

283

you and which I want to repeat: what was your relationship
with Madame Nahour?'

Oueni had an icy smile and his eyes were darker and brighter
than ever when he spat out:

'I had nothing to do with her.'

'Thank you, Lapointe. Will you call two detectives?'

He had got up and had gone round his desk. He stood in
front of Oueni, who was still in his armchair. Looking him
up and down the Superintendent asked bitterly:

'Revenge?'

Fouad then looked round the room to make sure they were
alone and the door was shut, and said:

'Perhaps.'

'Stand up.'

He obeyed.

'Hold out your wrists.'

He did so, without losing his smile.

'I arrest you on a warrant from Examining Magistrate
Cayotte . . .'

Then to the two Inspectors who came in:

'Take this man to the police station.'

CHAPTER EIGHT

IT HAD BECOME the 'Nahour Case'. For a week it was on the front pages of all the papers and had several columns in the sensationalizing weeklies. Journalists were permanently prowling round the Avenue du Parc-Montsouris, picking up gossip, and Madame Bodin, the charwoman, had her hour of glory.

Maquille went to Amsterdam, then to Cannes, and returned with an interview with the nurse, and a photograph of her and the children. He also questioned the casino managers and croupiers.

All this time the men from the records office went through the Nahours' house with a fine-tooth comb, in the hope of finding some clue. They also went through the garden and even searched the drains for the pistol which had killed Nahour.

The meeting with the solicitor had taken place on Monday afternoon before Pierre Nahour, his father and Lina.

Maigret was told about it on the telephone by Maître Leroy-Beaulieu. In his second will Felix Nahour did not leave his wife any more than the legal minimum. The rest went to the children and he expressed the desire that they be entrusted to the care of his brother and that if this were impossible he be appointed an alternative guardian.

'Didn't he leave Oueni anything?'

'I was amazed. I can now tell you that in his first will, which was cancelled by this one, Nahour left a sum of five hundred thousand francs to his secretary "in return for his devotion and services". Well, Oueni's name isn't even mentioned in the final will.'

Had Nahour found out in the meantime about Fouad's affair with Lina?

Thirty-six clients of the Saint-Michel Club, the manager and the croupiers, were questioned by the examining magistrate.

The journalists were waiting for them as they came out, and this provoked incidents after certain furious witnesses rushed at the photographers.

There were also some mistakes. A Cambodian student said he had seen Oueni sitting in the corner from eleven o'clock that evening. It took two days' patient investigation to discover that this student had never set foot in the club on Friday, but that he was mixing it up with the previous Wednesday.

Some neighbours, who came home at half past eleven after having spent the evening in the cinema, swore that they had not seen a car parked in front of the bar.

The magistrate Cayotte was a thorough and patient man. For three months he summoned Maigret to his office almost every day to ask him to make further investigations.

In the papers politics took first place again and the Nahour case was relegated to the third and then to the fifth page, before it disappeared completely.

Lina, Alvaredo and Nelly were not allowed to leave Paris without permission and it was only after the investigation was over that they were permitted to hide in a little house near Dreux.

The Grand Jury confirmed Oueni's indictment but the lists of the Assize Court were so full that the case was not tried until the following January, a year after Doctor Pardon had received the silent wounded woman and her lover in his surgery in the Boulevard Voltaire.

Curiously enough the two men never alluded to the Nahour case during their monthly dinners.

One day a slightly flushed Maigret had to give his evidence in court. Until then nothing had been said about Lina's affair with the defendant.

The Superintendent replied as objectively and briefly as possible to the Judge's questions. As soon as he saw the Public Prosecutor get up he knew that the young woman's secret was in danger.

'May I question the witness, Your Honour?'

'The Public Prosecutor may proceed.'

'Can the witness tell the jury whether he has reason to believe that there was ever an intimate relationship between the defendant and Madame Nahour?'

The Superintendent was under oath and could not cheat.

'Yes.'

'Has the defendant denied this formally?'

'Yes.'

'Nevertheless his attitude suggests that this is true?'

'Yes.'

'Did the witness believe in this relationship?'

'Yes.'

'Did this knowledge contribute to Oueni's arrest by throwing a new light on his motives?'

'Yes.'

That was all. The spectators had listened in silence but now there was uproar in the courtroom and the judge had to use his gavel. 'If order is not restored I shall clear the court . . .'

Maigret had the chance to sit next to Cayotte, who had kept a place for him. But he preferred to leave.

When he was alone in the deserted corridors in which his steps echoed he slowly filled a pipe without realizing what he was doing.

A few minutes later he was at the bar in the Palais de Justice and ordered a beer in a surly voice.

He didn't have the courage to go home. He drank another beer, almost in one draught, and then walked slowly towards the Quai des Orfèvres.

It wasn't snowing that year. The air was mild. It was like early spring and the sun was so bright that one expected the buds to burst into flower.

Back in his office he opened the door of the detectives' room.

'Lucas! . . . Janvier! . . . Lapointe! . . .'

It was as though all three were waiting for him.

'Take your coats and come with me . . .'

They followed him without asking where they were going. A few minutes later they went up the worn steps of the Brasserie Dauphine.

'Well, Monsieur Maigret, how about the Nahour case?' said the owner.

He regretted his question because the Superintendent looked at him and shrugged his shoulders. He quickly added:

'There's chitterlings today, you know . . .'

The couple could no longer go to Bogota. And would the relationship between Lina and Alvaredo ever be the same after the morning's session?

The Nahour case was back in the headlines. For the evening papers it was the story of a *ménage à quatre*.

Without the new motive on which the Public Prosecutor based his case, the jury might have acquitted Oueni.

The weapon had not been found. The charge was only based on the evidence of more or less interested parties.

The next evening Fouad Oueni was sentenced to ten years' imprisonment while Lina and Alvaredo, who had been let out through a side door, got into the Jaguar and drove off to an unknown destination.

Maigret never heard about them again.

'I've failed,' he admitted to Pardon, with whom he dined on the following Tuesday.

'Maybe if I hadn't run you that night . . .'

'Events would nevertheless have taken their course, after a slight delay . . .'

And Maigret added, reaching for his glass of Marc de Bourgogne:

'Oueni really won . . .'